THE DARK SIDE OF HONOR

Also by S.T. Phillips

The Dark Side of Death
A Jack Dublin Novel

THE DARK SIDE OF HONOR

A JACK DUBLIN NOVEL

By

S. T. PHILLIPS

THE DARK SIDE OF HONOR Copyright 2016 by Scomar Press.
All rights reserved. Printed in the United States of America.

ISBN-13: **9781540589552**
ISBN-10: **1540589552**

Cover design by damonza.com

First Edition December 2016

This book is dedicated to
Margaret Bleistine
also
Julio, Jorge, Paquito and
Yolanda Don

Honor is simply the morality of superior men.

H. L. Mencken

1

Washington D.C.

Jack Dublin stood in the shade, under the canopy of a restaurant table on M Street, and watched the killer casually walk across the street. He lingered there, just long enough to make sure he wasn't seen.

Contrary to his sixty-plus years and past history, the killer moved with guile, seemingly devoid of detection. Jack felt behind his back to make sure his Glock 26 was concealed.

"Excuse me, sir. Can I help you?" an approaching waiter asked.

"No thanks," Jack said. He waved the waiter away, then crossed the street to meet the man who had killed his mother twenty some years ago.

For now, his attention was on the young man walking with the killer, who appeared to be about college age. Tall and lean, the young man was wearing a pair of tan slacks with a white shirt open at the collar, no tie. His hair was neatly groomed and fairly short. They laughed intermittently as they crossed the street.

When the killer put his arm around the young man, Jack felt duty-bound to save the young man by walking up to the killer and blowing his brains out. But patience brings chances, and Jack knew he would have his.

Jack continued to surreptitiously follow them. They walked off M Street, the main street in Georgetown populated with restaurants, art galleries and bars. He watched them enter and go through a small alleyway bordered by an eclectic collection of stores, then down some steps to an open courtyard area where a large triangular planter was situated in front of the restaurant. People congregated here to wait for their name to be called.

The Sea Catch Restaurant used to be one of Jack's favorites. The food, wine list and service were impeccable, but the last time he was there, he was targeted by an assassin. While meeting a woman in front of the restaurant to get information about a case he was working on, an assassin standing on a walkway two floors up had decided to end Jack's life.

Fortunately for Jack, the man pulling the trigger was lacking in accuracy. Unfortunately for Peggy Garber, the woman sitting next to him, the bullet struck her, killing her instantly.

As Jack approached the entranceway, he paused and contemplated what he was doing. Deciding to continue, he cautiously descended the steps into the courtyard area, looking for signs of the shooting, but there weren't any. No blood, chalk outlines or other remnants of Peggy's death, just lots of people with an appetite.

Jack moved closer to the killer and young man, but judiciously remained in the background, some distance from them. He watched an attractive, bountiful hostess greet them.

"Hello Mr. Dublin, your table is ready," the buxom young woman said with a friendly smile revealing perfect white teeth.

"Thanks, Chrissy."

The killer and the young man followed her as she escorted them through the front room, the bar, and into the next room which had a decor of stone and brick, with lighting providing a generous accent. The place was packed. Not an empty table or chair in sight. Jack had worked in the kitchen of a busy D.C. restaurant when he was a student at Georgetown. He hated it. *If people only knew the mayhem that goes on in a restaurant kitchen.*

Jack remained behind them at a safe distance, satisfied with observing for now. Chrissy was passing out menus as the killer and young man sat down. When Chrissy left, Jack decided not to wait any longer. He walked up to the table and stood there looking glacially— at his father.

"Well, Jack!" Ben Dublin said with a proud smile and stood up. "Glad you could make it, have a seat." He gestured with his hand, pointing to the space next to the young man who was seated in one of those semi-circle, wraparound, leather booths. Jack sat down next to his son, Connor, whom he hadn't seen in years, and across from his father, who sat on one of two chairs facing them.

He took his menu, but remained fixed on his father who had the smile of a car salesman trying to convince you the car you just bought was only $100 over the dealer's cost.

Jack could feel Connor examining him between glances at his menu.

"You know, I've been waiting for this day for over twenty years," Ben boasted. "Now I get to sit with my son and grandson at the same table. Jack, I know this has to be awkward for you. I know it must be for you too, Connor," he said, re-directing attention to his grandson.

A waiter showed up at the table and began filling the glasses with water.

"Daniel, how are you today?" Ben asked.

"Splendid, Mr. Dublin," he answered jovially. "How 'bout yourself?"

"Daniel, I think this is one of the greatest days of my life."

"Really? Why's that?" Daniel asked while finishing up.

"I finally have the chance to sit with my son and grandson at the same table."

"I take it it's been a long time?"

"This is the very first time! It's a long story I won't get into, but I'm just happy it's finally happened."

"Congratulations Mr. Dublin. Congratulations to all of you. May I get anyone something from the bar?"

"I think this calls for champagne. What do you two think?"

"It's fine with me," Connor said.

"Jack?"

"Sure, why not?" Jack said reluctantly.

"How about a bottle of Veuve Clicquot?"

"Excellent choice, sir."

Daniel left to retrieve the champagne. Jack began to feel more pressure. He really wanted to talk to his son, but what do you say to someone you gave up for adoption when he was four years old? With his father there, it was more difficult. He looked at his father, still harboring the disgust of what he believed was his father's guilt in his mother's death. As he continued to stare, he imagined his mother sitting next to her husband, wondering what she might look like today. Somehow, she'd seen something in Ben Dublin she loved. There must be something redeeming about him.

Ben turned serious for a moment and looked at Jack. "Jack, I just want to say how sorry I am about Marnie. I know it must trouble you deeply. Let's hope she's on her way to a full recovery," he said.

Ben was referring to Jack's most recent girlfriend. She and Jack had been following a group of radical extremists who were tied to the corrupt Senator Rothschild. Since Jack killed his only son, Rothschild wanted him dead.

Several attempts were made on Jack's life without success. The last time, in St. Lucia, they blew up a boat Jack had momentarily left to retrieve his bag of guns and ammunition onshore.

Unfortunately, Marnie was still onboard when the explosion occurred. Now she was in critical condition at Walter Reed Hospital. The senator had a vendetta against Jack, who, months earlier, justifiably killed the senator's only son in self-defense. Currently, the senator was under indictment for laundering campaign money, among other things.

"Listen, I know you two probably have a lot to say to each other and don't know how to get it started. Hell, Jack, you probably have a lot to say to me too!" Ben paused to gauge Jack's response. "But today, let's all put our differences aside and get to know each other. Jack, you're probably wondering how Connor and I have stayed in touch, and how Connor happens to be in D.C."

"I'm sure if he wants to tell me, he will."

Connor remained quiet and didn't offer any comments. Jack didn't know how to read the young man's reaction, but his mind was working overtime.

Ben Dublin looked back and forth at Jack and Connor waiting to hear one of them talk, but neither did. It was if they were two people on their first date, which in a way, they were.

"Connor, would you like me to fill your father, I mean Jack, in?"

Connor looked sternly back at his grandfather.

"No, I think I can do that," he said before turning to look at Jack without emotion. "I attend college here. I go to Georgetown."

Jack cleared his throat. "What are you majoring in?"

"I'm working on my doctorate in Law."

"That's pretty impressive. You must have gotten your bachelor's degree pretty young," Jack said, impressed.

"I did. I was twenty years old."

"Jack, you'd be impressed to know how intelligent Connor is," Ben said boastfully. "He graduated at the top of his class in high school when he was only sixteen. He's a lot like you, a true Dublin."

"I'm glad to hear it," Jack responded truthfully.

Daniel returned to the table in short order and placed three champagne flutes in front of them. He opened the bottle and poured. Placing the bottle in an ice bucket, he said he would be right back.

Ben raised his glass, then Connor and Jack slowly raised theirs.

"To my grandson and son"—Jack noticed he took second billing— "and to us, may we all enjoy each other's company for many years to come." Ben brought his glass forward to clink with Connor's and Jack's. Jack dutifully brought his forward too, looking at Ben Dublin indifferently, thinking about how Connor was being used as bait.

After they each sipped their champagne, Ben reached into his pocket and pulled out his phone. It vibrated audibly. He looked at it, then asked Jack and Connor to excuse him for a moment so he could take the call. They watched him leave the table and walk toward the bar.

Jack and Connor continued to drink their champagne while trying to think about what to say. Jack began to straighten his silverware unnecessarily. "Do you want to ask me why I gave you up for adoption?" he finally asked.

Connor stared at him. There was something deep about his eyes. Something that indicated he wasn't an ordinary young man. He was wise beyond his years, yet there was innocence living beneath his protective shell. He wanted—needed—to find the answer to some questions all adopted children have.

"Why did you leave me? How could you? What did I do?"

Sometimes the answer was better left unsaid.

"Connor, I want you to know it was the most difficult decision I ever made in my life, and I've thought about it every day since. I know you probably hate me, but I did it for you," Jack assured him, looking at Connor for some affirmative reaction.

Connor just looked at him impassively.

"Are you trying to convince me, or yourself?" Connor asked coolly.

Score one for Connor.

"I'm trying to convince you."

"Y'know, Jack, and I say Jack because you're really not my father. It takes commitment to be a parent, and that's not a commitment you were willing to make."

Jack sighed. Connor's words cut him to the core. Jack wanted to tell him his side of the story, but it would be futile.

Before Jack could respond, Ben returned. His color was pale and he seemed troubled. Jack and Connor looked at him with raised brows.

"Jack, that was Mr. Prescott." Mr. Prescott was Marnie's stepfather. "You're needed at the hospital. It's Marnie!"

2
Washington D.C.

"Jack," Ben said, "I called Roosevelt, my driver, and he's waiting for you on M Street. He'll take you to the hospital. Don't worry about Connor and me. We'll wait for Roosevelt to come back or we'll take a taxi home."

Jack just sat there, trying to let all that happened in the last twenty minutes saturate into his brain until he could make some sense of it all.

"Jack, did you hear me?"

"Yes. Yes, I heard you," he responded, then stood up as if in a stupor.

"Are you going to be okay?" Ben asked.

"Yeah, I'll be okay," Jack answered while looking at Ben and then Connor as if they were apparitions.

"Do you want us to come with you?"

"No. I'll talk to you later." He nodded a brief farewell to both of them, then walked away.

Still somewhat stupefied, Jack quickly made his way to M Street as soon as he cleared the restaurant. As promised, the black limo was waiting curbside for him. Roosevelt, a large black man in an ill-fitting suit, was standing there with the rear door open. Jack glanced at him before sliding into the back. Soon they were headed to Walter Reed Hospital.

During the ride, Jack had plenty of time to play the mental tapes of the past few days. Not too long ago, he had been in a Black Hawk helicopter at Montserrat, fighting Pakistani terrorists who were trying to blow up a cruise ship. Earlier that day, he narrowly escaped being blown up at St. Lucia in the charter fishing boat where Marnie had been waiting for him.

Until she met Jack, she had been a happy, productive woman working in a lucrative, respectable position at a law firm. Her position was undefined, but determined by the law firm on an as-needed basis. In short, she was like the utility player for a ball team. With Jack, who at the time had been indicted, she was initially his paralegal, assistant investigator, confidant and ultimately his lover. She restored Jack's faith in the true meaning of relationships. Now, because of him, she was dying.

To top it off, his father had re-entered his life after being away for twenty years. Jack was still convinced Ben Dublin knew something about his mother's death, either directly or indirectly even though he professed his innocence. It also mystified Jack how his father knew Mr. Prescott and Marnie. There was something secretive about his father, and he planned to find out.

Then Jack saw his son for the first time in twenty years. It had been a long time since Jack released his parental rights. For what it was worth, Connor had grown up into a handsome, intelligent young man who seemed to be fairly grounded, in spite of his absentee father. It gnawed Jack. He was happy for his son, but remorseful that his son could grow up so well without his guidance. Now it was evident his son loathed him even more than Jack loathed his own father.

Right now, Jack felt like his life was in a cesspool of vortex proportions. There was only one person who could save him and she was lying in a hospital, in a coma…or dead.

They pulled up to the entrance. Charlie, a friend Jack had made in St. Lucia, was waiting for him in the lobby. Jack could see the ominous look on his face.

"What's the latest?" Jack asked.

"I'm not sure. They wouldn't tell me. They told me to wait for you down here, and then bring you up when you got here," he said, obviously hiding the truth.

"Cut the crap. Is she alive?"

Charlie shrugged. "I don't know."

They took the elevator up and when they arrived, Archibald Prescott, was there looking imperious as ever in his two thousand-dollar suit with a flower in his lapel. He didn't walk towards Jack. In fact, he walked away, toward a more private area. Jack and Charlie followed.

"Sit down, Jack." Mr. Prescott gestured toward an oversized comfy chair that must have occupied thousands of mourners through the years. This was where family members found out about their loved ones who returned from war missing body parts. It was where lives changed forever, where the reality of war became the elephant in the room. Jack knew once he sat in it, he would feel the depth of emotion those before him had felt.

"Jack, Marnie passed away a little over an hour ago." Jack thought Mr. Prescott was going to show emotion for the first time. "You'll be pleased to know, your name was the last word she ever spoke." Mr. Prescott bowed his head and placed his hand to his forehead, managing to maintain his composure.

Jack sat there with his hands clasped, looking at the floor in a wide-eyed stare. He took a deep breath as he began to realize the enormity of the moment.

Marnie had broken down his walls of insecurity about love, and gave him hope for the future, their future. He had never felt so comfortable and safe with any other woman in his life. She had healed the wounds of his past. There was nothing they wouldn't accomplish together. If he had remained at the hospital with her when she came out of surgery, maybe he could have talked to her, revived her. Now she was gone and he felt responsible. He should have stayed here instead of going home to rest. He owed her that, and now he felt like he let her down.

Mr. Prescott spoke. "I haven't made any arrangements, yet I believe she will have a Catholic funeral service and burial. I'll let you know when I have completed the final preparations."

Mr. Prescott then stood, all five feet seven of him, and put his black derby bowler hat on. Jack continued to sit for a moment, looking up at him in stunned silence. He felt the greatest respect for this man.

"Mr. Prescott," Jack said as he stood up, "I don't think there are words to describe how devastated I am. And I know I can't measure your loss, but if it's anything like mine, and I believe it's probably worse than mine, I hope you'll accept my condolences and my regrets. I know if you had not taken my case, Marnie would still be alive today."

Mr. Prescott looked at Jack and finally gave a weak smile. "I don't blame you, Jack. You were unlawfully framed. My life has always been about providing for those who have innocently received the short end of the stick. That's how Marnie came into my life. Her parents were dear friends of mine and my wife's. When they met an untimely death, I looked after Marnie. I had promised her parents. It was a completely unnecessary promise because I would have never let that child travel down a dark road." He paused. "Funny, in the end I guess I did."

He held out his hand and Jack shook it. "I will contact you soon."

Jack watched as Mr. Prescott walked toward the elevator. Charlie said something to Jack, but he wasn't listening.

"Mr. Prescott," Jack called out as he ran to catch him before getting on the elevator. "One thing has been bothering me, and I'm hoping you have the answer." Jack searched for the words before deciding to just ask him directly. "How do you know my father?"

Mr. Prescott smiled earnestly. "Jack, your father has been a friend of mine for years. Marnie worked with him at WISE International."

"His security firm? She…. Marnie worked for Dad?"

"He's the one who hired me to defend you. Your father put up your bail."

The elevator doors opened and Mr. Prescott soon disappeared.

Jack stood there feeling like he had been punched in the stomach by Joe Frazier. The bail his father paid when he was under indictment was one million dollars. And to think Marnie had worked for his father. It was more than he could comprehend.

3

Bethesda, MD

Marnie's funeral was held at a small Catholic Church in Bethesda, Maryland, not far from the prolific Mormon Temple, whose gold spires against white marble soar out of the trees along the Beltway. Whenever Jack saw it, he thought of *The Wizard of Oz* and flying monkeys, visualizing a witch flying over the spires on a broom.

Jack walked slowly up to the church, strong but grief-stricken, and deep in contemplation. Until he met Marnie, he had resigned himself to the single life. After his divorce, most of his relationships with women were shallow, empty and fleeting. Physically, Marnie was stunning. It was certainly what attracted him at first, but as he began to know her, he was charmed by her intelligence, wit and sense of humor. She was the total package and he fell deeply in love with her. Now, he felt responsible for her death.

It would take some time to get over her, but one of Jack strengths was resiliency. He would never minimize her importance, but he knew he would move on, eventually. He had no choice, and he knew Marnie would've demanded it.

Jack hadn't been inside a church since he became disillusioned with religion. It began with his divorce. He was no longer allowed to receive all the sacraments of the church. He found this hypocritical when he knew police officers who had been married for years, had children, got divorced, but were able to annul their marriage by paying cash to the Church. The reason these divorcees would do this, was so they could remarry in the Catholic Church and receive all the rights and privileges. The fact the Church would allow this caused Jack to become a lapsed

Catholic. Yet, as the son of Catholic parents who attended church regularly with him in his formative years, he couldn't escape the presence of God in his life. Now he felt more spiritual than religious, and being spiritual negated his presence in a pew each Sunday.

Three entrance doors under arches welcomed congregants from the mostly-brick façade. Once inside, Jack felt a rush of old childhood memories that, for the most part, were pleasant. Rows of fifty pews lined each side of the nave. The stained-glass windows depicted various biblical events, and the crucifix hung over the altar with Jesus nailed there. Some crucifixes had Jesus nailed in the palms of his hands, while others were in the wrist. Jack always looked up curiously, to see where the nails were placed.

There were only a handful of people in attendance at Marnie's service. Mr. Prescott planned it that way, knowing Marnie was not one for pomp and circumstance. Also, Marnie didn't grow up in the area, and didn't have a lot of friends outside the office.

Jack walked up to the front, taking a seat alone in the fifth pew, behind the last occupied pew. The priest, who appeared to be Jack's age, was already into the service. After surveying the crowd, Jack looked closer at the priest and realized he knew who it was, though they hadn't kept in touch. Michael Delledonne, who had been a Metropolitan police officer, shot and killed a man who had robbed a liquor store. It happened several years before Jack's shooting. Even though he was exonerated, Michael anguished over the death of the victim and resigned from the department. Jack heard he had entered a seminary, but had no idea he was local.

Jack looked around at the rest of the people, and realized his father was in the second pew behind Mr. Prescott. He was beginning to realize how close his father and Mr. Prescott were, as friends. There was also a lot he didn't know, but hoped to find out.

Sitting there listening to the eulogy, Jack relived his moments together with Marnie. He bowed his head, then said a prayer asking for forgiveness.

Someone tapped him on the shoulder. Opening his eyes, Jack was surprised to see his friend Billy D, who worked with Jack in the department's criminal investigation unit. When Jack was indicted, Billy put his job in jeopardy, providing valuable information for Jack's defense. If anyone from the department found out, Billy would have lost his job, his pension and perhaps his freedom. He was probably the only true friend Jack had on the department.

"What are you doin' here?" Jack whispered after they shook hands.

"I heard about Marnie. Couldn't get a hold of you, so I thought I would find you here," Billy whispered back. "How you holdin' up?"

"All things considered, I guess I'm doin' okay."

Billy just nodded and they sat in silence for a while. Billy began surveying the crowd.

"Holy shit!" Billy said, keeping his voice low, as he looked at the former police officer, now priest. "Is that Mike Delledonne?"

"Yeah, it sure looks like him."

"I never pictured him for a priest, did you?"

"Mike Delledonne?" Jack asked skeptically. "Not really. He always had a different woman with him whenever I saw him. It seemed the party life agreed with him."

"I can't believe it, three sneaker Mike, a priest," Billy said smiling and shaking his head.

"Why'd you call him that?"

"You don't know?"

"No."

Giving Jack a look of disbelief, Billy said, "They say his dick is so big, when he bought shoes, he had to buy three!"

Jack gave Billy a smirk.

"That's how he got the nickname, 'Three-sneaker Mike' "

Jack shook his head. "Now is not the time to try and make me forget where I am, and why I'm here."

They sat in silence for a while longer listening to the service.

"Did you hear the latest?" asked Billy, who then stopped and asked, "Do you mind if I talk, or do you want me to shut up?"

"No, you're alright," Jack said. "Go ahead."

"I don't know if you heard or not, but apparently your friend Bob Lewis is coming out of his coma."

Bob Lewis was the former FBI agent who set Jack up for the murder of the terrorist's courier, who turned out to be a Pentagon official's son. Lewis was shot in the head during a confrontation with the terrorist group he had been selling SAMS (surface-to-air missiles). A slow death would have been perfect for him as far as Jack was concerned.

Jack grimaced.

"Jack, this might be a good thing. He can testify against Senator Rothschild."

Senator Rothschild was the father of the young man Jack shot and killed in self-defense. The ruthless senator used Bob Lewis to set Jack up for a murder he didn't commit, and tried to have him killed several times. It was he who was ultimately responsible for Marnie's death. Now, the senator faced his own problems. He was about to be censured by the Senate for illegally funding his campaign.

They both turned their attention to the service and listened until it ended. The procession began to come down the center aisle. Jack was seated closest to the aisle, and could look at each person as they walked by. Father Delledonne, whose hands were prayerfully held to his chest, glanced at Jack and Billy, slightly nodding. He was followed by Mr. Prescott who looked at Jack for a brief moment. Shortly afterward, his father walked by, looking at him as if he had something to say, but couldn't.

As the last person passed, Jack turned to Billy and asked, "Are you going to the cemetery?"

"Not a chance. I don't like to get too close to an open grave. I just wanted to come and support you. We need to get together and talk."

Jack nodded.

"Give me a call."

"I will, and thanks for coming," Jack said, then added, "and thanks for saving me from a life in prison."

Billy just looked at him as they shook hands.

As soon as they exited the church, Ben Dublin was standing there waiting. He came over to Jack and Billy. "Jack, I need to talk to you."

Billy said, "I'll catch you later," and walked off.

"When and where?" answered Jack answered, who had questions of his own.

Ben handed him a business card. "Tomorrow at my office, nine o'clock."

"See you then." Jack put the card in his shirt pocket as he walked off to his car and headed for the cemetery.

4

Belize

There wasn't much in the way of mountainous terrain in this part of the world, which would have provided a naturally secure, protective perch for one of the world's most notorious drug dealers. Certainly with his wealth, he could have built his own mountain, but his compound was safely off the beaten path and unless you had business with "El Tiburon", The Shark, you would never know its location. The multilevel mansion was fortified by the fifteen-foot wall around its two-hundred-acre compound within the one thousand and forty acres he owned.

The private airstrip beyond the walls of the compound provided Jorge DePeralta with quick access to the outside world.

He initially thought about placing barb wire on top of the wall around his compound, but didn't want to give his property any obvious sign of illegal activity, so he relented on the advice of his lieutenants and placed broken glass cemented into the peak of the perimeter wall.

Strategically located next to the jungle, not four miles from the border of Mexico, and along the Rio Hondo, which provided a border between Belize and Mexico, "El Tiburon" had alternate plans of escape if necessary. He was close enough to direct his business, but far enough away to seem innocent, and beyond the reach of the law or those who sought revenge.

The compound yard area was vast enough to accommodate a helicopter, which it had on a couple of occasions. He owned a Bell Huey which achieved a dual purpose. It could evacuate him and his family quickly, if required, and also transport thirteen troops into a drop zone for eliminating his adversaries.

He didn't want the helicopter near his home unless it was absolutely necessary. It sat in a hangar just outside the compound. After all, the good people of Corozal had been talking about him since he arrived two years ago. He rarely made trips to town, but when he did, his tips were generous and the people discreetly loved him, although he was the subject of gossip due to his mysterious ways. Underneath his kind appearance was a natural darkness that commanded respectful terror.

The town of Corozal didn't have much of a police attachment. The population was only a few thousand. Most townspeople scraped by with menial jobs, mostly tourist-related, but there were many service-related jobs.

"Bella," Jorge called out. "I am going to town to get supplies. Do you want to come?"

It was unusual for Jorge to go to town, especially lately. Recently, there had been some murders between his family and the Navarro family. The wars were intensifying. Casualties were felt on both sides. Still, fate had to be tested every once in a while.

"Bella, did you hear me?" he called to his sister.

She was a mere shell of the woman she once was. Now in her sixties, her only surviving family member had tortured her, primarily mental, to a point of unsure compliance. Her identity was no longer meaningful. Older than her brother, the benefits of sage advice were no longer heeded. She was now subservient.

"Yes, I hear you," Bella responded weakly.

"Well, do you want to go?"

She contemplated the question, despising his company, but having the opportunity to interact with others was too much to pass up. "Yes."

"Well, c'mon. We're leaving in ten minutes."

Three fully-armored black Suburbans readied to go into town, each equipped with a team of security. DePeralta had suffered a gunshot wound to his leg several years ago from a dissatisfied customer who was quickly neutralized, and then sent on his way to hell by "El Tiburon" himself. The man was thrown alive into the pool of sharks kept on the compound. His screams were soon silenced as the sharks thrashed around, ripping him apart. The water turned blood red in a matter of seconds. The spectators were reminded; betrayal to DePeralta could become a life or death matter.

Jorge DePeralta was a handsome man with strong features, deep-set brown eyes, dark eyebrows and a full head of salt and pepper hair. When he smiled, his teeth were luminescent white, conveying a false image of warmth and grace. He was the ruthless king of the Cuban cocaine cartel, picking up where Pablo Escobar had left off.

Like Escobar in the 1980s, his cocaine labs produced, literally, tons of the white powder. He utilized a network of indigent peasants from poverty-stricken cities in Latin America, who worked in the labs and transported it, while willingly killing and dying for him. They were seduced with material riches beyond their belief, and intimidated with horrifying death, to keep them honest.

If DePeralta had problems finding pilots, he cultivated the most promising men and had them trained. His landing strip was long enough to accommodate large planes for heavy loads. Other drug lords thought he was crazy to have his operation so close to his home. He felt he had better control, and since he was a paranoid control freak, he had cameras, alarm systems and weapons to ensure his safety. It was like an army base. The only way to penetrate the compound was by air, but with anti-aircraft artillery and radar capabilities onsite, it was nearly impossible to breach. DePeralta had a fortress.

The Suburbans pulled up to the portico. Luisa, Jorge's wife, got in the second Suburban. She was a beautiful woman of Cuban descent, twenty-four years younger than her husband. Her parents were from Camaguey. They immigrated to the United States in the early sixties when Castro took all of their property and belongings. Humbled by their fall from wealth, they lived a quiet but happy life in freedom. Luisa was a surprise birth for her parents. They were in their forties when she was born. She had two older brothers whom she didn't know well. They were both married and out of the house by the time she was old enough to remember. Now living in different parts of the world, she had little contact with them.

Luisa was tall with long, beautiful legs, moderate breasts and a small waist. Her lips were full and naturally pouty. Her eyes were brown and seemingly large. Perfectly coiffed and manicured, she always dressed suggestively. Every man and woman, regardless of sexual orientation, stared at her. She was breathtaking.

"Juan." Jorge motioned to one of his main confidantes. "We need to talk when we get back. I need to know the status of the ether and acetone."

There had been a recent slowdown getting the ether and acetone from suppliers. They were two important ingredients needed to process the coca leaves into cocaine.

"We had a problem but I think we are back on track," he said. "We educated the right people and now the flow has started again."

"Good. We can't afford to slow down."

Bella came to the front door and looked at her brother for direction.

"Get in the car in the back," Jorge said, pointing to it.

She looked at him with an ambivalence she cultivated from years of hate and fear, before going to the rear vehicle.

Turning his attention back to Juan, Jorge asked him about the advance team they sent into town as a precaution.

"I just heard from them and the coast is clear."

Satisfied, Jorge got in the car with his wife and the convoy left the compound.

Their arrival in town didn't go unnoticed. The townspeople became electrified with the potential to make money from the generous man known as "El Tiburon". Whenever his motorcade rolled into town, the word spread like a match to a fuse. Those watching for entertainment's sake kept their distance, knowing he attracted the potential for danger.

After his bodyguards got out of the vehicles to look around and determine it was safe, Jorge and Luisa exited. Shortly thereafter, Bella got out too.

They walked to The Parrot, a secluded restaurant with an outdoor café. Walking inside they took a table in the back. There were only two people sitting at another table, who looked like tourists enthralled with each other.

Bella and Louisa sat down opposite each other with cold indifference. Neither one liked the other. Bella was only there because she had no choice. If Luisa had her choice, her sister-in-law would be dead.

Jorge gave some instructions to Juan, who went outside to supervise the others. Soon, one member of the entourage came in and sat at a table up front, to keep an eye out for any suspicious meddlers.

Before sitting down, Jorge reached under his shirt and adjusted the large knife he always carried. He left the guns to his bodyguards.

The waitress came over to hand out the menus and fill their glasses with water.

Jorge waited until she walked away. "Bella, you look very good today," he said.

"Thank you, Jorge," she replied indifferently.

"How do you feel?" he asked.

Looking up from her menu, she answered without emotion. "I feel good."

Once very vibrant, Bella had become almost lifeless for the last twenty years. She was forced into an existence she didn't want, leaving behind her husband and son. Her megalomaniac brother had threatened to kill both of them and she knew he was capable. She wasn't worried about her husband; he could take care of himself. It was her son that caused her the greatest concern. Bella had seen firsthand the violent, torturous acts of her brother. She had to make a choice between risking her son's life, or come and live a life of an indentured servant to her brother. It was a difficult choice, but sometimes to save the life of a loved one, you have to give a life, your life.

"How 'bout you, Luisa?" Jorge asked, turning to his wife.

"What about me?"

"Don't you think Bella looks extremely good today?"

Turning to Bella, she answered derisively. "Terrific."

"There is something I want to talk to you about," Bella said.

"What?" Jorge asked firmly.

"I have been with you for the last twenty-some years. I am old and I have nothing of value to offer you. Why don't you let me go back to America? I would like to see my son before I die."

Jorge sat back in his chair. His sister was the only living relative he had left. Their parents died when he was a young man. He never really knew what a close family was. Bella was gone by the time he was ten. Jorge never had anyone to admire him for who he was. There was nobody to cheer for him when he played baseball. All he saw around him were other kids with their families, laughing, hugging and loving each other. He swore to himself that someday he would know the true meaning of family.

Feeling abandoned, Jorge forged a friendship with a group of local drug dealers. Soon he was recognized for his bloodthirsty executions and the sadistic pleasure he took creating different manners of death. It wasn't long before he was the wealthy, powerful equivalent of a don in the mafia. His drug empire made him a billionaire.

"Bella, is this the way you disrespect me?" he asked. "After all I have done for you!"

"I mean you no disrespect," she answered somewhat fearfully, yet resolute. "You have taken me away from my son and my husband. I have stayed with you and been a good sister, a good friend. The least you can do is let me go back in the winter of my years and be with them. You have Luisa and your children. Just think if you were unable to see them for twenty years, how would you feel?"

Jorge listened without giving much credence to Bella. Over the years she had tried to escape his reach, but never made it any further than just outside his various compounds. Until now, it had been years since she mentioned her son, and how much she missed being with him. Jorge had told her he was dead, but she never believed it.

"I'll think about it," Jorge said, trying to placate her. "Is there anything good on the menu?" he asked, changing the subject.

Neither woman answered.

"I hear their fish tacos are delicious," he added.

"You can have that later. Why don't you try something else?" Luisa said with a smile.

"I love it when you're playful, *mi amor*!"

Bella didn't allow her revulsion to show for the two pigs sitting with her. She had been subjected to their disgusting public exhibitions of sexual innuendos for years. What they couldn't do in public, they would openly do at home, on display. Around the house you had to be careful not to walk in on them having sex. It didn't matter what room, or time of day. They were like animals. And Luisa was not quiet with her orgasms, but it allowed Bella to navigate her way around the house to avoid them.

The waitress returned to take their order. After they ate, they went out a side door which led into an alleyway that Juan had blocked off for privacy and security. Once outside, a little boy about eight years old was playing catch with one of the bodyguards. A distraction like this and lapse of security would typically result in severe penalties, but not this time.

"Oh my God!" Bella said while putting her hands to her mouth.

Jorge and Luisa turned to look at her. She had not shown that much emotion in years.

"What's wrong?" Jorge asked, concerned.

Almost in tears, she said, "He looks just like Jack when he was that age."

Jorge turned back to look at the boy, and paused. "Juan, take Luisa back to the car," he said.

Juan gave him a puzzled look before delegating the task to the guard playing ball with the boy.

Bella continued to look at the boy and remember her son, whom she had not seen since she had given up her freedom to spare his life.

Bella, Juan, Jorge and the little boy stood in the alley. There was an old rickety chair from the restaurant where apparently, the kitchen help would sit while on break. Jorge went over and sat down.

"C'mon over here, young man," Jorge said, holding out his hand.

The little boy looked frightened, not knowing what to do.

"It's okay, c'mon over."

He walked over timidly, holding the worn baseball. The stitching was frayed and coming apart.

"Do you like baseball?" Jorge asked.

He looked up at Jorge sheepishly with his big brown eyes, and nodded slowly.

"What's your name?"

"Diego."

"Diego, it looks like you need a new baseball."

Diego nodded, still afraid to say anything.

Jorge patted his lap and asked Diego to sit. Reluctantly, he did. Jorge glanced at Bella with a large devilish smile. Juan kept an eye out, hoping no one interfered. Bella looked on. She was not smiling anymore.

"Do you know about American baseball?"

"Yes, I like the Marlins," the boy said, feeling a little more comfortable.

"The Marlins. Wow! They're my favorite team too! They play in Miami, don't they?"

Diego nodded. "They're going to win the World Series this year."

Jorge threw his head back and laughed. "You're pretty confident, aren't you?"

"They have good pitching and hitting."

"Really?" Jorge said, still smiling.

Jorge reached to his side and pulled out his knife. Bella let out a gasp and Diegos' eyes got bigger as he stared at the knife.

"Let me see your ball. Maybe I can trim some of those stitches for you."

Diego handed him the ball, and Jorge began trimming the frayed stitches while holding Diego on his lap.

"Y'know Diego, my nephew used to play a lot of baseball, isn't that right, Bella?" he asked, turning back to look at her.

Bella didn't know how to answer. She didn't want to say anything to provoke her brother.

"I'm sorry Bella, I didn't hear you."

"Yes, he did."

He turned back to the boy. "What position do you play, Diego?"

"Right field."

Jorge started to laugh again. "Did you say right field?"

Diego nodded.

The ball fell out of Jorge's hand and rolled away. Turning to Bella to make sure she was still paying attention, Jorge asked her what position his nephew played as he took his free hand and placed it on Diegos' head.

"Second base," she said softly.

Jorge turned to look at the young boy. "Wrong answer, Diego."

Standing up and with a lightning quick motion, holding the little boy's head by the hair, Jorge took his knife and slit the young boy's neck, spurting blood into the alley.

Letting go of the lifeless little boy, he looked around for something to wipe his blade.

Bella cried out before Juan came to her and covered her mouth. She wobbled a little, then passed out. A couple more guards came down the alley to see if there was a problem. Juan gave Bella to Guillermo, a huge man, who took Bella back to the car. Still out, she was starting to convulse.

The other men secured the area, making sure nobody exited the one door leading to the alley.

"What do you want me to do with him?" Juan asked.

"Did you hear what he said?"

"No."

"He said right field," Jorge told him. "That's where they stick any-one who can't play. In right field. Little fuckin' loser."

"What do you want me to do with the body?"

"Throw him in the Dumpster."

"Boss, he'll be found in the Dumpster and we'll be identified."

Jorge thought for a moment. "Wrap him in a tarp and we'll take him back to the house. We could use some good fertilizer."

Finished cleaning his knife on Diegos' pants, Jorge strode back to the car.

6

Jack paused for a moment as he looked up at the Rollins Building. He had ten minutes before his scheduled meeting. He craned his neck back as a few passing wispy, white clouds moved into the azure blue sky. Always punctual, Jack was tentative about meeting with his estranged father. He took a deep breath and walked into the building.

Once inside, he saw the same security guard he had encountered the last time he was there to find Bob Lewis, the man who planted Jack's gun at the scene of a homicide. On that occasion, Jack was unceremoniously escorted out of the building and warned not to return. As it turned out, Bob Lewis didn't work for WISE International. It had been part of his ruse. Ironically, Jack was now going to meet his estranged father who *was* CEO of WISE.

As Jack approached, the guard's eyes showed a sign of recognition, but he didn't pick up the phone to call the police.

"Can I help you?" the guard asked.

"I'm here to see Ben Dublin."

"Do you have an appointment?"

"Yes, I do."

"What's your name?"

"Jack Dublin."

The guard picked up the phone and dialed the number. Afterwards, Jack was given a visitor's ID card and told to go up to the 30th floor.

When he got off the elevator, he walked straight ahead to a pair of large glass doors. After trying the doors and finding them locked, a secretary came to let him in. She appeared to be in her early forties, blonde hair, cute face, and large breasts accentuated by her dress.

"Good morning, Mr. Dublin," she said, smiling warmly. "Your father is waiting for you. Right this way." Jack followed her down the long hallway, enjoying the view from behind.

His father stood behind the desk in his almost cavernous office. "Good morning, Jack."

"Good morning," Jack answered formally as they shook hands.

"Why don't you have a seat?" Ben Dublin said, motioning to the couch.

The office was large and accentuated with dark oak. Several expensive Asian art pieces decorated the walls. The lamps on the end tables contained Asian script on their bases. Oriental carpets partially covered the dark hardwood floors. The view from where he sat encompassed a view of the Old Post Office Pavilion with the Washington Monument in the background. It was very impressive.

Once seated, Ben came over and sat down in one of the Queen Anne chairs next to the couch. Somehow, the clash of two styles worked with the décor.

"Can I get you anything? Coffee? Bagel? Donut?"

"Coffee would be fine."

"Betsy, please bring us some coffee, and some pastries too."

Jack examined his father while he gave the order to Betsy. Other than the short time they were together at the restaurant, it was the first time Jack really had a chance to take a good look at his father. He observed a man who had aged well. His gray hair was still full; his blue eyes still alert and penetrating yet warm. Lines had creased his face in a rugged, handsome way. It was difficult to think of him as a killer.

He and his father talked about the state of the world as it pertained to politics until Betsy returned a few minutes later with coffee and pastries on a tray.

"I guess you want to know why I asked you here today," Ben said while fixing his beverage.

Jack took a sip of his black coffee. "I do," he said.

"It's quite simple, really. I know you think I had something to do with your mother's death. I didn't."

Jack sat there looking at his father. He actually wanted to believe him, but the years of doubt and hate were hard to overcome. "If you didn't kill my mother, who did?"

"The investigation said it was an accident."

"I think we both know that's bullshit!"

"I found it hard to believe too, but your mother did have enemies."

Jack laughed diffidently. "My mother didn't have an enemy in the world."

"Jack, there's a lot of things you don't know about your mother, or me for that matter. Your mother and I worked for the CIA."

Jack looked at his father trying to understand what he had just said. It was the most preposterous statement anyone could have made. Growing up, his mother was always at home. He never had any reason to believe she was anything but the greatest mom in the world.

Before Jack could respond, Ben spoke up, "That's how we met."

"Wait," Jack said. "You were an international banker."

"That's what your mother and I had agreed to tell you, to keep my cover."

Jack set his cup on the table, looking at the floor for a moment with deep concentration. He brought his hand up to his face, rubbing his chin as he pondered the story. His eyes shifted back and forth while he tried to grasp the impact of what he had just been told.

"I can see from the look on your face that you find it hard to believe, but it's true, Jack. I can prove it. I…we…never wanted to deceive you, but we had no choice. It's why I was never home. I was always overseas on assignment. Look, it was a decision your mother and I made. She would leave the agency to raise you, and I would continue to work for the government. It killed me to miss your school events and things like that. I always wanted to be there, be a good father, but in the end, I knew your mother was fantastic. I knew she would pick up my end.

"I had to do it, Jack. The government owned me. It was the understanding we had, to allow your mother to leave, and be a stay-at-home mom for you. They released her from her contract."

Jack still had difficulty accepting it. If it were true, everything his life had been based on was now fiction. "Why should I believe you?"

"If I were you, I wouldn't believe me either, but it's true." Ben leaned forward, resting his arms on his knees. "I loved your mother, deeply. I was devastated when she died. I couldn't think straight. I didn't know what to do. I was catatonic. I know I should have been there for you. You had to be devastated too. I…I just couldn't help you. I was totally lost."

Jack continued to sit there, motionless. Even though his father was pleading for sympathy, there was a gut feeling, a doubt, that he was not being completely truthful.

"How did you know about Marnie and me?" Jack said, changing the subject.

"After your mother died, my contract with the government was no longer binding, so I left. I started WISE International as a small courier business. I had contacts around the world who knew they could rely on me to discreetly handle their affairs. In a few years it grew and never stopped. We now work with Fortune 500 companies and some very private businessmen, all legal. It's become quite lucrative.

"I met Archibald Prescott early on, through a client, and we became great friends. I hired his firm to do our legal work. That's when I met Marnie. I don't think I have to tell you, she was a treasure. Archie loved her just like a daughter."

"I know all about him, and how he became her father. How did you know about us?"

"When I heard about your troubles…" Ben said, sitting back. "Let's face it, Jack, I kept contacts on you. You're my son. I love you. I knew you didn't want anything to do with me, but I still cared deeply about what happened to you. When I read about your shooting, and Senator Rothschild's son, I knew there would be hell to pay. When you were at the scene of another shooting, I knew you were in deep shit. I called Archie and asked him to intercede, which he gladly did. I didn't know Marnie would be involved, but I was glad she was."

"So you arranged for my bail?"

"Absolutely!"

Jack sat there, his thoughts disorganized.

Ben smiled for the first time since Jack had arrived for their meeting. "You'd be surprised how many people I interacted with on your behalf. How come you never took the promotional exams? You would've certainly been promoted."

"I don't know. I guess I just didn't want it bad enough. Anyway, what can you tell me about my son?"

"Connor is a great kid. Hell! He's not a kid anymore. He's grown into a fine young man. You should be very proud about that. Y'know, I think I have an idea how you're feeling right now. You have no reason to feel guilty about anything. You made what you thought was the best decision for Connor. As it turns out, it probably was."

"What do you mean by that?"

"What I mean is, Connor was better off spending his time in one location. Let's face it, Jack, do you think you could have given him the love and guidance he needed while he lived three thousand miles away?"

Jack gave his father an icy, cold stare, even though he knew Ben was right.

"I know. You probably think I have no right to say that, because I was never there for you. But that's exactly why I can say it."

"I don't want to talk about this now. You still haven't told me why I'm here."

"I want to hire you."

"To do courier work?"

"No. I want you to investigate your mother's death."

"What?" Jack asked, raising his eyebrows.

"You think I murdered her, here's your chance. Prove it."

"Kind of late, don't you think?"

"I have all the money and resources you need to get to the bottom of it."

"That was a long time ago. People have died, moved on, et cetera. How am I going to get to the bottom of it?"

Ben reached for his coffee and a pastry. "I'm disappointed, Jack. I thought as an investigator, you would be up for the challenge. I'm giving you the opportunity to solve the mystery of your mother's death. Not just that, but I am giving you an open checkbook to spend as much money, within reason, to solve the case. Consider it a cold case file. I killed your mother and got away with it. Prove it! Bring me to justice."

Jack stared at his father. "How come *you* never tried to get to the bottom of it?"

"Like I said, I was devastated. I was useless. The CIA said they would investigate and get to the bottom of it. I had faith that they would. Don't forget, DNA was not available back then."

"What did they say?"

"They said it was an accident, which is the same conclusion reached by the police. I had to believe them."

Jack thought for a moment. Investigating his mother's death would be heart wrenching. He didn't know if was prepared to look at her autopsy pictures, or read the report. Maybe it was best left alone. Maybe he should remember her as he last saw her. Yet, Jack knew the evidence would convict or exonerate his father. The opportunity to find the truth was more compelling. "Okay, I'll do it. Can I hire some-one to help me and pay him a salary?"

Ben smiled. "Like I said, Jack, you can do whatever you want, hire whoever you want, I don't care. Just find the truth."

7

Washington D.C.

While heading over to the Metropolitan Police Headquarters, Jack had time to reflect. Having a chance to investigate his father and solve the mystery around his mother's death was an irresistible opportunity. At least, the distraction would help him get over the loss of Marnie.

Jack parked his car on the street in front of Headquarters. It felt strange. For twenty long, arduous years, Jack had put on his uniform and reported for duty. He truly believed in the cause of keeping citizens safe from thieves, thugs, rapists, and murderers. The camaraderie of police officers was unique. The closest comparison would be soldiers at war. While Jack enjoyed the esprit de corps, he kept a safe distance from department friendships. When he was off duty he didn't mingle with other police officers. His personal interests were different. Jack had a private pilot's license, enjoyed attending symphonies, could play classical piano, went to museums, and traveled the world.

He occasionally went to FOP-sponsored sporting events, but generally kept to himself. The only person Jack connected with was Billy D. They worked as a team in the criminal investigation unit and respected each other's privacy off the job. Jack had complete reverence for Billy.

When Jack was arrested on the spurious charge of conspiracy to commit murder shortly after he retired, he came to realize what a true friend Billy D was. He was the only officer on the department who had helped him, and now Jack was going to pay him back.

As he stood at the front desk, people who had pissed all over him were now smiling, saying hello, and shaking his hand. Jack had recently

33

made international news as a hero for saving the lives of everyone on a cruise ship in the Caribbean. He prevented terrorists from blowing it up.

"Hey Jack, how's it going?" asked Lou, the pint-sized corporal behind the desk.

"Good, Lou," Jack responded. "I'm here to see Billy D. Is he in?"

"Just saw him ten minutes ago, going up the steps. Hold on, I'll give him a call."

Five minutes later, Billy D came down and escorted Jack upstairs. They went to a small, empty office to avoid Lieutenant Merrill, the man in charge of the criminal investigation unit. The animosity between Jack and Merrill was deep. It went back to the days when he was Jack's supervisor. Jack saw him as the department sycophant. When he pushed to get Jack arrested, it was the final straw.

"What's up?" Billy asked. "You okay? I know you just came from Marnie's funeral a couple of days ago, but you gotta be feelin' pretty good these days. I've never seen anyone go from the slammer to bein' a hero in what seemed like thirty seconds!"

Jack smiled.

"You should've seen it. Lieutenant Merrill was as proud as a peacock about having you arrested. Now he just sulks in his office and makes himself scarce. Everybody in the office is lovin' it. It's like you took a dump right in the middle of his desk! It was great!" Billy eased back in his chair. "So what are you gonna do with the rest of your life?"

"I just came from my father's office."

"That can't be good. You hate him more than Merrill."

"I know, but he wanted to talk to me, so I decided for whatever reason to go hear what he had to say."

"What did he say?"

"He just told me he didn't kill my mother and I should believe it." "Do you?"

"It's funny. After all these years I've suspected him, there was something pretty believable about him today. Anyway, he is the owner of WISE International and he wants me to investigate the case."

"What case?"

"My mother's death."

Billy sat up straight. "Your mother died over twenty years ago, and it's already been investigated."

"Yeah, but there seem to be some question about how thorough the investigation was."

Billy D leaned forward. "What does it mean exactly; he wants you to investigate it?"

"He basically told me he would sign a blank check. He would allow me to use everything and anyone I can to find out if my mother died in a car accident or if she was murdered."

"Last thing I remember, you thought he killed her."

"He may have, but it would be nice to prove once and for all how she died, and whether or not he was involved."

"Sounds complicated. You may need help."

"That's why I'm here, Billy. I'd like to hire you to help me investigate my mother's death."

"Whoa, wait a minute. I've got a job, remember?"

"I'm thinkin' it's time for you to put your papers in and retire. I need your help. I'll pay you a salary you'll be pleased with. I can't promise you'll be home every night with Gloria, but you'll probably be home more than you are now."

Billy D leaned forward. "Gloria and I just separated."

"I'm sorry to hear that," Jack answered in disbelief. "You think it's temporary?"

"Nope. This is for good. She ran off with the mailman, if you can believe that!"

Jack didn't know what to say.

"She told me she wouldn't mess with my pay or my pension as long as I give her the house."

"Are you going to?"

"Hell yeah! I can always find a place to stay."

"It sounds like you have a lot of time on your hands. Will you help me then?"

"I've gotta think about it," Billy said. "You've caught me by surprise."

"Look Billy, working here will kill you. How many guys put in their twenty and then die five years into their pension?"

Billy nodded.

"This way, you come work with me, you'll get to travel some, eat better, sleep better, and get paid more. What's not to like?"

"How long, though?"

"I don't know how long it will take to wrap it up, but when we're done, I know I can ask my father to keep you on the payroll. You may not make as much money as I'm paying you for this assignment, but you'll make good money. WISE International is the best in the world. They have accounts all over the world *and* they subcontract with the military and Interpol."

"But if your dad is guilty, there won't be a job for either of us."

"I thought about that. Part of the deal will be, I take over the business if he's guilty."

"Wouldn't that be a little strange to be taking over a business from the man who killed your mother?"

"If he's guilty, at least I'll get something out of it!"

"When do you want me to start?"

"How soon can you put your papers in?"

"Jack, I love you like a brother, but I have to have something in writing. I can't just leave this job without knowing I have some job security. I have to know how much I'm gonna make, and how long I'll have a job. I need some guarantees."

. . .

Jack went back to WISE headquarters and began his orientation. Since his father was the president of the company, Jack was spared the trivial indoctrination and received his company paraphernalia to allow him access to the building. He decided to go to his father's office to interview him further.

First, Jack requested a contract outlining his understanding of their agreement. He also requested and received a contract for Billy D which provided him with a healthy salary and guarantees. When the company attorney was finished, Jack returned to his father's office.

"I need to ask you some questions," Jack stated plainly, standing in the doorway.

"C'mon in and sit down," his father said ambivalently, taking his glasses off and placing them on his desk. "Did our attorney provide you with the agreeable contracts? I felt they were quite generous."

"They were," Jack said as he took a seat.

"So, if you find I'm guilty, then you get the business?"

Jack nodded.

"If that doesn't motivate you, I don't know what will. This company is worth over a billion dollars." Ben said proudly before continuing. "I want you to feel free to ask my any questions, any time. Ask away."

"How did you find out about my mother's death?"

"I received a call from a Lieutenant Conway of the Wilmington Police. He was able to find me through channels at Langley."

"What did he say?"

"He said he had some disturbing news he had to share with me," Ben told him. "He said they recovered a body from a vehicle that was involved in an accident. The vehicle was registered to both your mother and me. I asked if they had identification of the body and he said it was a woman, but identification was difficult." Ben stopped. He took a moment to reflect as he relived the memory. The impact had only slightly diminished with time.

He continued on. "He said identification would be difficult since the vehicle had caught fire and the victim was burned beyond rec-ognition. At that point I asked if they needed dental records and he said they didn't, which I thought was strange, but then he told me the victim had no teeth." Ben maintained his composure.

Jack sat there, listening pensively. It horrified him to think of his mother's last moments.

"What did you do then?"

"I...I didn't know what to do at first. I was stunned. Who would ever do that to your mother? But, as I thought about suspects, I realized there were many potential suspects who lived all around the world.

Jack, your mother and I were involved with many assassins and terror-ists through our years in the CIA. It was limitless who could have come back for retribution. I realized there was no way I could ever find the responsible party."

"Did you try, at least?"

Ben sat straighter in his chair. His mood changed. He became serious.

"Listen, you have no idea what was going on at the time. You went to college, had no responsibilities, and banged every coed in sight, while I paid your fuckin' bills. So don't sit there in judgment of me. I told you, the government investigated it. Now, do you have any more questions?" Ben asked, trying to hold his temper in check.

"Not right now."

"Well then, you have an assignment. You still think I had some-thing to do with your mother's death, prove it! You're the hotshot investigator; let's see what you're made of. From now on, if you need something, see Bonnie in Finance or Alice in H.R. If you need to ask me more questions, make an appointment!"

Clearly, the climate had changed.

8
Belize

When they arrived home, Francisco, one of Jorge's men, carried the tranquilized Bella to bed. She would sleep until the next day. It was not the first time she had been drugged.

Jorge and Luisa walked into the spacious kitchen and sat at the counter, while their *criada*, Alda, made them a snack.

"What happened back there?" Luisa asked. She wisely maintained her silence on the way home, because of the men riding with them.

"There was an accident," Jorge answered stoically.

"What kind of accident?"

Jorge looked at his wife evenly. "You don't want to know."

Luisa stared at her husband and understood the finality of his comment. She knew not to probe any further into his business. "Bella certainly freaked out," she added.

"Bella is easily upset about things. You should know that."

"I do, but I haven't seen her this upset in a long time."

"She'll be fine," Jorge said before changing the subject. "We need to leave on a holiday soon, what do you think?"

She looked at her husband in amazement since he had become somewhat reclusive. "Honey! I can't believe I heard those words coming out of your mouth!" She draped her arms around his neck and gave him a kiss.

"You can't just stay here with me all the time. Your beautiful face should be seen in the world."

"Where are we going?"

"Where would you like to go?"

"Miami," she told him, "to visit my mother."

"This isn't supposed to be a visitation. It's supposed to be just you and me, on vacation."

"Oh Jorge, you haven't seen my mother in so long. She would love to see you. She's not getting any younger, you know," she said sadly. "We need to go soon."

"I'll think about it," he said as he began to cough violently. Recently he had begun to cough up copious amounts of blood. It seemed to be getting worse. He was reluctant to see a doctor, but he knew one in Miami who could keep his visit anonymous.

"Are you okay?" Luisa asked.

"Yeah, I'm fine," he said as he wiped his mouth.

They began eating the snack Alda had prepared. Alda was of Cuban descent. She had lived near the DePeralta family. Her parents worked on the farm for Jorge's father who was an attorney. Jorge's father, Heriberto, had inherited a 2,000-acre parcel. They raised livestock that included horses, cows, pigs, and chickens. When Castro took power, their farm was taken away from them. The DePeralta's defected to Colombia, where SeñorDePeralta had some contacts. After a few years of practicing law, Señor DePeralta became a judge. He was later assassinated by the Escobar drug cartel.

Jorge remained there to be with his mother and keep her safe. His sister, Bella, was already in the United States attending college. Eventually she was recruited by the CIA and became an operative working all over the world.

When Jorge's mother died, his only remaining family was his sister. He longed for her to help him balance his life, which was now in shambles, but she had no desire to get with her brother because he was so heavily involved in the drug trade.

He came to the United States once to approach her, but they argued terribly. He left, but not before threatening to make her life miserable. Bella had heard stories from credible sources, how Jorge tortured and murdered his enemies. He was maniacal and ruthless. Although she took his threats seriously, she felt she could take care of herself, even though she was alone most of the time. Her husband was always away on business, and her son was at college.

Juan carefully poked his head around the corner and asked Jorge if they could talk once he was done with his lunch. Jorge looked at Juan and could tell it was a topic of importance.

"Meet me downstairs in five minutes," Jorge instructed, and Juan left.

"Jorge, darling," Luisa purred, "We really need to get away. You're always involved with business. You never have time anymore, for me or Miguelito," she said, referring to their five-year-old son.

"Luisa, I hear you, but you have to understand, I run a business. It requires my attention. It allows us to live in the style we're accustomed to. I don't want to hear another word. I will decide when and where we go. We need to be safe."

At that moment, Miguelito ran into the kitchen. "Mami! Papi!" he screeched with joy as he ran to his mother. She took him in her arms and held him tight while looking at Jorge with contempt.

"Miguelito, how's my boy?" Jorge said, holding his arms open. Seeing this, Miguelito ran to his father, who picked him up. "What have you been doing today, my little man?"

"Rosita taught me about the presidents of the United States, and then we went for a swim," he said enthusiastically. "Did you know some presidents were assas…assas…"

"Assassinated," Jorge said, finishing the sentence.

"Yeah, that's the word. There are some bad people in this world, Papi."

"Yes, there are," Jorge replied, looking at Luisa. "I'm glad to see how much you're learning. You're a very smart boy and you're going to grow up to be a very smart man, a leader who will be rich!"

"Just like you, Papi!"

"You'll be even better than me," Jorge said. "Listen, I have to go talk business with Juan. You talk to your mother and I'll see you later, okay?" he said as he placed Miguelito back on the floor.

"Okay, Papi." Once on his feet, Miguelito ran to his mother again.

"I'll see you at dinner," Jorge said to Luisa, who nodded her head.

When Jorge got downstairs, he didn't see Juan but he heard him outside. He opened the front door and saw Juan talking with Julio, Jorge's son by his first wife.

Julio was twenty-five years old. He stood about five-feet-ten, weighed about two hundred pounds, and was chiseled. Jorge was bringing him into the business. So far, he was not disappointed with Julio's acumen for details. Every assignment Jorge gave him was completed to perfection. There was never a trail left behind.

"Julio," Jorge said, "when did you get back?"

"Just now," he replied. "I'm sorry I didn't tell you I was coming home, but—"

"No problem, son" Jorge interrupted. "I'm just glad you're home, safe and sound. Come, let's talk in the study. Juan, show the men where they can get some food and drink at the cottage, then meet me and Julio in the study."

When Julio got to the front door, they hugged each other. They walked to the office, closely followed by Juan. Jorge went to the well-stocked bar and poured himself a scotch on the rocks. "Would you like a drink?" Jorge asked. Each of them nodded, satisfied with whatever they got. He handed them their drinks, retrieved his, went behind his desk and sat down. Julio and Juan sat in chairs facing him. Opening a desk drawer of his ornate mahogany desk, he pulled out a Cuban cigar and held it up to see if they wanted one. They both did.

After the cigars were lit, Jorge asked Julio about his visit to Mexico. "What did you find out?"

"Our production has been cut by the Navarro family. They are buying up our suppliers and killing those that don't comply. We have very good reason to believe they are destroying our couriers and stealing our product," Julio said.

"How did you get this information?" Jorge asked.

Julio's face twisted, like he was insulted by the question. "I spoke to people."

"Who?"

"We spoke with some of the Navarro fighters we took hostage."

"You took some hostages?" Jorge asked with raised eyebrows.

"Why not? They are killing our people, so I thought I would return the favor."

"You killed the hostages?"

"Let's just say they were convinced to tell us what they knew. Then, they were released."

"Released?" asked Jorge incredulously.

Julio smiled. "Actually, you might say they were shot while they tried to escape."

Jorge took it all in and then asked Juan his thoughts.

"I think we need to beef up security for our people. If they feel they can't operate safely, the Navarro family will be able to convert them. Then we reestablish our supply lines. In the meantime, we need to send a message to the Navarro family."

"What do you have in mind?" asked Jorge, puffing on his cigar.

"We need to eliminate some of their people. Some who are in decision-making positions. Just to let them know they're not going to break us down. If we could kill Pablo Navarro, we could eliminate our problem."

Pablo Navarro was the eldest son of Domingo Navarro, leader of the cartel. He was known to be reckless and fearless. This usually provided opportunity to access, since he was a security nightmare for his people.

"How do we do this? Do you have a plan in mind?"

"I'm workin' on it."

"What about our subs?" Jorge asked, referring to the submarines they used to transport cocaine. When Pablo Escobar was making his billions trafficking cocaine, it had mostly been done by using aircraft, fast boats, trucks, and fishing vessels. As the sophistication of technology improved, it became more difficult to get cocaine into the States. Now, the drug trade was using primitively built submarines at a cost of $500,000 to $1.2 million to get their drugs to the necessary people.

These fiberglass semi-submersible subs, 50 to 100 feet in length, were painted black or dark blue, making them invisible at night and easy to elude detection. Their streamlined deck reduced its radar signature, and its exhaust system funneled its heat signature down towards the ocean, so it was nearly impossible for thermal sensors to detect them. Clearly, these subs were built to avoid detection, not out-run the police.

Usually there were four men on the boat, including skilled navigators and mechanics. Temperatures sometimes reached 160 degrees below deck where they slept and ate. There were no latrines so the men would do their business in a bucket then toss it overboard. The submarine traveled underwater with the exception of a small, encased window for the pilot to navigate. The conditions were unimaginably poor, but each pilot received about ten thousand dollars per trip, which to them was like hitting the lottery. Each sub carried six tons of cocaine, a street value of three quarters of a billion dollars, and could travel three thousand miles without refueling. Along their navigational journey were fishing boats with food and water provisions for the four men.

Juan considered Jorge's question about their subs. "More bad news there."

9
Belize

"What's the bad news?" Jorge asked, turning in his chair.
"Two of our subs have gone down," Juan said. "One has
been intercepted by federal law enforcement, and the other sank
before reaching its destination."

"Forget the one intercepted by the government, how did the other
sub go down?"

"Heavy seas I'm told, but I'm not convinced," Julio said interrupting Juan.

"Why do you say that?" Jorge asked putting his cigar down as he
began to cough violently again. He spit out a large amount of dark red
blood and wiped his mouth.

"Because I think we have a skunk among us."

"Surely, you're not suggesting I'm the skunk, are you?" Juan said
defensively.

"No, but one of your men is," Julio said confidently.

"Which one?"

"Francisco."

"How do you know that?"

"I have a paid informant who told me Francisco was seen with one
of Navarro's men in town."

"That doesn't necessarily mean anything," Juan responded defensively. "Maybe he was working Navarro's man for helpful information."

"Did he ever say anything to you about it?" Julio asked with an
eyebrow arched.

"No, I can't say he did," Juan answered contritely.

"We need to set up a meeting with the Navarros," Jorge said. "I don't like hearing about shipments being lost." Both men nodded. "We don't need to be fighting a turf battle with them. Let's set up a meeting, in Miami, which is neutral ground. At this meeting we will talk about a merger."

Juan and Julio sat listening with their mouths agape. They could not believe what they were hearing. Julio tried to interrupt. Jorge held up his hand.

"Hear me out. At this meeting we will find out as much information as we can about their operation. They will, of course, want to know about ours. We can tell them anything we want because it won't matter."

"What do you mean?" Juan asked.

Jorge deliberated. "I think they're the ones who have been setting us up and intercepting our shipments."

"We don't have any proof," Juan argued. "There are other groups forming who are trying to make a name for themselves. Maybe they're taking our shipments. If we start taking the Navarro shipments, we can expect an all-out war." There was a silence in the room. "I'm okay with that if you are," he added.

"Juan, you're starting to sound like we should just let them steal from us. What more proof do you need? This isn't a court of law. The other groups you're talking about, don't even know how to tie their shoes! Who else could be stealing our shipments?"

"Shouldn't we find out more information before we meet?"

Jorge turned his attention to his son. "Julio, this man you've been talking to, is he in a high enough position to get us more information?"

"I think so," Julio answered. "I'll need to talk to him in person, because he won't meet me in town anymore."

"Why not?" Jorge asked.

"He said it's getting too risky. I still have a way to contact him, but I will have to meet him somewhere in Mexico, near the border."

"Can he set up a meeting between us and the Navarros in Miami?"

"Probably."

"See if you can set it up for the end of next week. I need to go there and get some things checked out." Jorge drank the rest of his scotch. "I don't like the sound of him wanting to meet you in Mexico. Take some good people with you."

"Papi, I know what I'm doing. I always take a few of my men to watch my back."

"Good. I don't want anything to happen to you." Jorge began to cough uncontrollably. Julio and Juan just watched with concern. After the coughing subsided, he asked, "When can you do that?"

"I can leave tonight, and probably know something more within the next couple of days."

"Good, get back here as soon as you can. I want to know you're safe. Things seem to be heating up."

Julio looked at his father with deep concern. "Papi, it's dangerous for you in the States. You're a wanted man. If they find you, they will lock you up, and throw away the key."

"That's why I think the Navarros will meet with us. They know if I'm willing to take a risk and meet them in the States, then it has to be a safe meeting."

"They could set you up, Jorge," Juan said worried.

"I'm sure we can find out ahead of time what their game plan is, particularly if we have one of them with us."

"What do you mean?" Juan asked attentively.

"Julio, I want you to contact your informant and find out where Pablo is. Get him to the meeting. He has a wife too, doesn't he?" Jorge said smiling.

"Jorge, we have never messed with innocent family members, especially women and children," Juan said emphatically. "If you take one of them before the meeting, they will know, and it will be a bloodbath!"

"Times are changing, Juan. We need to change with them. We won't harm her; we'll just keep her for insurance."

"They won't negotiate on good terms. They'll lie to you and then wait to get revenge."

"I'm not worried. Whoever comes to the meeting will die," Jorge said calmly.

Juan sat there worried, knowing there soon would be a torrent of blood in the streets of Miami.

Julio smiled. He liked his father's idea.

"Do you have an escape plan?" Juan asked.

"I'm going to go on my yacht. We'll stay at the Epic Hotel in Miami. They have a dock there that will accommodate. If it becomes necessary, we can make a quick exit."

"It won't be quick enough. The Coast Guard and other federal police will chase you, and they will follow you in the air."

"Leave that to me," Jorge said. "It's a risk, but I'm taking Luisa with me to visit with her mother. I also have a doctor's appointment for some tests."

"I recommend you get your doctor's visit done a couple of days before the meeting," Juan said.

"Juan, I appreciate your concern. You have always been a good friend, a trusted friend. I know you will have the right people in place for the meeting. We will take down the Navarros. They won't be able to fuck with us anymore!"

10

Washington D.C.

J ack and Billy met at the offices of WISE International. Billy had already reviewed and signed his contract. He had gone through his orientation, received his appropriate badge and access information.

Jack now had his own office, two floors below his father's. Although spacious, it was sparsely furnished. Even so, his father had ensured he had an office with a view. It was nothing like the cubicles he and Billy were used to, in the Criminal Investigation Unit at Headquarters.

Billy came in and sat down in a hard back chair, facing Jack, who was sitting behind an ornate desk.

"You want coffee?" Jack asked.

"Nope, I'm good," Billy replied, looking around. "For a big-time corporation, they sure gave you a shitty office."

"Wait 'til you see your office."

Billy sat up straighter. "You mean, I get an office too?"

"Yep," Jack said. "You're in it."

"Where's my desk?"

Jack was organizing some items on his desk. "Don't worry about it. We're not gonna be here that much anyway. When we are, we can use a conference room."

"Speaking of work, what are the plans? Where are we starting and what are we doing?"

"I thought we would go up to Delaware and get some reports."

"It's the technological age, Jack. Why don't you just have them sent?"

"I don't think it's going to be that easy. We're talking about an accident that occurred twenty- some years ago. I think we'll have to go up, show our faces, flash a badge and kiss ass."

"Then what?"

"We'll see what we can find out and then make our next move."

. . .

Within three hours, they presented themselves at the Wilmington Police Headquarters in New Castle County, Delaware. They went to the front window in the public information center. After speaking with a Corporal Rosser, they waited for five minutes until a Detective Drexel met them in the foyer. They identified themselves, and told Drexel what they wanted. After further discussion, Drexel got them I.D. passes and took them back to a conference room where they waited for him to return. When he did, he had bad news.

"I've spoken with my superiors, and they said you need to get a court order for us to release any information," Detective Drexel said ambivalently.

Jack and Billy looked at each other. Jack suspected it wouldn't be easy, but now he would be delayed, and he wasn't happy about it.

"You have any ideas who I could hire to get a court order?"

"I could tell you our FOP attorney might be someone you could hire, but I'm not sure if this is his kind of work."

"Could you give us his name and number, or make a call on our behalf?"

"Okay. You ready to copy his number?"

Jack took out his phone and entered the phone number and name of the attorney; he repeated it to make sure he entered it correctly. "Could you call him, let him know we're going to call him, and put in a good word for us?"

"Sure, no problem. In fact, let me try to get him on the phone now while you're here, and then you can talk to him direct," Drexel said as he dialed from a phone in the conference room.

The attorney was Andrew Black and his office was on King Street, near the courthouse. He agreed to meet with Jack and Billy as soon as they could get to his office. As fortune had it, his schedule was clear for the afternoon.

The law office of Andrew Black was within a huge stone and marble building that had formerly housed the Superior Court of Delaware. Once the state built a new courthouse, Black's law firm bought the old building and modernized it. It was quite impressive with five Corinthian columns at the front of the building.

His office was paneled in dark walnut and furnished with tobacco-colored furniture. Black was in his mid-fifties. He was tall, with short wiry hair, bottle-black with grey at the temples. His lean frame looked like a jogger's. With deep-set eyes recessed in hollow orbits and a long nose peeking out over a mustachioed upper lip, Black gave the appearance of a well-established, capable attorney.

Once inside his office, Black sat and listened attentively to the situation Jack presented to him, taking occasional notes. "How soon do you want this?" he asked the men.

"As soon as possible. We don't want to stay here any longer than we have to. It's not that I don't like Delaware—I grew up here. It's just that we have a lot of work to do, and this is holding us up from getting started. We'd like to get back to Washington tonight."

Billy just sat and nodded.

"It will take me about an hour to put a motion together and if we're lucky, I can get before a judge today since it's Friday and they normally do sentencing, which"—Black looked at his watch—"they should be finished by now. I'll call over there and try to catch Judge Boynton before he heads out for the weekend. He's a friend of mine, and I've got another matter to discuss with him."

"That would be great," Jack said, enthused.

"Do you have a number where I can reach you to give you an update?"

Jack gave it to him.

"I wouldn't go too far, in case the judge wants to talk to you."

"We'll probably just go somewhere close to get something to eat and then come back to your office, if that's alright."

"Sounds good to me."

Jack and Billy went to the Washington Street Ale House on the recommendation of Black. Jack ordered a salad and an iced tea. Billy had a burger and a craft beer.

"What do you think our chances are?" asked Billy.

"I don't know, but I'm staying optimistic."

"Have you ever worked a cold case?"

"No. How 'bout you?"

"Nope. They put together a cold case unit, but I wasn't chosen. After all, I wasn't one of the fair-haired children."

"It'll be interesting to take a look at the file. They had to miss something and we're gonna find it."

"I'm looking forward to working with you again, Jack. Like old times. And I know how much this means to you."

After lunch, they returned to Black's office and waited. Shortly thereafter, he returned with good news: he had obtained a court order allowing them access to the file of Jack's mother's accident. After settling Black's fee, Jack and Billy headed back to Wilmington Police Headquarters.

Detective Drexel had left for the day, but fortunately had told another detective by the name of Folsom about the situation. Anticipating a court order, Drexel had researched the files, found them and had them available. Detective Folsom took the men to the same office they were in earlier and presented the files. It was late, but Folsom was working the four-to-twelve shift, and was content to sit with them until his shift ended since he was getting caught up on some paperwork at an adjacent table.

First, Jack separated the narrative, pictures, and diagrams. He decided to examine the pictures and diagrams first, while Billy reviewed the narrative. They were permitted to make copies of anything they wanted so long as they left the originals intact.

They made copies of everything, but also took the time to quickly examine the documents while they were there. By 10 P.M. they left with copies of the entire file. They were tired but decided they could make the drive back to Washington.

Once they returned to the office, Jack told Billy to get some rest and meet back at the office at 9 A.M. In the meantime, Jack went to his office and took out the autopsy pictures. Looking at the charred remains of the victim, he still couldn't bring himself to think it was his mother. Suddenly, his mind drifted to Marnie and her ghastly burns from the explosion. The pain she must have endured was unbearable. After a few moments, his thoughts returned to the task at hand.

He peered closer at the image. What struck him first, even though his father had forewarned him, was the victim in the picture.... She didn't have any teeth. Even in a fire, the teeth of a corpse remain fairly undamaged. This allowed for positive identification by obtaining dental records from the decedent's dentist. The only way it made sense for the teeth to be absent was if the victim had dentures. But his mother had beautiful original teeth. Jack neared the conclusion the victim was deliberately placed in the car to confuse the police, making them *believe* it was his mother.

Jack continued to stare at the picture trying to believe it wasn't his mother which led to another problem. If in fact it wasn't his mother, then who was it, and where was his mother after all these years? Intellectually, he knew it had to be her, but instinct told him otherwise. Perhaps after he read the report again, he would understand what happened, proving it was her. That was only half the battle.

Regardless, he had to find out who the sick, depraved person or persons were who did this. Locating the original investigator was paramount. Until Jack could talk with him to see what he remembered, he would have to risk making assumptions.

11

Washington D.C.

The next morning, Saturday, when Jack arrived at his office, Billy was already sitting on the couch in front of a coffee table where he had a cup of coffee and some papers spread out.

"You're here early," Jack said.

Billy looked up briefly from the paper in front of him. "I couldn't sleep, so I thought I would get started."

"Yeah? When did you get here?"

"About a half hour ago."

"Find anything interesting?"

"I don't know. It seems it was a slipshod investigation if you ask me, but I have to get further into it."

"What makes you think it's a slipshod investigation?"

"I don't know exactly yet, but when I do, I'll tell you."

Jack chuckled. "Thanks for the useless information."

"Haven't you ever had that cop instinct telling you something's fucked up?"

"You've been reading reports for a half hour and already you have a feeling something's not right?"

Billy just nodded.

Jack went to get a cup of coffee and then returned to his desk. "Let's take this stuff into the conference room," he said.

Shortly afterwards, they had reconvened in the conference room, laying files on the table while taking seats on opposite sides. They sat in silence for the next couple of hours, only interrupted a few times with minor questions and comments to each other, along with coffee and restroom breaks.

They wrote down pertinent questions, but didn't share them until shortly before noon.

"Did you find anything to confirm your suspicions?" Jack asked.

Billy met Jack's eyes. "I thought it was doubtful how they reached the conclusion it was an accident...and that the victim was your mother."

Jack raised a brow. So his buddy had come to the same conclusion? "Really?" he asked, his curiosity piqued.

"Yeah, I mean, where is the scientific data? What was the BAC of the victim? Were there any road defects? Were there any vehicle defects? Were there any witnesses? Maybe I missed it, but it seems this was the report of one officer. Don't you think there should be some other reports from other police officers?"

Jack sat there nodding his head while Billy talked and then said, "I did see a report that indicated the BAC was point one five, but the toxicology report didn't say whether there were any drugs or not. I also saw in the report that the vehicle appeared to be structurally sound but the tow truck driver said he smelled a fire accelerant. The investigator dismissed it, though, saying it was gasoline from the explosion of the gas tank."

"I don't know how he dismissed the gas so easily."

Jack nodded. "The thing that bothers me most is the autopsy report. It said they attempted to get the dental records from my mother's dentist but there was no further information. I would think that would be critical, don't you?"

Billy shrugged.

"I think we need to find the officer who did this investigation and see if he remembers it. We need to find my mother's dentist and see if he sent the records."

"Well, we know the officer on the report is Conway but why should we be concerned with your mother's dentist? It said in the autopsy, the victim had no teeth. Clearly, the autopsy picture shows the victim had no teeth."

"True, but I think the size of the mouth and the jaw would lend itself to positive identification, don't you?" Jack said.

Billy nodded thoughtfully.

"Also, it clearly states in the report, they requested the dental records. But it never indicates whether or not they received them, and whether or not they used them."

They sat in silence again.

"There's a lot missing from what I can see," Jack finally said. "The fact they found my mother's identification and the vehicle was registered to her is not conclusive enough for me."

"I have to agree with you, Jack, but where the hell is your mother if she wasn't killed in this accident?"

"I don't know but I'll feel a lot better if we can talk to her dentist and Officer Conway."

"I think there was another officer's name mentioned somewhere in the report. I wrote it down..." Billy quickly referred to his notes. "Here it is, Officer Waverly."

"My mother's dentist was Dr. Guzman. I went to him once when I needed a tooth pulled. His office was off of Pennsylvania Avenue in Delaware. I'll Google it and see if he's still there. Why don't you call Detective Drexel and see if we can locate Conway and Waverly? They're probably retired but Drexel seems to have an FOP connection, and they'll know where their pension checks are sent."

They took a break and met back in Jack's office. Once there, they worked the phones.

"What did you find out?" Jack asked.

"Conway retired as a major and is currently working as Vice President of Security for the Bellagio Casino in Las Vegas. Waverly left the department and doesn't receive a pension check."

"Shit!" Jack said. "He may have some good information."

"Don't worry, he's in New Orleans."

"How'd you find that out?"

"Drexel said he stays in touch with another officer still on the department."

"Did he say anything else?"

"Yeah, he said Waverly left shortly after this investigation. The officer he stays in contact with said this accident really bothered him and now he works at a bar in the French Quarter."

Jack frowned. "How'd he end up in New Orleans of all places?"

"Don't know," Billy said. "What did you find out?"

"Guzman doesn't have an office anymore. He may have retired. I couldn't find a listing for him, business or personal."

"Do you think we got all the information?"

"You mean, did we copy everything?"

"Yeah."

"I think we got everything in their files, yes."

"What now?"

"I think we have to go out to Las Vegas and talk to Conway."

Billy's eyes lit up. "I've never been to Vegas, but I've always wanted to go."

"Don't get too excited, we're not going there to gamble or see a show. We're working."

Billy looked disappointed, but with hope said, "Okay, but if we have to stay over, we should do something fun while we're there."

"We'll see, but I'm not planning on staying overnight. It's gonna be fly in, talk to Conway, fly out."

"Man, you're no fun!"

Jack just smiled. "Do you have something to do for the rest of the day?"

"Why?"

"I'm gonna work on gettin' us some tickets to Vegas. Most likely we won't leave until tomorrow, but if it changes, I'll call you. Why don't you get some of your personal stuff done, and then tomorrow we'll head to Vegas."

"Sounds good to me."

Billy took off and Jack sat in his office checking the Internet for flights. He wanted to get round-trip flights for the same day but soon realized it wasn't realistic. The flight time was about four and a half hours for a direct flight—round-trip would be about nine hours—so he made reservations for Monday with a return on Tuesday. He called Billy and told him about the travel arrangements, and they agreed to meet at 3 A.M. at the office for their 6 A.M. departure on Monday.

Jack didn't have anything else on his agenda so he decided to get Guinness, his chocolate lab, and take a ride to Wilmington. While he was there he could check out Dr. Guzman's address and see if he could find out any more information. The Internet is great, he figured, but nothing replaces checking out things in person.

A couple of hours later, Jack was in Wilmington along with Guinness. He drove to the former office of Dr. Guzman, whose office was in an upscale condo building. After walking Guinness for a few minutes, Jack kept her in the car since he was parked in front of the building and she would be in his sight.

An elderly doorman waited to ask him some questions before allowing him entry. Jack showed him his badge knowing it would gain him access.

"Can I help you?" the doorman asked.

"I hope so. Can you tell me how long you've worked here?"

"About six months, why?"

"I'm trying to find out what happened to a dentist who had an office in this building, but it was over twenty years ago."

"You need to talk to Bennie."

"Bennie?"

"Yeah, Bennie's worked here for over twenty years."

"Is he here?"

"No, but he's coming in around two."

"You're sure he's not off today?"

"No, I checked this morning to see who was relieving me and it's him."

"Okay, thanks. I'll stop back here after two."

Jack returned to the car and decided to take Guinness for a walk at Bellevue State Park in North Wilmington to kill some time. When he got back to the condos on Pennsylvania Avenue, a different doorman stood to greet him.

Jack went up to the door and the elderly gentleman approached and let Jack in. "Can I help you?"

"Yeah, are you Bennie?"

"Sure am. You must be the guy who was here earlier talking to Earl."

"I didn't ask him his name but I guess we're talkin' about the same guy. He said you've been workin' here a long time."

"Yep. About twenty-three years."

"Do you remember a dentist by the name of Guzman who used to have an office here?"

"I sure do. A shame what happened to him."

"What do you mean?"

"About twenty years ago, he was found dead in his office, right here in this building. Apparently he had a drug problem and they found him with a needle in his arm. He OD'd."

Jack remembered Dr. Guzman. He didn't seem like someone with a drug problem. "Did you know him?"

"You mean, did I talk to him? Yeah," he said, answering his own question.

"What did you know about him?"

"Enough that it came as a shock to me. He was the last person I would have thought had a drug problem. He was in good shape, always seemed happy. From what I heard he had a good family, strong marriage. There was nothing to indicate he was an addict. Nothing."

"Was there any publicity surrounding his death?"

"I think there was an article about it in the paper."

Jack nodded, pondering the information for a moment. "Is there anything else you remember?" he asked.

"No, not really."

Jack grabbed a piece of paper and borrowed Bennie's pen. He wrote down his name and phone number and slid it over to Bennie. "If you think of anything else, please call me."

Looking at the paper, Bennie glanced up and asked, "What's goin' on? That was a long time ago!"

"Probably nothing, but I'd like to know anything you can think of, okay?"

With puzzled eyes, Bennie replied, "Sure, okay."

"Thanks, Bennie," Jack said and then left to return to D.C.

12

Washington D.C./ Delaware

Jack returned to his condo in Rosslyn. He paused to look out the patio doors and admire the view of the Washington Monument before pouring himself a Glenmorangie on the rocks. Heading into his study, his thoughts meandered back to his father and mother. With his mature eyes, they now seemed to be an unlikely match. As he recollected, he couldn't recall very many acts of affection between them.

Once his computer was fired up, he examined the web for information about Dr. Guzman. After some diligent searching, he found an article in the *News-Journal* about his death. It described how police found his body with a hypodermic needle still in his arm. There were no signs of foul play. Toxicology tests would be performed, but unless there was significant information to refute the belief it was an accidental death due to overdose, it would remain closed.

The article quoted several people from the condo building, both patients and non-patients alike who knew Dr. Guzman. He was described as a kind, unassuming man who was polite, engaging and always willing to help out the less fortunate.

One employee, Sally Goodman, said she was still in a state of shock. She never had a clue about his alleged addiction. The article said she worked for him for almost eleven years.

Jack grabbed his drink, leaned back in his chair, and pondered the article. There was nothing he could discern that connected his mother's death with Dr. Guzman. After taking a sip, he returned to the article, and found the date of Guzman's death was only a couple of days after his mother's accident. Using the Internet, he found a

Sally Goodman living in the city of New Castle. She appeared to be the same age of the woman who was quoted in the article. It was late and Jack was tired. He decided to drive to Delaware in the morning. He contemplated calling Billy but decided against it. He wanted time to think about the case by himself. It was hitting close to home.

The next day, Sunday, after feeding Guinness and taking her for a walk, Jack drove again to Wilmington to locate Sally Goodman. This time he took his new BMW, a white metallic M6 Gran Coupe. He still had his Jeep, but today he preferred the BMW. It had 550 hp and could go from zero to sixty in four seconds. He loved the power and the feel of driving what felt like a jet. It was the model Marnie had always talked about.

Even though he had lived in Wilmington, Jack had never visited New Castle, a small city situated along the Delaware River. It was an old town still with original cobblestone streets. It was first settled by the Dutch in the 1600's. It's thought to be the first place William Penn landed when he came to the continent. Now it was a quaint little town with shops, bars, restaurants, Bed and Breakfast homes, and a small police department.

He stopped by the New Castle City Police and showed his badge to the officer at the front desk. He asked about Sally Goodman. Typical of small town police, they knew her.

The officer said she was a widow who was retired and usually could be found walking her dog around the Strand. When asked, the officer said he thought she had worked in a medical profession, but wasn't sure.

Encouraged, Jack got back in his car and used his GPS to find her address. He parked a short distance from her modest house and watched it for a while, trying to gain some familiarity with the surroundings. Except for the sound of horse hooves and the *clackety-clack* of a carriage passing by, there was minimal activity due to a light falling rain.

After about fifteen minutes, he decided to get out of his car and approach Goodman's house. Before he could get out, he looked in his passenger side mirror and saw a woman matching Sally Goodman's description walking a small dog up the uneven brick sidewalk. Not wanting to frighten her, he decided to let her pass before approaching her. After she went into her house, he gave her five more minutes.

Knowing from years of experience, door bells hardly work, he knocked on her door with authority, then rang the doorbell anyway.

A spry woman who appeared to be in her seventies, cautiously answered the door, opening it slightly. Peering out at Jack, she asked what he wanted.

He showed his badge and asked if she was Sally Goodman.

"She doesn't live here, why do you ask?"

"I need to talk with her about when she worked for Doctor Guzman."

"I think I need to call the police," she said defensively.

"If you feel more comfortable doing that, go ahead, but I was just there before I came here," Jack responded calmly. "Listen, the reason I'm here is because I am investigating my mother's death. My mother's name was Isabella Dublin."

Once he said his mother's name, he could see a visible sense of relief.

She opened the door with a sad smile. "Your mother was great! I'm so sorry about her death," she said as the smile left her face. "Please, come in," she said opening the door.

Jack stepped into her modest living room. She turned off the T.V. and walked toward the dining room. He followed her through the living room. Her furniture was dated but appealing.

"Can I get you a cup of coffee?"

"That would be great!"

She disappeared into the kitchen. "Do you want regular or decaf?" she yelled out.

"Regular is fine."

"I've got one of those Keurigs. They're great! I used to make a whole pot of coffee and ended up throwing half of it away," she said as she brought their coffees to the table. "There's cream and sugar if you want," she said.

"Sugar's good enough for me."

They fixed their coffees.

"I read the article about Doctor Guzman, and it said he overdosed on heroin. What can you tell me about that?"

"What does that have to do with your mother?"

"Probably nothing, but I'm trying to cover all the bases."

"I didn't believe Doctor Guzman had a drug problem then, and I don't believe it now."

"So, you think he was murdered?"

"Yes, I do."

"What makes you think that?"

"I knew Doctor Guzman very well. He was a fitness freak. He ran in marathons, ate healthy and chastised me and others for eating junk food. There is absolutely no way, in my mind, he could have been taking any drugs, let alone heroin."

"Did you tell that to the police?"

"Yes, I did," she said before blowing on her coffee.

"Who do you think would want to kill him?"

"I'm sure each one of us makes a lot of enemies over the course of our life, but I can't think of a single soul who would've wanted to harm him. He was a kind and gentle man." Ms. Goodman stood up. "Can I get you a muffin or something to eat?"

"No thanks, I'm fine."

"Are you sure? I have some delicious banana nut muffins," she said smiling.

"No, really, I'm fine." Once she sat down, he asked, "Was there anyone in particular you can remember who may have been capable of killing Doctor Guzman?"

She paused before speaking. She clearly had someone in mind.

"I don't know his name but he was Spanish. He came into the office with another man and a woman, a few days before Doctor Guzman died. He had a very intimidating way about him. He didn't have an appointment, but he said Doctor Guzman would want to see him. He insinuated they were related."

"How long were these men in his office?"

"As I think back, I think they were in there for about an hour, but I can't be sure."

"Where was the woman during this time?"

"She sat in the reception area."

"Anything in particular you noticed about her?"

"She stood out because she didn't look like any of our other patients. By that I mean, she looked like she was off the street, a drug addict. Here teeth were extremely decayed. I could smell her breath from fifteen feet away."

"What was Doctor Guzman's demeanor afterwards, do you remember?"

"Actually, I do. Y'see, Doctor Guzman was always in a good mood. He never had a bad word to say about anybody. That's why I remember. After the men left, Doctor Guzman called the woman into his office. When he looked at me, he was somber, almost withdrawn. I asked him if everything was alright and he said it was, but I knew he was lying."

"Was she on the schedule?"

"No. She was an add-on. He told me to take off the rest of the day, which I thought was odd since he was going to examine the woman, but I didn't question it. It was the last time I saw him."

"Were you able to identify these men who came into the office?"

"Like I told the officer then, I wouldn't remember them. I just saw them for a quick minute. I do remember them being sinister looking."

"Ms. Goodman, who questioned you, do you remember?"

"Yes, as a matter of fact, I do. His name was Waverly. The reason I remember is, before my husband died, I lived on Waverly Road in Fairfax. That's how I remember it," she said, proud of herself.

"Is there anything else you can think of that would be helpful?"

"That was a long time ago. I'm surprised I remembered as much as I did."

"One more thing, actually two. How long before Doctor Guzman died, did my mother visit the office?"

"I don't remember."

Jack nodded.

"You said there were two things."

"Oh yes, did my father ever come to the office?"

"I don't think so. I don't think I ever met him."

"Do you know if Doctor Guzman ever had the opportunity to send my mother's records to the medical examiner?"

"That makes three!"

Jack looked puzzled.

"You said you only had two more questions. That makes three!"

They both chuckled before Ms. Goodman answered. "He didn't have a chance, but when I was allowed back in the office, I tried to clean things up so his wife could sell the practice. One day there was a certified letter on the desk which I opened. It was the request from the medical examiner."

"What did you do?"

"I thought I would get your mother's records and send them."

"Did you?"

"I went to the filing cabinet to get them but they were gone."

"Did you tell the police?"

"I told Officer Waverly, but he didn't seem too upset about it."

"Were there any other files missing?"

"I don't know."

"When you went to the cabinet, did it look like it always did or were they in disarray?"

"They looked like they normally did."

"I guess that's all I have for now. Can I give you my phone number in case you think of something?"

She agreed and they exchanged phone numbers. As they were walking to her front door, she said, "Mr. Dublin, I thought your mother was great. She was very proud of you. She talked about you all the time. I was so sad when I heard about her accident, but I didn't have time to dwell on it because Dr. Guzman died a couple days later."

"Thank you, Ms. Goodman. It's very kind of you to say those nice things. I'm happy to hear she was proud of me."

"Y'know Doctor Guzman was Cuban too. They talked about Cuba all the time."

Jack walked out the door and down the steps. He turned to Ms. Goodman and asked, "What size was the woman who came in that day?"

"You mean the last patient? The one with the bad teeth?"

"Yes."

"She was about five feet six. Petite. I hate to say this but she was… how can I put this delicately…she was very unattractive," she said reluctantly with a half-smile.

"Thanks. You take care, Ms. Goodman."

13

Jack and Billy met at the office at 3 A.M. as planned. Jack felt bad not taking Billy with him the previous day, but at the time, he felt he'd handle it alone because he didn't want Billy to influence his perspective.

"You got everything we need?" Billy asked.

"Yep, got everything," Jack answered. "We'll take my car and park at the airport."

They loaded their bags into Jack's Jeep and started for the airport.

"What'd you do the rest of the weekend?" Billy asked.

Jack hesitated as he took a turn into the light morning traffic. "I went to New Castle."

"Delaware?"

"Yeah."

"You go to visit some old haunts?"

"No. I went to follow some leads," he said, glancing at Billy.

Billy frowned.

"Look, I figured you had shit to do, and I didn't think it would amount to much."

"Well, did it?"

"Yeah, it did." Jack then recounted every detail.

Billy just looked out the window, not saying anything.

"I know, in retrospect, I probably should have let you know I was going, and let you decide whether you wanted to come or not. Sorry."

"Y'know Jack, when you asked me to help you, and offered me the job, I was truly honored. I was honored that you thought of me as someone important enough to help you get to the bottom of your mom's death. Now I'm not so sure," Billy said as they started to turn for the airport. "I don't need charity, Jack."

"That's not why I asked you to join me. I need your help. You have good intuition. Like I said, I should have asked you to come with me."

Billy smiled. "I'm actually glad you didn't. I was busy gettin' laid."

"You asshole!" Jack said. "Bustin' my balls for nothing!"

"Well, you really should have asked me, so I could have said no, but it's alright," Billy said laughing.

After a few moments of silence, Billy asked, "Did you ask that woman, what's her name, Sally Goodman?" Jack nodded. "Did you ask her what size the woman was, who was in the office?"

"Yeah, I did."

"Was she the same size as your mother?" Billy said with raised eyebrows.

"She was. See, that's exactly why I need you. You have great instincts!" Jack said to placate Billy.

Jack parked the car and they headed for the terminal. Once they were airborne and settled in, they began talking more about Conway. They wanted to pick his brain as much as possible then find Waverly and talk to him. Most likely, they would head for New Orleans when they finished with Conway.

After discussing the case and getting some food, Billy turned to ask Jack about his dad. "You still think he had something to do with your mom's death?"

Jack sighed. "I don't know, I'm keepin' all the options open. If he had been around more when I was growin' up, I may feel different, but we didn't have a great relationship. I really don't think he had a great relationship with my mother, either. Most of the time he was around, and it wasn't much, he seemed preoccupied, like we didn't matter."

"Didn't you say he said he worked for the CIA, and wasn't a banker?"

"Yeah."

"Maybe that's why he wasn't around, and maybe it was his way of protecting you and your mother. Did he ever tell you anything about his job? Y'know, it had to be pretty intense. Unless he was a desk-jockey."

"No, we never got that far."

"Maybe you should give him a chance."

"Like I said, I'm keeping all my options open," Jack said. "What about you and your dad?"

Billy grimaced. "Not a lot to tell. My mom was a saint and my dad was a sinner. Mom cleaned houses and went to night school to become a nurse's assistant. Dad was never home, kinda like your dad. He worked in the sanitation business. He gambled, drank, and womanized."

"How do you know he was cheatin' on your mom?"

Billy looked at Jack in disbelief. "It doesn't take a rocket scientist to figure that out."

"Maybe you should give *him* a chance."

"Can't."

"Why not?"

"A couple of years ago, he found out he had cancer. He circled the drain for a couple of months, and then he died."

"Oh," Jack said, without going any further.

"Jack, y'know, if the woman in the car wasn't your mom, it seems odd your mother hasn't surfaced. So it's probably not good news no matter how you look at it," Billy said.

"Logic tells me you're right, but my instinct tells me it doesn't have to be bad news. That's what we're going to figure out. If she's still alive, I'll find her. If she isn't, I'll find out how she died and where she's buried. If my father had anything to do with it……he'll pay, one way or another."

Billy nodded. "Do we have an appointment with Conway?"

"Yeah, I thought the element of surprise wasn't necessary. It's been a long time, so I wanted him to have time to think back to the accident."

"Did he remember it when you asked him?"

"He was vague."

They sat in silence, then Jack opened up a book he brought with him, and Billy started to read the magazine in the pocket behind the seat in front of him.

When the plane landed, they rented a car and headed for the Bellagio Casino. Once they got there they checked in and went to their room. Their appointment was for 1 P.M. and since there was a time change they had a little time to spare, and decided to order something to eat from room service.

At 12:45, a man in a suit presented himself at the front door of their room.

"Mr. Dublin, Mr. Dawkins?" asked the gentleman at the door.

"Yes," Jack answered.

"Mr. Conway sent me to take you to his office. My name is Dave," he said as he held out his hand. After the men shook hands, Jack and Billy followed him to Conway's office. They small-talked on the way about the flight, accommodations, and weather.

Conway's office was located on the first floor of the hotel, down a hall where you needed a special card for entry. Once inside, they were directed to an outer office, and took seats on a leather couch.

"I feel like we're going to see the principal," Billy said.

Jack just nodded his head methodically. He was already starting to get his game face on.

They sat there for less than a minute before a tall man with a healthy tan walked in. His smile revealed glowing teeth that would make Jack Nicholson envious. He wore a suit that looked like it cost several thousand dollars and expensive-looking bright shoes to match. He was handsome, charismatic, and engaging.

"Gentlemen, I'm Evan Conway," he said, looking at Jack. "And you are?"

"I'm Jack Dublin and this is Billy Dawkins."

He firmly shook both their hands, then took a seat in a chair facing them. They did not go into his private office.

"Thank you for taking the time to meet with us. I know your time must be valuable," Jack said.

"Not a problem, although other than being intrigued by your visit, I'm somewhat perplexed as to why you want to talk to me," he said curiously.

Jack explained how they came across his name during the course of their investigation. Then he went further, telling him why it was important to reopen the case.

"So what do you remember about the investigation?" Jack asked.

"To be perfectly honest, I don't remember anything about it," Conway said, laughing lightly. "It was over twenty years ago. I can't even remember what I had for dinner last night!"

"What did you have for dinner last night?" Billy asked plainly.

Conway gave Billy a dismissive look.

"Perhaps I can refresh your memory," Jack said as he showed the accident pictures, which clearly displayed the accident scene with Conway standing in the street, next to the vehicle.

They watched him carefully review the photographs. When he was done, Jack handed him the accident report. Conway glanced at it briefly, then said, "Y'know, if I remember correctly, Officer Waverly was the primary. He handled this investigation; I just assisted."

"Do you remember how the identification was made in this case?" Jack asked.

"We ran the tag, and the woman in the car was the owner of the vehicle. She also matched the description of the victim."

Billy took a sip of water and cleared his throat. "How did you determine that?" he asked.

"We checked with some of the victim's neighbors and they described someone her size."

"That's it?"

"We didn't have DNA at that time, it was still new, but she was wearing a religious medal that was positively I.D.'d as hers."

"Who identified the medal?"

"Her husband," Conway said, turning his attention from Billy to Jack, "which I guess would be your father."

"Was there anything else particular about her identification?" Billy asked.

"She was missing her teeth. We requested dental records but they were never sent, as I recall."

"Did you determine the cause of the crash?"

"Yes, it was concluded she was traveling at a high rate of speed and was unable to negotiate the turn causing her to crash, glancing into a tree, going over an embankment, rolling over a couple of times before the car caught fire.

"We had the vehicle checked out by a mechanic to eliminate the potential of any tampering with the integrity of the vehicle."

"And?"

"There was nothing. In fact, I remember the tow-truck driver thought he smelled an accelerant, but that was unfounded."

"The brakes were good?"

"Yes, there were no problems."

They talked some more and then Jack asked Conway about the remainder of his career. He said he retired as a Major, and came to Las Vegas for a security supervisor position before moving up to Director within a few years. He said he came out west because his wife had respiratory problems and the low humidity was helpful. Jack said he hoped it worked for her. Conway told him it did for a while but she died of breast cancer shortly after they bought a house.

Jack and Billy shared condolences, then returned to business. Billy asked him if Officer Waverly had risen in the ranks as well.

"No, Joe always thought he was too good for the job," Conway said. "He was going to become a millionaire. I like Joe, but he always thought he knew more than everyone else. He had all the answers, so he left and took a job somewhere in New Orleans. I don't know what he does now."

"Is he still in New Orleans?" Billy asked.

"Don't know, but I think so." Conway looked at his watch and stood. "I hope that helps you. Here's my card. If you need anything, just give me a call."

"Thanks," Jack said, taking the card as he and Billy stood up.

"Take care gentlemen, and have a good flight. If you'd like to see a show here, I can get you some complimentary tickets."

Jack and Billy exchanged a glance, then Jack said, "No thanks, but we appreciate the offer."

"Take care," Conway said, and they shook hands.

Jack and Billy waited until they got to their room before they spoke.

"For a guy who couldn't remember shit, he sure remembered a lot of shit!" Billy told him.

Jack just nodded, lost in thought.

14
Las Vegas/New Orleans

Jack and Billy discussed the interview and came to the conclusion that Evan Conway was just grandstanding and didn't have any deceitful involvement in a cover-up. He probably let Waverly handle it, and then went about his business. Still, they left their options open.

They went out to dinner, walked around doing some people watching, and then went back to the hotel. The next morning they packed up and left for the airport. They decided to go directly to New Orleans and find Waverly, instead of going back to D.C. Thankfully, Jack had Carla, his dog sitter, watch Guinness while he was gone.

Once they arrived in New Orleans, they went to the Marriott on Canal Street. Jack decided it would be better to keep some distance from the French Quarter. The Marriott was two blocks away from Bourbon Street. Since neither one had been to New Orleans, they checked into their room, and then walked around the French Quarter to get a feel for the layout.

Their information indicated Waverly owned a topless bar on Bourbon Street. They had a physical description of him but no picture. Walking down Bourbon Street, Billy asked Jack, "Got any ideas on how we find Waverly?"

"We're going to find him tomorrow," Jack said. "I have a contact on the NOPD who is going to meet us at the hotel."

"Who's the contact?"

"A guy I went to high school with by the name of Gus Cooke. He was the last person you'd figure would become a police officer."

"Why, because he was always in trouble?"

"No, nothing like that. He was like a worm. He wore horn-rimmed glasses, was skinny, had a big nose, dressed funny and was very quiet. Everyone made fun of him. His nickname was "Beaker." After high school, he came to New Orleans on spring break, fell in love with the city and a girl, then decided to stay."

"How'd you find out he was a cop down here?"

"Stroke of luck, actually. I saw him at a conference in Chicago. It was a drug conference."

They walked into Rick's on Bourbon, a topless bar where Big Daddy's operated for forty years. Big Daddy's was infamous for its gaudy interior and the mannequin legs that swung through a window to attract attention. It had been seen in a couple of movies. Topless women paraded on stage while thirsty men, young and old, tried to imagine what it would be like to get one of them in bed. Rick's was now a man cave. It had big-screen TVs to watch sports, cold beer, and plenty of young, beautiful women who took care of your needs.

As they walked in, Jack told Billy to order him a beer while he went to the men's room. When Jack walked past one of the bouncers, a young heavyset, burly man with tattoos all over his body and large gauges in his ears, he gave Jack a defiant look. Jack looked at him and smirked, while shaking his head.

While Jack was using the urinal, he observed the same man come into the men's room and stand at the wall behind him. They were alone.

"What the fuck is your problem?" the bouncer asked belligerently.

Jack looked straight ahead into the mirror in front of him, looking at the reflection of the tattooed man. "I don't have a problem," he said.

"Why'd you look at me that way?"

Jack said, "Oh, now I understand. You think I was making fun of you. Actually you reminded me of somebody," Jack said as he pulled his zipper up and turned around.

The bouncer was now somewhat appeased, and his angry demeanor seemed to calm down.

"He looked like an asshole too!" Jack said.

As the bouncer realized what Jack said, he moved forward and grabbed Jack's shirt.

"You got one minute to get out of here!" he said furiously.

"That sounds reasonable," Jack said. With a lightning quick move, Jack brought both of his open hands up and smashed them into the bouncer's ears. The bouncer, now in pain, and slightly bent over, held both his ears while Jack gave him a quick uppercut to the jaw. The heavyset man fell to the floor. Jack grabbed his shirt and dragged him into the stall. He slammed his head on the commode, just hard enough to make it count, but controlled enough not to kill him.

Groans emitted from the bouncer who was now laying on his back. His eyes were unfocused, looking aimlessly at the ceiling, and his mouth was open. Jack leaned over and felt his carotid. His pulse was still strong but his forehead had a huge welt that seemed to be swelling rapidly. Jack got close to his face and whispered, "Hope you like your new tattoo, asshole!"

Just as Jack was getting ready to leave the men's room, Billy walked in, and surveyed the aftermath of Jack's work.

"What the fuck are you doing?" Billy asked in astonishment.

"Just giving some douche bag a little education. By the way, I don't think we better stay for the beer," Jack said as walked past Billy.

Jack walked out of the bar and Billy followed, but not before throwing some money on the table where two cold beers sat waiting for them, in frosty mugs.

"Man, you kicked the shit out of him!" Billy said, pumped up. "I hope you didn't kill his punk ass!"

"Nah, he'll be okay in a few days," Jack said nonchalantly, as they got out to Bourbon Street.

Jack was walking fast with Billy hurrying to catch up.

"Where to now, killer?" Billy said sarcastically.

"Let's go to Pat O'Brien's," Jack said. "I think it's right around the corner."

They walked to Pat O'Brien's, a New Orleans iconic bar, and sat in the piano bar section. It was occupied with tourists. Each of them ordered a beer.

"What are we gonna do now?" Billy asked.

"Have a couple of beers, look at the scenery, go someplace else and get some dinner, then go back to the hotel" Jack replied.

"What time is your friend meeting us tomorrow?"

"One o'clock."

"What are we goin' to do 'til then?"

"I don't know, sleep late. Just relax will ya?'

At 1:00 P.M. the next day, Jack received a call from the concierge stating someone by the name of Gus Cooke was in the lobby waiting for him. He and Billy went down to the lobby and didn't see anyone there who resembled a police officer or Gus Cooke. Jack went out the front door of the hotel and looked both ways when he felt someone tapping him on the back.

Jack turned around. "Are you Gus Cooke?" Jack asked.

"Jack, how are you?" Gus replied in a distinctive voice Jack recognized immediately.

"Holy shit, Gus! I can't believe it's you?" Jack asked flabbergasted, while looking at a man who had a ponytail, wire rim glasses, and ruddy complexion. He looked like he had plastic surgery on his nose.

"Who the fuck do you think it is?" Gus retorted, smiling.

"I know I saw you in Chicago a few years ago, but man, you've changed," Jack said.

"Yeah, I got the scumbag look. A nose job didn't hurt either, what do you think?"

"You definitely look the part," Jack said. "Hey, I want you to meet my partner, Billy Dawkins."

They shook hands and then Gus directed them over to a corner in the lobby which was private. There were a couple of comfy chairs there. They pulled them close to each other where they could talk privately.

"Let me bring you up to date on my information," Cooke said. "Waverly is one tough son of a bitch to get close to. I got a snitch who may be able to get us into him. There are layers of security we need to get past, but my guy is good. Our intel says Waverly is into a lot of shit. We think he's tied to a drug cartel, but we're never able to close enough to nail him."

"Did you know he used to be a cop in Delaware?" Jack asked.

"I've heard something along those lines, but it don't mean shit to me."

Jack scrutinized Cooke's words along with his expression, particularly his eyes. It was common knowledge, or at least believed, New Orleans cops were big on payoffs, and even though he felt Cooke was a straight arrow, you could never be sure.

"Gus, I gotta bring this up," Jack said simply. "We're not in our comfort zone down here. We're relying on you. Some officers could be on the take. Is there a possibility, Waverly could be protected?"

Gus paused, "Jack, I appreciate your comments. You think I'm on the take?"

"No, I'm not saying that, but not only is our safety at risk, yours is too."

"I know this city. There are cops on the take. I know this to be a fact, but I'm not, and if I know people who are, I'll take 'em down," Gus said frankly.

"I just don't want to walk into a potential deadly situation."

"I understand. Believe me; I'm not going to allow any of us to be in harm's way. You have to trust me, or we should end this now."

There was a silence while everyone looked at each other. All this time, Billy never said anything. He just let Jack talk. Clearly, this was Jack's ballgame and he was following the lead.

"Gus, I have faith in you," Jack finally said.

"Good, now let's get down to business. Waverly is a scumbag, ex-cop or not. He's been dealing in drugs, prostitution and who knows what else. There's been a rumor for a long time that he's getting his shipments from Mexico. I want to bust his ass, big time. The problem is, he never shows his face. He's insulated, tough to get to. However, your visit may be timely. I have a snitch who says he can get us in."

"Is this snitch reliable?" Jack asked.

"I haven't used him in a while, but when I did, he was good."

Cooke then went over the plan.

They drove to Iberville Street near Katie's Restaurant. The snitch was nervous about meeting in the French Quarter. They found a parking spot in Cooke's unmarked, beat-up Taurus which still seemed conspicuous to Jack. There was a little foot traffic but not much vehicle traffic. Jack and Billy looked around taking in the New Orleans architecture. Jack sat upfront with Gus, and Billy sat in the back.

"Hey look," Billy said almost laughing. "There's a midget talking to a tall, hot blonde."

"Where?" Gus asked.

"Over there," Billy said pointing to the corner.

"That's our snitch," Gus said.

"Who's the babe he's talkin' to?" Jack asked.

"You won't believe it, but that's his wife."

"What?" Jack said in disbelief.

"I never could understand how tall beautiful women went for midgets," Gus said.

"I can't either," said Jack.

"I can," Billy said.

Gus looked at Billy in his rearview mirror and Jack turned around to face him.

"How the hell do you know?" asked Jack.

"It's easy. When they're nose to nose, his toes are in it. When they're toe to toe, his nose is in it!"

Gus laughed and Jack smiled, shaking his head.

Gus pulled the car out of its spot and began driving in that direction. Pulling the car close, Gus called out, "Hey Shortstack!" The midget looked and then walked over to the car and got in the back, sitting next to Billy.

"These guys are from Washington D.C. and they want to talk to Waverly. You *know* I want to talk to him too, but for other reasons. Can you get us in?"

The short man's real name was Carmen Immediato. He was an icon in the Quarter. He was always around the bars and known for his penchant for hookers. Usually, that's how Cooke paid him, by getting him blowjobs from hookers he kept from getting busted. They paid him back with favors. He said he never messed with them, but it was an innovative way that allowed him to get information without using Department buy money, which was always in short supply.

"I can get you in but it's goin' to cost you," he said.

"How much?"

"You need to set me up with Ruby."

Gus said Ruby was a stripper who sometimes went a little too far and would get caught hookin' and dopin'. She was about five feet six, slender build with a great body and pouty, ruby red lips.

"That can be arranged, but, you have to get us in. I want to know there are no weapons."

Shortstack started laughing. "You gotta be kiddin' me man. No weapons? Fuck, there's always gonna be guns. Man, how long you been around?"

"Don't fuck with me Shortstack! You know what I mean. We have to get in there before they can get to their guns. If they start shootin', I'm gonna shoot your little ass first!"

"Calm down, man. Ain't gonna be no shootin'. I'll take care of it. You think I wanna get shot. You gotta protect me. After this goes down, I may have to disappear for a while. Waverly could kill me."

"Not if he's dirty. If he's dirty, he's going away for a long time."

15

New Orleans

They dropped Shortstack off on Canal Street and then went to the Quarter. This allowed them to get set up. Shortstack was visibly nervous about being seen with Gus before the meeting. Waverly had long tentacles working in the city, and no doubt, some were cops.

The three of them took positions down the street from where Shortstack would come out of Rick's. If he wasn't wearing his hat, Waverly was not there.

They waited for an hour before Shortstack came out into the street. He was wearing his hat.

Gus, Jack, and Billy started for the crowded bar. They walked in and asked to see Waverly. Nobody remembered Jack, but they seemed to know Gus without acknowledging him. It was a different time of day from when Jack and Billy were there before, and a different crew was working. They were told to wait.

Finally the man at the door got their attention and pointed to another bouncer in the back who was waving at them. They walked back to him and he opened a door that led to a stairway. They ascended the stairs and knocked on another door at the top. The door was opened by a large man with tattoos and a ponytail who ushered them in. They were led into a landing where the windows, which appeared to be open from the street, were actually façades. You couldn't see out to the street. They followed the man down a hallway to yet another door. He knocked on and another large bouncer opened the door and let them in. They walked into a room that was like a large living room and were told to take a seat anywhere. Cameras from all four sides of the room discreetly monitored their moves.

They waited a few minutes before a tall, slender man walked in. He was wearing tan pants with a Caribbean-style shirt. He wore a pair of shaded glasses and had a pencil-thin moustache, but what stood out was his toupée. It was wiry and seemed like someone had just plopped it on top of his head. He pointed at Jack and asked him to join him over at a bar that was at the other end of the room.

Jack stood up, looking curiously at Gus and Billy, and went over.

"Sit down," the tall, slender man told Jack.

Jack pulled up a barstool and sat facing Waverly. He found it difficult not to look at the toupée. It appeared as if it was made from pubic hair.

"Would you like something to drink?" Waverly asked as he poured himself a Glenmorangie scotch over ice. Jack wondered if Waverly's choice of drink was coincidence.

"No thanks," he replied.

"I understand you want to talk to me."

"I do."

"I didn't do it," Waverly said, looking at Jack stone-faced as he held his hands in the air. He then started to laugh. "I'm sorry," he said, calming down. Waverly got a serious look on his face. "You're the man who almost killed one of my bouncers."

Jack looked Waverly dead in the eye. "Maybe your bouncers should know who they're fuckin' with before they open their mouth."

"I don't appreciate anyone who fucks with any of my men."

Jack sat calmly and listened. Waverly was important to him. "I apologize if I offended you," Jack said while deliberating. "If I had it to do it over...I still would have kicked his fuckin' ass!"

They stared at each other for a few moments before Waverly started to laugh. "I like you. You're a tough motherfucker! What would you like to ask me?"

Jack looked over at Billy who sat there waiting for a cue. Jack held out his hand and Billy came over with a folder and handed it to Jack before going back to sit down.

"You used to be a police officer, right?"

"That was a long time ago," Waverly said, "before I got smart."

"Well, it was a long time ago there was a fatal accident that you investigated, and that's what I want to talk to you about."

Waverly continued to give Jack the cold stare of a man who placed no value on life.

"In 1991, you and another officer investigated a fatal accident on Rising Sun Lane."

"If you say so."

"Well, you did," Jack said before handing him the accident report. "Maybe this will help you remember."

Waverly took the report, still staring at Jack. Finally, he began to look at it with disguised interest. "I don't remember this. Hell, it's been over twenty years and three wives ago. What's the big deal, anyway?"

"The big deal is," Jack stated with an edge in his voice, "the victim was my mother."

"Sorry about that, but to me it was just another fatal accident," he said callously.

Jack's eyes pierced Waverly. "You must remember something about it. How many fatal traffic accidents did you investigate? I'm gonna guess and say, maybe two."

"How'd you come up with that number?"

"Because shortly after this accident you quit the police department. You only had nine and a half years on."

Waverly pondered the statement. "Anything else?"

"Yeah, you left because you felt you were better than everyone else. You felt there was more money to be made here in New Orleans. Why work shiftwork and make a peasant's salary, right?"

"You got that right. Those poor bastards putting their lives on the line, working shiftwork, gettin' paid next to nothing, and then havin' their personal lives all fucked up. Why? So Joe six-pack can go to his meaningless job, drink and barbeque on weekends while raising a family? Do you think people appreciate it? If you do, you're living in a fantasyland."

"Is your mother still alive?" Jack asked.

"No."

"Hopefully she didn't die in an inferno like mine did, where the only way they could hope to identify her is through dental records."

"What is it you want to know?"

"The woman identified as my mother had no teeth in her head when they did the autopsy. She was identified by a religious symbol she wore around her neck, and the registration from the car. Do you remember anything about that?"

"Vaguely."

"What can you tell me?"

Waverly began to look at the ceiling as if the answer was hidden there. "Let me look the report over again," he said, then read the report in earnest. "I think I clearly stated everything I knew then, in the report. The tow-truck driver said he smelled an accelerant, like gas, but it was determined the smell came from the gas tank explosion. An examination of the vehicle revealed the brakes were faulty and may have been the leading cause of the accident."

"The brakes caused the accident?"

"I didn't say that. I said they *may* have been the cause."

"And the identification of the victim, don't you think it was weak? I mean, c'mon, the victim had no teeth. How could anyone really know who it was? Dental records wouldn't mean shit."

"Let me ask you this, Sherlock. The car was registered to your mother. Nobody else was reported missing. The physical description matched your mother. The religious medal around the victim's neck was your mother's. I'm gonna take a wild-ass guess, but I bet you haven't seen your mother since. Am I right?"

Jack just looked at him.

"I thought so. So tell me, Einstein, who the fuck could've been in that car, if it wasn't your mother?"

Jack looked into Waverly's face and eyes, hoping for some type of clue. His police intuition told him Waverly was lying about something, but he didn't have any way to prove it.

"Maybe you have some ideas about whose body was in that car," Jack said.

"You think I'm clairvoyant? Let me tell you something, I think it was your mother in the car. Why do I say that? Because there is nothing else that points to anyone else."

"What about Doctor Guzman?"

"Is that the drug addict dentist who happened to die with a needle in his arm?

Jack nodded.

"How does that relate to your mother?"

"You tell me."

"I don't have a fuckin' clue."

"I think you do," Jack said.

"Man, it's been years ago. How would I know?"

"Because you were the primary investigator."

"So?"

"You seem to be a reasonably intelligent man. So a woman dies in a fiery accident. There are no plausible means to identify her body. How would you identify her?"

"Teeth."

"Exactly! But wait, this woman doesn't have any teeth. So let me ask *you*, Sherlock, doesn't it seem a teensy, weensy bit suspicious?"

Waverly sat without responding, looking at Jack.

"Wouldn't a reasonable, prudent investigator think to himself, *Holy shit! Why is this woman with no teeth out driving on back roads?* Answer that question, you fuck!"

Waverly's men started in their direction until Waverly held up his hand.

Waverly just smiled at Jack. "Y'know, you seem a little upset and I'm going to overlook those last comments. I'm sorry your mother died in an accident, but I have nothing further to say."

Jack stood. He took a card he had with his name and phone number on and handed it to Waverly. "I would appreciate it, if you come to your senses and remember anything, to give me a call. You need to do the right thing."

Waverly took the card and placed it in his pocket. He waved to one of his bouncers. "Show these gentlemen out."

Jack, Billy and Gus walked back to the car. Nobody said anything until they got in. Gus drove them back to their hotel.

"I'm gonna nail that guy," Gus said, "one way or another."

"Jack, I think I heard most of your conversation," Billy said. "I heard a couple of things I found interesting."

"Like what?"

"Well, for starters, he contradicted Conway. He said the brakes were faulty. Conway said there was nothing unusual about the brakes."

"Yeah, that's true," Jack replied.

They pulled up in front of the hotel and Gus let them out. "What's next on the agenda for you guys?"

"I think we'll head back tomorrow," Jack said. "I don't think Waverly's gonna call me with anything."

"Don't worry, I'll stay on it. If anything develops I'll get in touch with you."

"Thanks, Gus."

"Billy, nice meeting you."

"You too," said Billy.

16

Belize

Jorge and Juan were sitting in Jorge's office discussing the state of the drug trade. They were doing well even with the recent cost suffered from the loss of the two submarines. They had wisely invested money in businesses, mostly in South America, but also in Europe. The United States was not receiving any of their investment dollars. The trail could lead back to them no matter how many shell companies they had. It was too risky. For now, they were content with profits supplied by the drug-hungry Americans.

Jorge's cell phone buzzed. He reached into his pocket and saw it was Julio calling.

"It's about time you called," Jorge said, answering his phone. "You had me worried."

"It's nice to finally talk to you, Jorge," the voice of Pablo Navarro said. "I'm a great admirer of yours."

"Where is my son?" Jorge demanded, looking at Juan whose face reflected shock.

"He's here. He's fine."

"I want to talk to him."

"In a minute. He tells me you want to meet with me in Miami next week. Is that correct?"

"Yes."

"I think that's a good idea. Any particular day or time?"

"Next Thursday," Jorge said.

"I think I can do that. First, some ground rules. You can bring one person and I will bring one person. I don't want any trouble.

Your reputation precedes you, Jorge. No guns. If I get wind that you are planning something other than a peaceful meeting, I will not be there. Let's not bullshit ourselves—I think we have a lot to offer each other."

"Let me talk to my son," Jorge said through gritted teeth.

"Just a moment."

Within a minute, Julio came to the phone.

"Papi?"

"Julio, are you alright?"

"Yes, Papi, yes, yes."

Before Jorge could ask anything else, Pablo Navarro took the phone.

"As I said, Jorge, Julio is fine and being treated well. He'll be returned to you at the meeting," Pablo assured him. "What time and where are we going to meet?"

"I will call you on this phone, Thursday morning, and let you know," Jorge said, mindful he could be set up if he mentioned the venue early. "If anything happens to my son, you will be sorry you were ever born."

Pablo laughed. "Jorge, you have nothing to worry about. I don't want to do anything to jeopardize our meeting. I think we're going to make a lot of money together. Talk to you next Thursday," he said, then hung up.

Jorge looked at Juan, pausing before he spoke. "Julio and I had a signal. If he was ever detained by anyone or any group, and I was able to speak to him, he would say the word 'yes' three times to alert me he was in fear for his life. We felt this was one way to communicate without suspicion from the captors. He said it three times."

"What are we going to do?"

"First, I want you to assemble everyone out at the shark tank. Make sure Francisco is there."

"Then what?"

"I'll take it from there."

Shortly afterwards, Jorge walked outside to the shark tank. There was a high level of excitement mixed with fear from the thirty or so men waiting. "El Tiburon" had the look of death on his face. They stood away from the shark tank, fearful they would be thrown in.

The shark tank was a large aquarium submerged in the ground approximately fifty yards from the main residence. There was a four-foot-high Plexiglas wall around it with an access door at both ends. Jorge wanted to protect Miguelito from climbing in. Four tiger sharks were lurking in the water, no doubt interested in the human activity. Buckets of chum were placed next to the tank. It was close to feeding time.

Jorge walked over to the men and began pacing back and forth, occasionally glancing at each of their faces. Juan stood to the side with a roll of duct tape in one hand and several ten-inch strips of medical rubber tubing in his other hand. Next to him was a chainsaw.

"There is one thing I will not tolerate and that is disloyalty. You men are well taken care of and so are your families. Every once and a while, I will ask you to do me a small favor, and when you do, you are compensated very well for it. Most of you lived in poverty when I found you. Now, you and your families are living a good life. Why would any one of you decide to betray me? There is a price to pay for this disloyalty." Jorge turned his stare at Francisco. "Why would you do this to me, Francisco?"

"Boss, I don't know what you're talking about," Francisco said nervously. He had a wide-eyed stare and was sweating profusely. He started looking around for someone, anyone, to defend him.

"You were seen talking to the Navarro family and now my son is being held hostage."

"I didn't have anything to do with that, I swear!"

"Take him over to the shackles," Jorge directed the men standing next to Francisco.

"NO, NO!" Francisco shouted as several men wrestled with him, happy to no longer be suspects.

Francisco, kicking and fighting, continued to scream. He knew what was coming next. The men placed him face-up in shackles in a pit. It had been used many times before. It was only three feet deep and about twenty feet in diameter. Sometimes Jorge would place the condemned man face-down, take his knife and make several incisions on the man's back, drawing blood to attract the vultures. Then he would leave the man there to be eaten.

Vultures are very meticulous. They leave no meat on the bone.

Today, Jorge was impatient. He wanted to exact an immediate revenge and he wanted to send a message to everyone assembled: Hell exists on Earth!

"Juan, tape his mouth," Jorge instructed as Francisco continued to beg for mercy, calling Juan's name. "Put tourniquets above the elbows and knees."

Juan did as he was told, and the men began shouting and cheering in a bloodthirsty frenzy. They chanted, "No mercy, no mercy." Jorge pulled the chord and the chainsaw came to life. With each squeeze of the throttle, it sounded like that of a bloodthirsty predator, gnashing its teeth, salivating in anticipation of tasting flesh and blood, while tearing through to the bone. The sound of the chainsaw made the men even more ravenous.

"Here, Juan, you can have the honor," Jorge said shouting, while looking at him intensely. Juan took the chainsaw, returning the stare without reservation. "Start by cutting him below the right elbow, then below the left knee."

Juan moved into the pit, looking down on Francisco who was writhing in the shackles. His eyes were wide open as if they were going to pop out of their sockets; his screams were muffled behind the tape. His chest heaved up as if he had the strength to break the bind that would temporarily keep his soul tied to the Earth.

Without hesitation, Juan moved in like a barbaric surgeon cutting into the flesh and bone below the right elbow. Blood and small splinters of bone took flight, and like flock, sprayed Juan's clothes as the men continued to cheer. The blood didn't flow from the opening now visible in Francisco's arm. The tourniquet was serving its purpose. After all, Jorge didn't want Francisco to die yet. There was more to come.

Juan looked at Jorge for permission to proceed. Jorge nodded. Juan continued with the left leg below the knee. The muffled screams were now less extreme. Francisco was losing consciousness. He had become delirious.

Jorge walked over and shouted in Juan's ear to turn the chainsaw off. Once that was done, Jorge kneeled next to Francisco whose eyes were now staring unfocused at a heaven still out of reach. The blood vessels were bright red from the straining he did, trying to resist. Jorge didn't want him unconscious. He wanted him to be aware of what was happening. He took a syringe and injected Francisco with a drug that brought him back to a conscious state.

Once Francisco came to, he was unshackled. There was no fight left in him. A few men carried him over to the shark tank as instructed. Jorge grabbed the ragged, detached arm and leg by the wrist and ankle, and carried them over to the tank. Francisco was propped up so he could look into the tank where the sharks were gathering, occasionally breaking the surface with more than their fins.

Jorge had a demonic look on his face. It was a look that had become a constant reflection of his twisted, monster psyche. He loved these moments. He was invincible. He was the Devil!

"Do you see the sharks, Francisco?" he asked, smiling. "They have come to greet you. Can you say hello?" He took the ragged end of the man's detached arm and starting waving at the pool of sharks. "Hi there, Mister Shark. How are you today?" Jorge said, imitating a little boy.

Francisco slowly closed then opened his eyes. He was desperate to die, to end the agony.

"I think they're smiling at you, Francisco!" Jorge said mockingly before throwing the arm into the tank. As he did, the sharks thrashed and fought for the appetizer. "Oops, sorry 'bout that, Francisco. At least you're still a leg up!" Jorge laughed madly at his own sick, twisted joke. The men watching began to laugh carefully as well.

"Say goodbye to your leg, Francisco," he said as he threw the leg in. A second appetizer.

Jorge then looked at Francisco like a man possessed by Lucifer himself.

"You are a scum-sucking traitor, and you are going to die a death reserved for people like you." Jorge turned to the crowd. "What should I do?"

"Feed him to the sharks!" they shouted in unison.

"Do you hear that, Francisco? They agree with me. Now you are going to hell!" Jorge said maniacally. "Take the tape off his mouth. I want to hear him scream!"

The tape was removed, but Francisco had no pleas for mercy. He appeared to try and gather enough spit to project at his executioner, but his mouth and throat were desiccated.

"Throw him to the sharks!" Jorge shouted.

Francisco's body was hoisted and thrown into the tank. The tiger sharks moved in and began fighting for every morsel of flesh. The pool turned red with blood. There were no screams. The only sound was that of the thrashing water. Within minutes the water calmed down. Body parts floated to the surface. Soon, the men returned to their posts.

"Get cleaned up and meet me in the study," Jorge told Juan as he walked quickly toward the house.

17

J uan met Jorge in his study.

"I think that went well, don't you?" Jorge asked, smiling, while lighting a cigar and propping his feet up on the desk.

"I think if anyone is thinking about helping the Navarro family, they'll think twice," Juan answered.

Jorge nodded. "What are your thoughts about how to proceed with the Navarros?"

"We have to be careful. They have Julio and we don't want to do anything to put his life in any more danger than it already is."

"Those are my thoughts exactly." Jorge took a puff of his cigar and offered one to Juan, who accepted.

"The meeting in Miami. I think we should stake out a place and keep an eye on it. Even though I won't tell them where it is until the day we meet, I think we need to send some people down to Calle Ocho to listen to any talk."

Calle Ocho, or Eighth Street, is a street in Miami famous among exiled Cubans, where plots to overthrow Castro were the daily topic of conversations. It's also known as Little Havana.

"Do you have an idea where we're going to meet them?" Juan asked.

"I was thinking about Versailles but I'm also thinking about La Carreta," Jorge said. "What do you think?"

"I think La Carreta would be better," Juan said as his phone rang. "Who is this? Oh! Mr. Waverly, what's goin' on?" Juan listened intently, looking at Jorge occasionally. "Okay, let me get back to you," he said as he ended the call.

"What did he want?"

"You're not going to believe this, but he had a visitor today."

"Who?"

"Your nephew."

"What did he want?"

"Waverly said he and another guy were there to ask questions about your sister's death."

Jorge paused while looking at his cigar as he rolled it between his fingers thoughtfully. "What did Waverly tell him?" he asked.

"He said that he told him nothing, even though they had police reports to contradict him."

"Y'know, Juan, I think Waverly has outlived his usefulness. I can't risk having him talk to my nephew and the other investigator, or any investigators for that matter. We need to send some of our people in New Orleans over to visit with him. I want him dead by the end of the day," Jorge said, coughing between puffs off his cigar. "Can you handle it?"

"No problem. I'll make sure he's dead before the sun comes up. Any idea how you want it done?"

Jorge took a moment to consider. "He always seemed to enjoy trying out new shipments. Make sure they give him a hot load, one that's pure enough to send him on his way. I don't want a mess or questions from the local police. Make it look like he did it to himself."

"I've got just the right guys to do it."

"One more thing. My nephew is not gonna stop there. I don't want to kill him yet, but he needs to be distracted. I heard he has a son who lives in Washington, D.C. Last I heard, he was college age. I want you personally to go there, find him and bring him back here."

Juan look overwhelmed. "That's not the easiest thing to do," he said. "I mean, you can't just go into the United States, pluck somebody off the street and bring them back here. It's not that simple."

"It's not simple," Jorge acknowledged, "but it can be done."

"It can be done, but I'm gonna need some time to find out about him. You know, where he lives, where he goes to eat, things like that."

"There's a ten million-dollar bonus for you, if you can get it done."

Juan seemed disinterested in the bonus. "What about Miami? Am I going there with you?"

"Yes, I want you there."

"Holy shit, Jorge! I can't be in two places at the same time. Don't forget, you said something about getting Navarro's wife and bringing her here, too."

"Forget about her. They're gonna have her guarded to the max now that we know they have Julio," Jorge said, putting out his cigar. He went over to the bar and fixed himself a Gentleman Jack on the rocks. "We'll have to wait for her. If they fuck with Julio, we'll get her, and she won't be the only one who'll suffer."

"We only have a week's time."

Jorge nodded. "Here's what you'll do. Give the instructions to our New Orleans people. Then get on a plane to Washington. Take a couple of our best guys with you. Find out what you can about my nephew as quickly as you can. Set up a trap and get him. Charter a private jet; I don't want our jet to be seen in the States. It'll draw attention. Get him on it and bring him back."

"You make it sound so easy. It won't be. There could be complications."

"What complications?"

"It's endless, Jorge. And you know it."

Jorge smiled. "Juan, you are my most trusted friend. We've been through a lot together. We've seen this business grow beyond our wildest dreams. Do you remember the time we rode our motorcycles up to the judge's limo in midday traffic and emptied our machine guns? Then we had to hide out in the jungle for a week!"

Juan couldn't help but smile at the memory.

"Nobody has bigger balls than you! You can do it!"

"Those were different days, Jorge. We were much younger. Now my balls hang down to my knees!" Juan said, half laughing. "Why me? Why can't we send some of our best guys to get the job done?"

"Because you need to supervise. You don't need to get your hands dirty. I just want you to make sure it's done right."

"Why do you want your nephew's son? You know that once we get him, it's only gonna make your nephew more eager to find you."

"Exactly!"

"That's what you want?"

"Absolutely! I want him to come here so I can see the look on his face when he finds out his mother is alive, and that she's been here for twenty years! And after all I've done for her; I want to see that miserable, ungrateful fucking bitch watch as I feed her son to the sharks!"

18

New Orleans

They entered the hotel and decided to have a drink at the bar. Jack ordered a Glenmorangie on the rocks and Billy ordered a Dixie beer. They sat there for a few moments taking in the surroundings. The bar was not crowded. At the other end of the bar was an overweight man in an ill-fitting suit talking to an attractive woman half his age and one-third his weight. She continued to smile as he bought her top shelf drinks with the intention of taking her to his room. It was destined to become an ill-fated seduction.

"What's next, boss?" Billy asked while sipping his beer.

Jack ran his hand through his hair. "I really don't know at this point. I know Waverly's dirty, but I don't know if he knows more about my mother's death that he's just not telling."

"I'm telling you that dude's got so much dirt on him, it would take a jackhammer to hack it off."

"I know, but what can we do at this point? I doubt I'll get another chance to talk with him." Jack took a sip of his scotch. "Got any ideas?"

Billy pondered the question. "I don't know, but I think we gotta hang around a little bit longer. I feel like something's gonna break."

Jack smiled. "Thanks for sharing that voodoo bullshit piece of wisdom!"

"C'mon Jack, what've we got to lose? We may as well stay here a couple more days and see what happens. You know if Waverly is as dirty as we think, he's gonna make some calls, and there's gonna be some activity. We're gonna get a call. I feel it!"

They sat in silence for a few moments.

"Y'know, I find it very suspicious that they were able to get that investigation past supervisors. I mean, c'mon, how could a corpse drive the vehicle? It's a definite homicide," Billy said.

"People were paid off."

"Waverly definitely was. He's probably still working for the same guy who paid him off. I don't know what to think about Conway."

"As I think about it, an autopsy would have shown whether the victim was dead or alive when the vehicle caught fire. When we get back, we need to read the autopsy report again. I don't recall seeing that issue addressed."

"Me neither, but we had so much information to sift through in a short amount of time."

"Even so, I think it would have stood out."

"I tell you what," Billy said, "there's a lot of shit goin' on with this investigation."

"And Waverly is the key."

Billy nodded. "I wonder how far up the chain this cover-up goes?"

"Who knows, but we've gotta find out."

Jack and Billy got a table, ate dinner, and then went to bed.

. . .

At 3:30 A.M. the phone rang in Jack's hotel room.

He looked over at the clock and answered the phone. "This better be good, Billy."

"It's not Billy, its Gus. I'm out front of your hotel. You need to get dressed and meet me downstairs as soon as possible. I just got a call. Waverly's in some kind of trouble. I don't know the specifics but it doesn't sound good. Hurry up!" The phone went dead.

Jack called Billy and told him the situation and they both hurriedly got dressed. They made it downstairs in five minutes.

Gus was alone. As soon as they got in his unmarked car, they drove over to a beautiful home on St. Charles Avenue. They arrived within minutes of leaving the hotel. The house appeared dark. Once they got out of the car, Gus led them around back through a gate. Shortstack was standing at the back door and let them in.

"Where is he?" Gus asked.

"He's upstairs laying on the floor next to his bed," Shortstack answered.

They rushed up the stairs, turning on lights as they went. Waverly was lying next to his bed surrounded by drugs, syringes, and other paraphernalia. Lying on the bed was a once attractive blonde-haired woman, naked and beaten. Her body suggested she was a dancer at the club. Blood covered the sheets.

"Try not to touch anything," Gus said. "I'm gonna have to call this one in, but you may want to see if you can get anything out of Waverly. I think he's got one foot in paradise."

Jack looked at Gus and realized this would be his last chance. He kneeled down next to Waverly and pulled up into a sitting position. He was barely alive.

"Waverly, Waverly!" Jack said as he shook the body, trying to get a response.

Waverly just made a gurgling sound, but his eyes appeared to be focusing on Jack.

"Waverly, remember me? I'm Jack Dublin. I talked to you yesterday about my mother. Is she still alive?"

Waverly dropped his chin to his chest. Jack shook him again

"Waverly! Is my mother still alive?" Jack said louder, still shaking him so he could look into his eyes.

"Jack, try another question," Billy said. "Ask him where she is."

"Where's my mother?" Jack asked louder, losing the ability to hide his frustration.

Waverly looked at Jack and weakly said, "Puh-leez."

"Fuck you, you bastard. Tell me where my mother is!" Jack said as he shook him more violently.

Waverly gave Jack a final look and said, "Puh-leez."

Once it was apparent Waverly was dead, Jack lowered him to the floor and stood up.

"Well, I guess I'll never know. That scumbag is taking it to the grave," Jack said, pinching the bridge of his nose.

Maybe he wasn't saying 'Please,' maybe he was saying 'Police,'" Billy said.

"What difference does it make? I'm not any closer to the answer."

"Guys, we gotta get going. I'm gonna have to let dispatch know about this. It would be best if we weren't here when patrol arrives. Shortstack, you need to get out of here too. I'll just tell them I received a tip and that I'm on my way here."

"You giving us a ride back to the hotel?" Jack asked.

"You may want to take a taxi. I'm gonna be here a while. I'll call one for you."

"Tell them to pick us up at the corner," Jack advised.

Jack and Billy left the house, while Gus and Shortstack stayed behind to sanitize the scene. Jack and Billy walked to the corner and waited. A patrol car rolled up next to them and asked what they were doing in the area at that time of the morning. They told the officers they were waiting for a cab. After providing their drivers' licenses and retired badges, the officers asked how they ended up on St. Charles Avenue.

"We were on Canal Street and decided to walk around," Jack explained. "We continued to walk and before we knew it, we were lost. Finally, after trying to find our way back, we decided to call a cab."

"What brings you to New Orleans?"

"Just some place we wanted to see. We've never been here before," Billy said before adding, "We like jazz, good food, and Southern women!"

"Looks like your cab is coming down the street," the cop riding shotgun said as a Checker cab approached.

"You guys take it easy," the driver said, pulling away.

Jack and Billy got in the cab and returned to the hotel.

"Let's get some sleep, get breakfast, and find a flight home," Jack said morosely.

Billy nodded. "See you in the morning. What time?"

"Eight."

. . .

They left New Orleans on a direct flight to Washington, D.C. Both Jack and Billy were pretty quiet since getting on the plane. They talked sparingly about the case at breakfast. Neither one had anything encouraging to say. It was a foregone conclusion—Jack's mother would never be conclusively identified as deceased or alive, except legally.

Jack sat by the window and looked at the earth below, pondering his situation. His mother's case had hit a dead end, and he was estranged from both his son and father. Now he would have to move forward. Perhaps he would go to law school like he had considered years ago.

He glanced over at Billy in the aisle seat. He was looking at the travel magazine every airline stuffed in the pocket under the tray table.

Jack leaned back in his chair. Billy had been a true friend and he would help him secure a job with WISE International. It was the least Jack could do.

He glanced over again at Billy and noticed a strange look on his face. It was almost as if he had come under a trance.

"What's wrong?"

"Jack, your mother is alive and I think I know where she's at!"

"What, do you have a crystal ball?"

"No, it's just that I was looking through this magazine about retiring in Belize. Somehow Waverly popped into my head and it came to me."

"What? You're clairvoyant all of a sudden?"

"Jack, think about it," Billy said persuasively.

"Okay, Belize." Jack frowned. "I still don't get it."

"Remember when Waverly was talking to you before he died?"

"Yeah, not that he said much."

"You asked him where your mother was. We thought he was saying *Police* or *Please* when he said *Puh-leez*. Jack, I think he was saying 'Belize'!"

19

When they arrived back in Washington, Jack took Billy to the office where he could get his vehicle. They agreed to meet back at the office the next day. Jack promised Billy he would keep him in the loop with any information he gathered about Belize.

As soon as Jack returned to his office he went to the Internet and looked up information on Jorge DePeralta. He found a wealth of information about his drug operation and his legend among the various cartels. While he was researching, his father popped his head in the office.

"You just get back?" Ben asked.

"Yep, just this minute," Jack answered.

"You have any updates?"

"Yes and no."

"What do you mean?"

After a few moments to gather his thoughts, Jack said, "I don't have any conclusive information yet, but I think there may have been a cover-up in the investigation of Mom's death."

Ben came in and sat down in front of Jack's desk. "Fill me in," he said with a furrowed brow.

Jack told him about the trip to Vegas in detail and offered vague details about the New Orleans trip. He didn't want to get his father's hopes up, now that he was fairly certain his father had nothing to do with his mother's death.

"Who do you think killed her?" Ben asked, and before Jack could answer, he added, "Are you still considering me a suspect?"

"Right now, all options are still on the table," Jack said naturally. "I don't have any hard leads on a killer right now."

Ben smirked. "What now?"

"I keep looking."

"That's it?"

"I just started. The case is over twenty years old. Did you think I'd have it wrapped up already?"

"I guess not, but I was hoping you would have eliminated me as a suspect by now."

"All I can do is keep going. I feel confident the case will be solved without any doubt as to what happened that night. When I can be reasonably certain you had nothing to do with her murder, I will let you know."

Ben stood up and walked toward the door. Before leaving, he turned to face Jack and said, "Connor and I are going to get a bite to eat at Clyde's. Do you want to join us?"

Jack sat there in a quandary. He knew he needed to get in touch with his son, but he also needed to validate his new information. "What time are you going?"

"In about a half hour."

"I can't guarantee it, but I'll try."

"Jack, you need to mend the fence with Connor. I'm trying to help you. I'm not going to be around forever, y'know."

"I agree and I will, but for now solving my mother's death is priority."

"Okay," Ben said. "I understand, and I know that's why I hired you, but don't forget about your son. He's the one that's living."

Jack nodded his head slowly.

Once Ben left, Jack looked feverishly for the phone number of Brian Oliver who worked for the CIA. He was the man who saved Jack's life in St. Lucia, and then Jack helped him track down a group of terrorists. Realizing Jack's help had been crucial to the success of the mission, Brian had told him to call if he ever needed his services.

Jack located his number. He didn't put it in his phone or computer for safety reasons. Instead he had it written down on a 3-by-5 card. He was still antiquated in some of his ways, sticking with the tried and true.

"Hello," the voice answered.

"Is this Brian Oliver?" Jack asked.

"Who wants to know?"

"Jack Dublin."

"This is Brian Oliver. How are you, Jack?"

"Pretty good. I may need your help."

"If I can help without getting either of us in trouble with Uncle Sam, I'd be glad to. What do you need?"

"I'm investigating my mother's death. It occurred twenty plus years ago and I have uncovered some troubling information."

"Like what?"

"My mother was allegedly killed in an automobile accident in New Castle County, Delaware. The car caught fire and the body was never really positively identified—"

Oliver interrupted. "I know DNA testing was fairly new back then, but why don't you have the body exhumed and tested?"

"I would, but the body was cremated."

"Okay, continue."

"I went to police headquarters and obtained, by court order, the file pertaining to the investigation. What I found were a lot of inconsistencies. Anyway, jumping ahead, my partner and I tracked down the two investigators and spoke with them. One works for a casino in Las Vegas and the other worked at a bar on Bourbon Street."

"Were they helpful?"

"In a way. The one in Vegas didn't seem to remember much, and the one in New Orleans was murdered after we spoke to him."

"Do you think the one in New Orleans was murdered because of your investigation?"

"Instinct tells me yes, but I can't prove it."

"What was another inconsistency you uncovered?"

"The body in the accident had all of her teeth removed."

"I think you and I both know someone didn't want the true identity of the victim revealed. What did the guy in New Orleans tell you?"

"Not much until I talked to him right before he passed away."

"How did that happen?"

"I have a friend on the New Orleans police department. He made the introduction. The night after we talked, my friend took us to his house where he had overdosed on heroin, probably a hot load. Shortly before he died, I asked him if he knew where my mother was. At first, it sounded like he said 'Police' or 'Please,' but my partner thinks he may have said 'Belize.' Do you have any information on a Jorge DePeralta?"

"Why him? Did one of them mention him by name?"

"No, but he's my mother's brother, my uncle."

"Jorge DePeralta is one of the most notorious, treacherous leaders of a drug cartel in South America," Brian explained. "There is no end to the murders he commits. He doesn't just assign his people to kill; he takes delight in carrying out some of the murders himself. He recently moved to Belize, to be close to his operation in Mexico."

"I'm not sure, but I think my mother is living there."

"You think she's part of his business?"

"God, I hope not. Number one, I hope she's alive. Number two, I hope she's not involved with him. If she is, it's because she's been doped up. Number three, I want to get her out of there."

"Let me see what I can find out from the DEA. They're not always forthcoming with information for another agency, but let me get back to you."

"How long do you think it will take?"

"Give me a day."

"Sounds good. I'll be waiting to hear from you, Brian."

They both hung up.

Jack looked at his watch, then stared at the door for a few moments. Taking a nervous breath, he started for Clyde's.

20
Washington, D.C.

Ben and Connor Dublin met at the entrance of Clyde's restaurant on M Street in Georgetown.

"Hey Connor, you hungry?" Ben asked.

"Starved!"

They went inside and shortly thereafter the host seated them in a booth near a window. It was busy on M Street as usual; however Clyde's didn't seem to benefit from the foot traffic. There were only a few diners and a trio of Hispanic-looking men were just coming in and taking seats at the bar.

Ben enjoyed this restaurant and came here often for breakfast and lunch. The server, Michelle, arrived at their table shortly after they were seated.

"Michelle," Ben said happily looking up at her. She was about the same age as Connor. "I'm so glad you're our server today. I want you to meet my grandson. This is Connor. Connor, this is Michelle."

"Actually, I think we met before," Michelle said. "Weren't you at Ryan Mitchell's party last weekend?"

"Yes, yes I was." Connor smiled.

"That was a great party, wasn't it?!"

"Yeah, it was."

They both just stared dreamily at each other when Ben interrupted. "Connor, are you ready to order?"

"Oh! Yeah! Of course," Connor answered, returning to his menu. "I think I'll have the Reuben."

"Good choice," Michelle said. "Fries okay with that?"

111

"Yes."

"How about you, Mr. Dublin?"

"Y'know Michelle, I think I'll have a chicken Caesar salad."

Michelle took the menus. A smile never left her face.

"Oh! I almost forgot," Michelle said, looking embarrassed. "What would you like to drink?"

Ben ordered a Black and Tan and Connor ordered a Diet Coke with a slice of lime.

Once she was out of view, Connor turned to his grandfather and said, "Man, she is hot!"

Ben laughed. "It's nice to know the tradition of healthy sexual appetites among the Dublin men continues!"

Connor smiled. "Did you have any doubts?"

"Hell no," Ben said, "but I haven't seen you with a girl or heard you talk about one for a while either."

"I don't like to talk about my conquests," Connor said, chuckling.

Ben laughed heartily. "That's good. Keep it that way."

Connor got serious. "What was Jack like?"

"What do you mean?"

"I mean, what was he like as a child?" he asked. "Or as a kid, y'know."

"To be honest," Ben said thoughtfully, "I don't know how to answer that. I was never around, so I can't give you an honest answer. I know he loved your grandmother. They were very close. I'm glad about that, since I wasn't much of a father figure. Also, your father was very athletic. He played a lot of sports, like football, and baseball was his main sport. Your grandmother didn't want him to play football. She was afraid he might hurt his hands."

"Why did that matter?" Connor asked.

"Your father was a trained pianist. In fact, he was quite good. I did get to see him perform once at a recital. He probably could have played with a symphony orchestra, he was that good," Ben said with pride. "Your grandmother was an amazing mother. She kept him focused. Your dad could also speak several languages and it was all because of her."

"Do you know how he and my mom met?" Connor asked. "Mom never talked about Jack."

"They met at college is all I know," Ben said, somewhat annoyed. "Y'know Connor, you need to start referring to your father as Dad, not Jack."

Connor chose not to respond, looking at his grandfather respectfully.

"Connor, listen," Ben said diplomatically. "Your father didn't run out on you. Think about it. He's not the one who moved to California. He had a job here. He couldn't have gone out there."

Michelle returned to the table with their drinks. "Your food should be out in a minute," she said before leaving, sensing she had interrupted a private conversation.

"When you were born, your father doted on you like crazy."

"No offense, but how do you know?"

"I saw him with you at the park," Ben answered without offense. "He couldn't wipe the smile off his face."

"What happened between him and my mother?"

"I only know what your mother told me," Ben said. "She said it was just as much her fault as it was your father's. They just grew in different directions. Your dad was wrapped up in his job, and your mother wanted more out of life."

"Wrapped up in his job," Connor said. "That sounds familiar."

"The difference between me and your father is, I was never around. He was."

"Why did he allow me to be adopted by my stepfather?" Connor asked, stirring his lime and soda.

"He knew, or at least he thought, it would be better for you in the long run. If you think about it, he sacrificed for you." Ben took a sip of his beer.

"That's what he said."

"When did he tell you that?"

"At the Sea Catch, while you were on the phone."

Ben nodded.

Michelle reappeared with their meals. "Can I get you anything else?" she asked, smiling.

"I'm good," Ben replied. "How about you, Connor?"

"I'm fine," Connor said, smiling up at Michelle.

"Okay." She nodded. "I'll check back on you."

"Connor, I have to use the men's room," Ben said. "I'll be right back." He was hoping to give Connor and Michelle some time to talk without him being there.

Ben walked over to the bar where the three Hispanic men were still drinking. His favorite bartender, Jake, was working. Jake was in his thirties with a few tattoos on his forearms. Stylish, at least for people his age, he wore his long hair in a ponytail. Yet, he knew his sports!

"Hey Jake, how's it goin'?" Ben asked from a position close to the other three men at the bar. As usual ESPN was on the TV behind the bar.

"Oh hey, Mr. Dublin," Jake answered. "I didn't see you come in."

"I came in with my grandson," Ben replied. "So, what are your thoughts about this year?"

"You mean the Nationals?"

"No, the Skins."

"I think they're gonna win the division!"

Ben gave him a skeptical look. "You really think Kirk Cousins can take them to the Super Bowl?"

"I think so. What do you think?"

"I think as long as they have that nutjob for an owner, they're not going to win anything."

Jake laughed. "I admit Snyder looks like he's trying to be the Steinbrenner of football."

"At least Steinbrenner's teams won World Series consistently," Ben stated. "Besides, I think Jerry Jones already has that honor!"

"Yeah, you're right, and they're always in the thick of things."

"I think we have to look out for the Eagles. Since they fired Kelly, they've turned things around. This Wentz kid looks pretty good. I hate to admit it, but Kelly's not the first Irishman to disappoint me," Ben said with a twinkle in his eye. With a farewell nod to Jake, he headed for the men's room.

. . .

Two of the men at the bar looked at the third man for instructions. He waited a few moments and then simply nodded. One of the men got up and headed for the men's room while the other headed over to Connor's table.

When the one man got to the men's room, Ben was washing his hands. They were the only two in there. The man pulled a pistol equipped with a silencer, aimed it at Ben, and fired once. Ben immediately fell to the floor. The man dragged him into a stall and sat him up on the commode.

Meanwhile, the other man went to Connor's table and sat down. Connor looked at him in disbelief.

"I think you're at the wrong table," Connor said to him.

"No, I'm at the right table," the man said, smiling. "I have a gun pointed at you under the table. If you want to live, if you want your grandfather to live, you'll get up now and leave through the front door."

"Fuck you," Connor said.

The man's facial expression became serious as he brought the gun from below the table to show Connor. "Now, let's get moving."

"What about my grandfather?" Connor asked.

"He's fine for now. I guess he'll wonder where you're at when he comes out of the men's room, but we're not sticking around to find out. Now move."

Connor got up from the booth and headed toward the front door. He glanced back at the men's room but didn't see his grandfather. As he looked, the other two men were headed toward the front door too.

Once outside, they got into a waiting car and drove away.

21

When Jack got to the corner of Wisconsin and M Street, he looked ahead to Clyde's. All hell had seemed to break loose. Police and ambulance personnel were out front where a crowd was gathering. Jack sprinted from the corner down to Clyde's.

Uniformed police officers had cordoned off the entrance and were establishing a perimeter. Jack approached one of the officers stationed out front and flashed his badge.

"What's going on?" he asked.

The officer looked around. "There's been a shooting," he answered.

"Who got shot?"

"I don't know, but they're getting ready to bring him out now."

Jack looked at the crowd, hoping to see his father and Connor standing there, but no luck. The entranceway to the restaurant was blocked by uniformed officers he didn't know. There was a sergeant on the scene. Jack didn't know him either. If detectives from the Criminal Investigation Unit had arrived, they were most likely inside already. He looked again to see if there were more officers arriving that he knew to intercept for information, or better, get him access inside.

Increased activity began forming at the front door. The paramedics were preparing to bring a stretcher through. Several officers cleared the way. People began pushing and jockeying for a better view, including Jack

"Get back, get back," an officer barked at the people standing by.

As the stretcher made its exit, Jack saw the pallid form of his father wearing an oxygen mask. A blanket covered him up to his chest. Jack could see blood on his shirt above the top edge of the blanket. The paramedics moved Ben past the throng of onlookers out to the awaiting ambulance. Jack moved down the stretch of people toward his father.

"Move back," an officer ordered.

"That's my father!"

"This man is your father?" asked one of the paramedics.

"Yes," Jack said, "what's his condition?"

"We're trying to keep him stabilized. He was shot once in the back. There's an exit wound in his chest."

"Have you seen my son?" Jack asked loudly, looking at his father hoping to get some response from him, but his eyes were closed. He was unresponsive.

"No, I have not," one of the paramedics answered apathetically, as they loaded Ben into the rear of the ambulance. "Do you want to ride to the hospital with us?"

Jack paused. He was torn between going to the hospital with his father or returning to Clyde's to look for his son. "Where are you taking him?"

"MedStar."

Jack was relieved to hear it. MedStar is a Georgetown University Hospital well known for its emergency and trauma care. "I'll meet you over there," Jack said.

He watched the ambulance pull away with its lights and siren. He turned to go to the restaurant to look for Connor. The officers at the door stopped him. "This is still a crime scene, sir. You're not allowed to go in."

"My son is in there. He was with my father when he was shot. I've gotta find him."

"I'm sorry, sir. You still can't go in."

"Who's investigating this?"

"You mean the name of the officers?

"Yes, the detectives."

"Here they come now," the officer answered, looking behind Jack.

Jack turned and saw Detective Bill Keane and an unknown detective walking across the street towards him. Keane was the detective who had interrogated Jack when he was suspected of homicide in the death of a man who was dealing with a group of Pakistani terrorists. Jack was still not happy with the way Keane treated him. He still burned with what he felt was a betrayal of the brotherhood of cops.

"Hello Jack. Why am I not surprised to see you at another shooting on M Street?" the humorless Keane asked.

"Where's Nick?" Jack asked, referring to Detective Nick Bucci, Keane's investigative partner.

"He retired last week."

Jack looked at Keane's new partner. "Who's this?"

"This is Detective Andy Fatek," Keane answered. "This is retired Detective Dublin," he said to Fatek.

"I've heard of you," Fatek said, holding out his hand.

Jack shook his hand. "I bet you have."

"I'd like to talk, Jack, but we have work to do," Keane said as he started for the front door.

Jack grabbed his shoulder. Keane turned around. "Someone shot my father, Bill. I think my son may be in there. Can I go in with you?"

Keane looked at him with wide, pensive eyes. "Your father is the victim in this shooting?" he asked.

Jack nodded.

"Let me get a pulse on the situation, and I'll come back out and talk to you."

Jack waited a few minutes before Keane came to the entranceway and waved him over.

"Let this man through," Keane said to the uniformed man at the door.

Once inside, Keane took Jack aside to give him an update. Crime scene technicians were working in the men's room area. Uniformed officers were talking to the manager, bartender, and a waitress who seemed very upset.

"Jack, from what I can gather so far, your father and son were here getting a bite to eat. Your father went to the men's room. Three Hispanic men were sitting at the bar. One got up, went to the men's room, and shot your father. Another went to the table where your son was sitting and convinced him to leave with him. He probably had a gun. The other guy paid the bar tab. The four of them left together. That's all I have for now. We're going to try and get some prints, look for surveillance video, to see if we can ID who they are."

Jack nodded.

"Jack, I'm sorry. They say your father is in pretty bad shape. Maybe you should get to the hospital, in case he'll be able to give some information. After we finish here, Andy and I will be going over to see if we can talk to your father."

"I'll head over now. Keep me up to date," Jack said, handing Keane his card.

Jack left the restaurant and walked down the street, where the pedestrian traffic had died down. He pulled out his cell phone and called Billy D. He brought him up to speed on what had happened.

"Billy, I need you to get down here to Clyde's," Jack said. "I want you to stay on top of Keane. You got along with him pretty well, didn't you?"

"Yeah," Billy answered. "He's a bit of an asshole, but I can get around it."

"I'm going to the hospital to check on my father. Call me as soon as you get any information on Connor."

"I'll be there as soon as I can. I'll find out what I can, and give you a call," Billy said. "And Jack?"

"Yeah?"

"I think our investigation kicked the sleeping bear!"

"And that bear is gonna die!" Jack said resolutely. "Billy, please find as much information as you can about Connor. He just came back into my life. I don't want to lose him."

"We'll find him," Billy said. "And we're gonna find your mother too."

Jack hung up and a squad car pulled up alongside him.

"Get in," the officer ordered.

22

Detective Keane hooked Jack up with a ride to the hospital in a patrol car. Once he got there, Jack went to the E.R. desk and was told his father was in surgery. Jack went up to the waiting room area on the fifth floor as instructed. He hoped his father would pull through, and be able to communicate. He needed him to provide information. If his father had been holding back all these years, now was the time to come clean. Once he could question his father, and get some answers, he would find his uncle. There, he knew he would find his son. If he was lucky, he would find his mother too, or at least solve the mystery of her death. Then he would kill Jorge DePeralta.

Jack paced as he surveyed the empty waiting room. It was a typical hospital waiting room, comfortable chairs, taupe painted walls with comfortable, relaxing pictures of scenic landscapes, and windows looking out to the streets below. On a table in the center of the room stood a sculpture of a doctor leaning over with his stethoscope on a little boy's chest. The little boy looked up at the doctor with wide-eyed wonder. At first, Jack thought he was mistakenly in the pediatric wing, but he looked around and saw a sign indicating he was in the right spot.

Jack walked over to the windows and watched people walking in and out of the hospital before he found a comfortable chair in the corner of the room. He sat down and stared at the floor. Glad that he was alone, he began to analyze his life.

It's amazing how one's existence winds through the serpentine rivers of life. Not long ago he was an ordinary cop mundanely doing his job before justifiably killing a young man trying to rape a woman. The next thing he knew, he became the target of a U.S. senator, father of the man he killed, and somehow his estranged father was lurking in the background.

Upon reflection, the thing that bothered him most was the repercussion of killing a man. No, it wasn't pulling the trigger, it was the fact that he allowed himself to feel guilty. It pissed him off thinking about it. He killed a low-life, silver-spoon piece of shit, while protecting an innocent woman about to be raped, and then wallowed in guilt for several weeks. Maybe that's what happens the first time you kill someone—you feel guilty. You question yourself, "Was there anything I could have done different?" Jack would never again allow himself to feel remorseful about cleaning up the scum of the earth.

His father's shooting was now the impetus of his thoughts. Until a few days ago, Jack didn't know his father was CIA. He wondered if his father was an operative who killed, and what his thoughts were when he killed. Jack figured a trained killer is somewhat of a lone wolf. It hunts down a valid target and eliminates it. It doesn't consider ramifications. It's motivated by righteous survival.

While he considered this premise, a shiver ran down his back. The thought of an innocent bystander in harm's way momentarily clouded his thinking. This was different. He was no longer working the street in patrol. Killing DePeralta would not be spontaneous where innocent people could wander into the kill zone. It would be the result of a well thought-out plan. It would be one against one. No spectators, no bystanders.

Jack reminded himself he would be killing with purpose, not pleasure. Any pleasure he reveled in was killing for the defensible, greater good. The quote about the meek inheriting the earth was bullshit! Someone needed to protect the unwitting, slumbering population.

That's why he knew when he tracked down his uncle, he would kill again. This maniac had ruined the lives of thousands by poisoning them with drugs. Jack's contact, Brian Oliver, had advised him DePeralta had tortured innocent people, raped young girls, and executed people in every way imaginable. One of his favorite methods was tossing them in a shark tank he had on his estate while they were still alive. Hence, "El Tiburon," the shark, became his nickname. Killing DePeralta became Jack's mission, his focus. Perhaps he and his father had more in common than he could have ever envisaged.

Jack returned to thoughts about his son's kidnapping. It was definitely a well-planned attack. They had followed his father and son to Clyde's. They knew they had to separate his father from Connor. Once they eliminated his father, Connor would be easy prey. Jack figured they would smuggle Connor out of the country, to where DePeralta lived. Jack would touch base with Oliver again to affirm the intelligence.

Jack clenched his jaws and ground his teeth. If the information was correct, Jack and Billy would go get his son back. He didn't count out the possibility that DePeralta may contact him. But he doubted it. Jorge was a hoarder of people, but not as if they were antiques and collectibles. People were expendable. He enjoyed using them, then disposing them without a second thought.

Oliver told Jack that an informant who used to work for DePeralta, but escaped, said that DePeralta once said to him, "I am like God the Creator. I can give life and I can take it away."

Jack looked at his watch. He was getting frustrated. He hated waiting. He needed to determine his father's condition, knowing it was futile to ask the nurses at the desk. He wouldn't find out anything until a doctor spoke with him.

Jack sat there for an hour trying to distract himself by reading mindless magazines, and drinking some watered-down coffee he bought from a vending machine down the hall. He had called Billy twice, but it went right to voicemail.

Jack got up and started pacing again. He walked over to the windows and stared. The sun was starting its descent. The sky was getting darker. It was twilight. Soon the street lights would come on. The night creatures, as Jack thought of them, would come alive as if they had been signaled, and begin finding their marks.

At this moment, he realized cops were truly powerless. The drug flow was out of control. Police could only sever the limb of the beast, but it would immediately grow new ones. Jack now knew, the only way to be effective is to kill the beast!

A young couple, probably in their early thirties, came into the room and sat down in the first available chairs. The male was trying to console the female. Jack sensed they were husband and wife, and from the distraught behavior of the woman, he figured it was a relative of hers that was in surgery.

Shortly thereafter, a man in surgical scrubs entered the waiting area. He looked around and went to Jack first.

"Are you related to Ben Dublin?" he asked.

"Yes, I'm his son," Jack replied.

The man in scrubs sat down next to him. He was a small man, medium build, maybe five-feet-eight, of Asian descent, appearing to be in his mid-thirties. He wore glasses, but otherwise he was pretty much non-descript.

"I'm Doctor Hiu. I'm the surgeon who attended to your father. The good news is your father is still alive," he said in clear English without an accent. "He suffered a gunshot wound to his back and chest. The bullet entered the upper left quadrant of his back and exited through his chest. Fortunately there was an EMT team parked down the street when he was shot. If they had not been there, your father probably would have died.

"They were able to get him intubated and start a transfusion. Unfortunately, we had to perform a pneumonectomy, which means we had to remove his left lung. We had no other option, since the bullet had pierced and shredded it. His breathing became so labored; we felt there was no way to repair it under the circumstances. Your father is in extraordinary shape. Another man of his age most likely would've died before he arrived at the hospital, let alone survive the surgery. Right now he is in critical condition. The next forty-eight hours are going to be crucial."

"Is he able to talk?" Jack asked.

"He is still in recovery and heavily sedated. He has an endotracheal intubation. That's simply a tube inserted to help him breathe. He can't talk and shouldn't be subjected to any questions. I don't want anyone talking to him until I reevaluate him. He needs to remain stabilized. He will have constant care, and will be under constant supervision. I'll check back on him in another two hours. After that, he will be evaluated every four hours and always under constant observation."

"Doctor, my father is Catholic. Does he need to have final rites? I mean, is it that serious?"

"I don't want to put a percentage on your father's survival possibilities, but it wouldn't hurt to have a priest look in on him."

Jack read between the lines. His father was close to death and there may not be an opportunity to talk to him before he passed.

"Thank you, Doctor," Jack said. "Can I see him?"

"When he is assigned a room, you may see him, but again, I'm cautioning you not to ask questions that could upset him. Even if he appears to be unaware of your presence, he probably can still hear you. If you want to talk to him with comforting, reassuring words, that would be fine."

Jack nodded. "Thanks again, Doctor."

Doctor Hiu stood up and Jack did as well. They shook hands and the doctor started to leave before Jack asked him, "How will I know what room my father is in?"

"I'll have a nurse come for you and take you to his room once he's assigned one."

"Okay, thanks."

As the doctor left the room, Archibald Prescott entered unexpectedly, accompanied by Father Delledonne.

With a raised eyebrow and a long face, Jack resigned himself to the fact there would be others involved in his nightmare whether he liked it or not. Jack was surprised to see them so soon.

23

"**H**ello Jack," Mr. Prescott said without displaying any emotion. "Jack," Father Delledonne said, holding out his hand.

Archibald Prescott was a man who never showed emotion. Perhaps that's why he was one of the best attorneys in Washington, D.C., if not the entire nation. He was straightforward and very astute. The ultimate courtroom card player. He knew when to hold 'em and when to fold 'em.

"Hello, Mr. Prescott," Jack responded plainly. He realized how close his father was with Mr. Prescott, but Jack was tired, irritated, and didn't have time for Prescott's pompous manner, but he would keep his frustration in check. He shook Mr. Prescott's limp hand and then shook Father Mike Delledonne's, whose hand was so big and strong it was the opposite of what he pictured a priest's handshake would be.

"How is your father?" Mr. Prescott asked.

"The doctor just told me its touch and go."

"Can we see him? Does he have a room?"

"No. Not yet."

"Why not?"

"Because he's heavily sedated, and he's still in recovery," Jack said, exasperated.

"What happened…specifically? I mean he was shot, that much I do know."

Jack cast a jaundiced eye at Mr. Prescott. He knew Prescott had contacts throughout the police department, and the news media for that matter. Just like in the courtroom, Mr. Prescott was coy. He probably knew just as much, if not more, than Jack.

Jack didn't want to spar with Mr. Prescott. After all, he had defended Jack when he was falsely accused of homicide. It was Mr. Prescott's imperious attitude that pushed Jack's buttons.

"He was shot in the back," Jack said. "He suffered life-threatening wounds. They had to remove one of his lungs. He's not out of the woods by a long shot."

For the first time since they'd arrived, Father Delledonne spoke. "Jack, does your father need to receive the Sacrament of Last Rites?" he asked earnestly.

Jack looked at him, trying to separate Mike Delledonne the cop from Mike Delledonne the priest. It wasn't easy.

"Do I call you Mike or Father Delledonne?" Jack asked respectfully.

"Call me Mike."

"Mike, perhaps he should receive the sacraments as soon as he gets a room." Looking at Mr. Prescott and Mike, Jack added, "How did you two get here?"

"We were meeting in Father Mike's office when I received a call about your father. I told him what happened and he insisted on coming to the hospital with me," Mr. Prescott said with apparent equanimity.

"What do you know about the shooting?" Jack asked.

"I know he was at Clyde's, and was shot in the back by an unknown assailant while in the men's room. I was further told he was brought here. As soon as I could, I got over here."

"Jack, I know it must be terribly difficult for you," Mike said. "If there's anything you need, please let me know. I'm here for you."

Looking at him, Jack could see the sincerity in Mike's eyes. He had no beef with Mike. In fact, he really had no beef with Archibald Prescott. Taking a moment, he realized he was stressed out, and didn't need to take it out on them. He just didn't like living in a vacuum.

Mr. Prescott closed his eyes as he slowly wiped his forehead with his hand. He appeared to be in deep thought. Jack watched him as he stood up and walked over to the windows.

"He's really upset," Mike said, his voice low. "He has always talked about your father with such admiration. I don't think you know how close they are."

"I have an idea, but I don't know why."

Mr. Prescott walked over to them and sat down. Looking directly at Jack, he said, "I think there's something you're not telling me."

"Like what?" Jack asked.

"Connor. Was he with your father at Clyde's?"

Jack hadn't thought to bring it up with Mr. Prescott. "Yes, he was."

"And where is he now?"

Contemplating his answer, Jack said, "He's been kidnapped."

Mr. Prescott showed emotion for the first time. He looked away from Jack and it appeared as if a tear had formed in his eyes. Prescott knew what it was like to lose someone. His daughter had died trying to help Jack defend himself against a serious but frivolous charge.

"I thought so. Ben told me they were going to dine at Clyde's and that you might join them. I know you're probably focused on getting Connor back from the kidnappers, but there is something you haven't considered."

Jack raised a brow. "Like what?"

"Like calling Connor's mother and letting her know what's happened. After all, she has a right to know."

Jack was dumbfounded. He hadn't even thought about her. It had been about twenty years since he spoke with his ex-wife. Meg had left Jack to move to the west coast because she wasn't happy being a cop's wife. She said he had become cold and indifferent. Jack was still in love with her, and had no idea about her unhappiness. He was devastated when she took Connor with her, and he felt helpless. Her family had money and any attempt to fight her in court would have been expensive and futile. Jack went out to visit Connor a couple of times, but when she married a Hollywood producer, he knew he no longer had a chance to be the father he'd wanted to be. When Meg asked Jack to surrender parental rights, he painfully conceded, thinking it was in Connor's best interest.

"You're right, I need to do that."

"I have her number if you need it," Mr. Prescott offered.

Though curious to know how he had her number, Jack decided not to ask about it. "Okay, I'll take it if you've got it."

Once he got the number, Jack went aside to make the call in private. He entered the number and then contemplated before hitting send. Once he did, he thought quickly about the past, and how it measured to the present. When she answered he would just come out and tell her the truth. There was no answer so he left a message. Within minutes his phone vibrated.

"Hello," Jack answered with hesitation in his voice.

"Hello, Jack," said the voice he remembered being married to. "It's been a long time."

Memories flooded his conscience as he tried to talk. Jack had become hardened with time.

"Jack, are you there?"

"Yes, I'm here. How are you, Meg?"

"I'm fine, Jack. I heard you've met Connor."

"Yes, I have," Jack said painfully.

"What's wrong? Something's wrong, I can hear it in your voice." There was obvious concern in her voice.

"Meg, I have some difficult news to tell you."

"Oh my God! What happened?"

"Connor has been kidnapped!"

"Kidnapped?" she asked emotionally.

"Yes. It happened a couple of hours ago. He was with my father at a restaurant here in D.C. My father was shot and is in critical condition. That's when Connor was taken."

"Oh my God!" she said again as she started to cry.

"Listen, Meg. I'm going to get him back. Don't worry."

She continued to cry. Jack didn't know what to say. Finally he said, "Maybe you should come here. Can you get a flight out today?"

"Yes, I can," she said, regaining her composure.

"Then get a flight, text me the information, and I'll make sure if I can't be there, someone will pick you up. I think it would be best if you were here."

She said okay and then she started to say something else, but apparently decided against it.

"If anything happens in the meantime, I'll let you know, okay?" Jack offered.

After she acknowledged Jack, they hung up. Jack didn't have time to think about the past. He needed to focus on Connor and his father. As soon as his father's status was determined, he could act on the information he had, and find his son. He hoped Billy would have more solid intelligence.

Just then, Billy entered the room with Detectives Keane and Fatek.

"**W**e've got him," Juan said to Jorge by phone.

Jorge smiled. "Tell me what happened."

Juan related the entire event. He told him how they shot and killed Ben Dublin. He further stated how Connor was now sedated, and wouldn't be presenting any problems for travel.

"Where are you?" Jorge asked.

"We're just coming up to the airport now."

"Have you had any problems?"

"None so far."

Jorge sat out on the upper deck of his three-level, luxurious yacht that cost over thirty million dollars, and he loved it. It had a sleek design, five cabins, decorated with imported marble from a quarry in Carrara, Italy. The same quarry had been used since ancient times and had produced more marble than any other place on Earth. Some of the most prolific structures in the world were created with Carrara marble, such as the Pantheon in Rome and Michelangelo's statue of David. The interior design was customized with bubinga wood from central Africa, one of the most expensive woods in the world. Jorge spent a couple extra million to have it specially outfitted with triple waterjet gas-powered turbine engines, providing it with a maximum of 12,500 horsepower. Jorge appreciated the speed of getting to, or perhaps more importantly, getting away from the port of call. His yacht could reach speed of 50 knots, the equivalent to 57 miles per hour, impressive for a yacht over one hundred feet in length traveling on water.

He was sitting under a canopy, shielded from the intense sun, overlooking the Caribbean ocean, smoking a Cuban and drinking Glenmorangie Ealanta scotch from a Baccarat glass. The yacht was currently occupied by the three-man crew, two bodyguards armed with M-10s, and himself. The bodyguards were stationed down by the dock.

Luisa and Miguelito would fly to Miami since it would take almost a day to sail there from Belize. Jorge wanted the peace and quiet of the yacht without Luisa meddling into his business. Besides, Luisa was anxious to see her mother.

"Are you boarding yet?" Jorge asked.

"Yes, we're on board."

"Great. When you get here, secure the boy away from Bella. Make sure he is watched and cared for. I don't want anything to happen to him, yet." Jorge took a pull on his cigar and blew the smoke into the still Caribbean air. "Let me know when you arrive. You need to take care of this as quickly as possible. Get down to the marina right away. We need to be in Miami by tomorrow."

"I will take care of it," Juan assured him. "You don't have to worry about anything. My men are already in Miami scouting out Calle Ocho for any suspicious activity. So far there hasn't been any sign of the Navarros or Julio."

"Tell them to use whatever resources they have to find out anything from the staff at La Carreta. The Navarros must have had some contact there by now."

"I will. By the way, why are you taking the 'Luisa' to Miami? How come you didn't fly?"

"When we leave Miami, it may have to be done quickly. The authorities will be thinking we're leaving by air. I want them to be as confused as possible. They won't think of the boat."

"Don't kid yourself," Juan said. "They will know you're in town, and they may know about your boat."

"I'll be out of their jurisdiction in no time. The 'Luisa' is lightning fast. The Coast Guard won't be able to catch up with me before I get into international waters."

"That won't stop them. They will stop your boat and board it. They will take us into custody, and bring us back to the United States as fugitives."

"I have a backup plan. They won't get us. Believe me!"

"I don't know what that could be, but it better be good because it's gonna be dangerous."

"You worry too much. This is what makes it exciting! I'll see you when you get here."

Jorge finished his cigar and poured himself another drink. He looked out into the harbor and thought about the empire he had built. It had brought him fortune, but he worried if his family would survive. The drug trade was lucrative, and full of scorpions. Assassins come cheap and money is abundant. There's always someone who will pay a higher price, but loyalty can't be bought. It's fear that makes people faithful. Occasional displays like the one with Francisco being thrown into the shark tank were good for keeping his people in line.

Julio was his oldest son. As a proud father, Jorge watched him grow up to be a strong and intelligent young man. Now he was being held by a family who knew their share of horrors.

The Navarros had always blamed Jorge for the death of their father, Pedro. He was their patriarch, their strength. Their family had prospered once Pedro broke off from working for Jorge. Although not quite as successful as Jorge, their family's presence was a constant, threatening reminder to Jorge that he was never safe.

Not long after Pedro started his own drug trade, it became apparent that his path would cross Jorge's and when it did, there would be a territorial dispute ending in bloodshed. Pedro had become strong, recruiting young people from Laredo, Texas and turning them into ruthless killers who carried out orders efficiently.

One day, Pedro made a foolish mistake. He had been traveling alone to the market. Since it was only a mile away from his home, he felt safe. His body was found the next day, his head posted on a fence close to his home. There was no note. The message was obvious: Don't fuck with Jorge!

"Excuse me, Mr. DePeralta." It was the voice of his captain.

"What?" Jorge asked as he turned around.

"I've been informed by security there is a young woman on the dock who would like to speak with you. She said her name is Alexa."

"Send her up," Jorge said reluctantly. He had not seen her in a couple of years and he was not looking forward to seeing her, but his curiosity got the better of him.

Shortly she appeared on deck. Alexa was as beautiful as her mother, if not more so. She wore a white dress that fell to her mid-thigh and accentuated her legs and posterior. The loose neckline plunged to her waist displaying ample cleavage. She wore white pumps with an open toe and four-inch stiletto heels. Her eyes were doe shaped. She looked radiant.

Alexa walked towards Jorge with a model's confidence.

"How come you disrespect me like this?" Jorge charged.

She sat down across from her host. "What do you mean?"

"I haven't seen you in at least two years, and I'm your father. So, for the first time you see me, you dress like a hooker."

"I thought I've dressed respectfully," she said, offended. "I tried to dress in a way that would be pleasing to you. I mean no disrespect. I want nothing but to please you."

Jorge disregarded her comments and stood up to signal he wanted a hug. She stood and hugged him.

"Can I get you something to drink?" he asked.

"Yes, I would like a Manhattan."

Jorge raised his eyebrows and pursed his lips as if impressed. He raised a hand and one of the deck crew presented himself.

"The lady would like a Manhattan," he said.

The crew man acknowledged and returned promptly with her drink.

"So, how is your mother?" Jorge asked.

"She's fine," Alexa answered.

"Where is she these days?"

"I don't know. I haven't talked with her lately."

Jorge smiled. "That's bullshit!"

"No, I'm not kidding. I haven't spoken with her since she turned fifty."

Jorge nodded in understanding. "So what brings you here?"

"I just haven't seen you in so long, I thought I would stop by."

Jorge smiled. "C'mon Alexa, don't bullshit me. You must want something. I haven't seen you in a couple of years. You don't just stop by to say hello. What can I do for you?"

Alexa frowned, then leaned forward to grab her drink from the table. She was obviously uncomfortable.

"I need to ask you for a loan."

"Are you in trouble?"

"Not exactly. Let's just say I have debts."

"Are you on drugs?"

"No," she answered emphatically.

"How much do you need?"

"Only one hundred thousand."

"*Only* one hundred thousand," Jorge repeated, laughing.

"Yes," she said plainly. "To you that is nothing."

Jorge smiled. He knew she was right. "Why should I?"

"Because I'm your daughter and I need your help."

Alexa was Jorge's oldest daughter. She was the only child of Jorge and his first wife, Yolanda. Yolanda was Spanish and beautiful when Jorge had met her. Within a week of courtship, they had married. Yolanda got pregnant and Alexa was born almost nine months to the day of their wedding. After two years of a volatile relationship, Yolanda left and left Alexa with Jorge. She knew she wouldn't escape with her. Since Yolanda was from a well-established and wealthy family, she was able to find sanctuary somewhere secluded from Jorge, who had threatened to have her killed. She knew how he had tortured people and was in fear for her life.

"Are you sure you don't know where your mother is?"

"Why is that important to you, now, after all these years?"

"I just want to send her a Christmas card." He laughed.

Jorge poured himself another drink and asked Alexa if she wanted something to eat.

"No. Thank you."

"Well, Alexa, I must say you have turned out to be quite a beautiful woman. I've heard you hang out at the local hotels. I hope you're keeping yourself clean. Virtue is a treasure."

"I'll try to remember that, and who told me," she said with half a laugh.

Jorge leaned forward. "I will give you the money, but there may come a time when I need a favor. I will expect you to carry out my request, whatever it may be."

"Like what?" she asked, concerned. "I'm not killing anybody!"

"No. It would be nothing like that."

"As long as I don't have to harm anyone, I'll do whatever you ask, within reason."

"You may be asked to extract information using your God-given skills." Jorge smiled.

"I'm okay with that."

"Good! Now let me get you the money. I'll be right back," he said as he got up and disappeared into the yacht. He returned in five minutes with one of his wife's Louis Vuitton bags. She had so many; he figured she would never miss it. Inside was $100,000 in cash. "I thought you would want to walk around in style, so I put the money in here. You can count it if you like, or you can take my word for it."

"I'll take your word for it," she said, standing up and taking the bag from him. She opened the zipper and looked in at the cash before closing it back up. "Thank you," she said, holding out her hand.

"What? I give you a hundred thousand in cash and I don't even get a hug?"

She went to him and hugged him.

"Don't forget our deal," he whispered in her ear before kissing her on both cheeks.

Then Jorge signaled one of his bodyguards. "Please show her out."

Alexa looked at her father, then left without saying another word.

25

As soon as Juan and his entourage boarded the boat, they began their journey to Miami. All in all, there were fifteen men aboard; more men would be available when they arrived. The yacht was equipped with more guns and ammunition than they would need, but Jorge felt it was better to have more than not enough.

Juan had checked in with his scout team, and there still was no sign of the Navarro family on Calle Ocho.

"Do you think they'll harm Julio?" Juan asked.

"For their sake they better not," Jorge said. "If anything happens to him, I will use all my power to destroy them. If it takes every dollar I have, every ounce of my strength and the last breath of my body, I will kill every last one of them, including their sons and daughters. No one will be spared."

"And if they don't harm him, and want to make a deal?"

"I'll kill them anyway," Jorge said with a laugh.

They planned a strategy, then began to relax and enjoy the comforts of their home at sea.

They arrived at the Epic Hotel located at the mouth of the Miami River and overlooking Biscayne Bay. The Epic had its own marina which could accommodate ships up to 900 feet. At times the aristocracy of the Middle East would dock their yachts here, and the sheikhs would take up private residence for long periods of stay. Guests staying above the twenty-sixth floor had their own area to enjoy meals and entertainment, if they didn't want to mingle.

Luisa and Miguelito had already checked in to the hotel. They were located on the thirty-second floor.

Jorge exited the yacht incognito as a member of the crew. He had fitted himself with a gray beard and glasses. Juan was dressed as a businessman carrying a suitcase. They entered the lobby, which had high ceilings and two restaurants. It wasn't crowded, yet there were enough people checking in to distract anyone from noticing him, unless, of course, someone was looking for him. Still, his disguise would make it difficult to be discerned.

Jorge headed for his room while Juan went to his room across the hall.

"*Mi amor*," Luisa cried out as she ran to Jorge who had just entered the room. She kissed him and hugged him. Stepping back, she started to laugh. "I love your disguise!"

"Where's Miguelito?"

"He's taking a nap."

"Good. I don't want him to see me like this," Jorge said as he began to peel off his beard and eyebrows. "Did you make my doctor's appointment?" he asked.

"Yes, it's for tomorrow at eight o'clock, just like you wanted."

"Good," he said. "Thank you my love!"

They hugged and then she asked, "How's your cough?"

"It's no worse than it was," he said, unconcerned. "Don't worry. It's probably just some kind of infection. The doctor will give me some antibiotics, and in a week or so it will be history." He started to cough violently again, bringing up more blood, which he spat into a handkerchief.

Luisa looked at him apprehensively. "Jorge, darling, I'll be glad when you get well again. Can I go to the doctor with you?"

"No, I don't think so. How is your mother? I thought she might be here when I arrived," he said, concealing his joy that she wasn't.

"You are so sweet!" Luisa squealed with delight. "With all your problems, you still ask me how my mother is. I love you!" she said as she came over to him as he sat on the sofa.

"Can you get me a drink, please?" he asked before she started to tell him about her mother.

"Sure, what do you want?" she asked as she headed toward the bar.

"Scotch and water."

He watched her walk over to the bar area. They had been married more than ten years and he never got tired of looking at her. She still had a perfect figure, small waist, smooth hips and 34D breasts. Her eyes were playful and her lips tantalizing. Yet, lately Jorge found it difficult to get an erection. He played it off, but he thought to himself, *Here I am, one of the wealthiest and most powerful men on Earth, with a wife that most men would die just to touch, and I am incapable of pleasing her sexually.* Of course, there were other ways to give pleasure to her, but it didn't do anything for him. He thought he may have cancer, and the effects were disrupting his sex life.

Mortality wasn't something he thought about in the past, but lately it had grabbed his attention. Most men in the drug trade usually died in battle, or by ambush. He had resolved it as a way of life. Now, as he considered his prognosis, he knew his death would come sooner rather than later. He laughed at the irony that he may die of natural causes.

Even so, he would leave his family well taken care of, which brought his thoughts back to Julio. It pained him to think of the harm that could come to him, particularly when he remembered all the various tortured ways men had died as a result of his orders.

He smiled briefly, lost in the reverie of his maniacal mind, thinking about the ten men several years ago who had worked for Navarro and were caught trying to sabotage one of his labs in Mexico. He had put them on crosses and lit them on fire along his driveway, five on each side, as if they were welcoming torches lighting the way for visitors at a party. Jorge sat on his balcony with a cigar and a drink, watching them burn as they screamed for a quick death.

He hoped Julio wouldn't face the same fate.

Luisa brought him his drink and sat beside him. She kissed him on his ear as he sipped his scotch. She started rubbing his arm, gliding her hand up and down lightly.

"I want you to make love to me," she cooed in his ear.

Jorge took another sip and put his drink on the table. "What about Miguelito?"

"He's asleep."

"What if he wakes up?"

"He won't, but even if he does, we'll have our door closed," she said soothingly. "What's wrong? You never used to worry about that before."

"It's been a long day, Luisa. I have my appointment tomorrow, and I have to get Julio back."

"Is he going to be okay?" she asked, not really caring about the welfare of her stepson.

"He better be!"

"I'm sure he will."

Luisa continued the seduction, rubbing his arm and kissing him. She progressed to rubbing his crotch, trying to arouse him. Jorge sat there, quietly wondering if he would rise to the occasion. She began telling him how much she wanted to feel him inside her, how she couldn't wait. Slowly, Jorge felt himself becoming stimulated. Luisa started to breathe heavier.

She stood and took his hand to lead him into their bedroom. Jorge followed, anxious to perform—not for her, but for him. Once inside the bedroom, Jorge closed the door and began to undress before she came over to him and loosened his belt. Then she unbuttoned his shirt, kissing him on the chest while her hands made sure he was still in the game. Once he was naked, he tried to begin undressing her, but she stopped him and led him to the bed.

Slowly, she began to seductively remove her blouse, revealing her bulging breasts held captive by her bra for a brief moment. She reached behind her and undid the snaps, sliding the bra slowly away, spilling her breasts and button nipples, erect and waiting. She then lowered her skirt to the floor, confessing the absence of panties. She stood proudly before him wearing only her smile.

Luisa slowly moved toward the bed, looking at his crotch.

"I can't wait to feel you inside me. I'm going to make you feel so good."

Jorge just watched, hoping and praying his semi-erect penis would rise to the occasion.

"Oohh! You look so good. I bet you taste good too," she said, starting to touch him.

At that moment his phone rang. Jorge jumped up and retrieved the phone from his pants, which were on the floor next to the bedroom door.

"Hello," Jorge said anxiously.

"Hello, Jorge."

It was Pablo Navarro.

26

Washington, D.C.

Billy walked briskly over to Jack, while Detectives Keane and Fatek stopped to talk with Mr. Prescott and Father Mike.

"Jack, we don't have much," Billy said, irritated. "Clyde's has cameras, but they weren't working. They had new cameras scheduled for install tomorrow. What we've determined is the perpetrators were of Spanish descent. There were at least three of them, possibly four. One was driving a getaway car."

Jack interrupted. "Has Keane been cooperative?"

"Yeah, he hasn't been a problem. He let me talk to the manager, bartender and waitress after he did. We shared information. It was all pretty much the same."

"You don't think the restaurant people had anything to do with it, do you?"

"What do you mean?"

"Like, did the bartender tip off the kidnappers?"

"No, I don't think he had anything to do with it. I think the Spanish dudes followed your father and son into the bar. They've probably been tailing your dad for a couple of days. Even if they lost sight of him, they would know to go there. You know how much he loves that place."

"Did you ask if they were already there when my father and Connor came into the restaurant?"

"I did, and they said your father and son got there first. The waitress was pretty upset. Apparently she knew Connor, but not intimately."

Jack gave him a puzzled look.

"I don't think he banged her yet, but he probably would have," Billy said innocuously. "She's pretty hot!"

"Jesus Christ, Billy! What the fuck does that have to do with anything?!"

"You never know, but anyway, she was able to give a pretty good description of one of the guys. He came over to the table and talked to Connor, after your father went to the bathroom to drain his donkey."

"What about the bartender? What did he have to say?" Jack asked, ignoring Billy's irreverence.

"He said the one guy who paid the tab was older than the other two. You'd think he could have given great descriptions since they were his only customers at that point, but he didn't."

"Anything peculiar?"

"He said the older dude just drank diet soda, and the others drank Modelo beer."

"That's a Mexican beer. Maybe they're Mexican."

"I don't think so—get this, they first asked for Hatuey beer."

"So?"

"Hatuey beer is made in Cuba."

"How'd you know that?"

"'Cause I'm smart!" Billy answered. "Actually, I had a Cuban friend in 'Nam who talked about how he'd die for a Hatuey beer. The name of the beer sounded pretty shitty to me, so I asked him about it. He told me it was kinda like, the national beer of Cuba."

Jack nodded. "What about DNA or fingerprints? They had to touch glasses and the counter."

"When they got up, the bartender immediately put their glasses in the sink and washed 'em. Apparently, he's pretty anal about being clean. He also wiped down the counter."

"Does Keane know this information?"

"He knew about the bartender cleaning everything, but he didn't know about the Hatuey beer. I decided to share it with him. You never know, he might be able to share better information later. I figured if we keep him in the loop, he'll do the same for us."

"Good thinking," Jack said. "Did you ask if anyone saw the getaway car?"

"I did, and they didn't know, but a witness outside said it looked like they piled into a dark-colored van of some type with Maryland tags."

"Direction of travel?"

"The witness said it looked like it was headed toward the Scott Key Bridge."

"So, unless they were deliberately throwing us a curve," Jack said, trying to consider all the angles, "they're probably southbound in Virginia."

"Yep, that's what I'd say."

Keane and Fatek started walking over toward Jack and Billy. Prescott and Delledonne remained where they were and continued talking.

"Did Billy fill you in?" Keane asked.

"Yeah, he did. Have you notified VSP?" Jack asked, referring to the Virginia State Police.

Keane looked at him with contempt. "Of course! Give me some credit."

"Sorry, I know you know how to do your job. Consider me a checks and balances type of guy."

"Look, Jack, we're sharing information here. Don't act like you're my supervisor."

Jack moved up close to Keane until they were a foot apart. "In case you didn't hear, my father got shot, and is a couple of breaths away from death. My son has been kidnapped and God knows where he's at, or even if he's alive. So don't give me any shit about asking some questions."

Keane glared back at him. "Y'know, Jack, I don't have to tell you shit! In case you forgot, you're not a cop anymore," he answered through clenched teeth. "So why don't you go fuck yourself!"

The tension of the moment was temporarily relieved when Keane's phone vibrated. He didn't answer it right away. He wasn't finished glaring at Jack, but finally, he walked away to pick it up. Detective Fatek walked away too.

"Holy shit, Jack! I thought you were gonna punch his lights out!" Billy said.

Jack regained his composure. "That would've been pretty stupid. He's right. He doesn't have to tell us anything."

Keane walked back to Jack and Billy. "That was VSP. A van was found in Annandale," he said, controlling his emotions. "It was scorched. Nothing much left of it. I doubt we'll get anything out of it evidence wise, but it may provide a clue. We're checking the local airports close to where the car was found for anyone matching the description that's flown out within the last couple of hours."

Jack nodded. "Listen, I'm sorry. I'm just a little stressed."

Keane waved a dismissive hand through the air. "Forget it, Jack. I can't imagine what you're going through. We're going to do everything we can. You know that." A moment later, he added, "Your father might be a help, if he can talk to us."

"I don't think that's possible. He's still in recovery. They told me that when he gets a room, he'll be heavily sedated."

"What are his chances?"

"You mean of staying alive?"

"Yeah."

Jack related in detail his conversation with the doctor. Detective Keane listened intently while Detective Fatek and Billy stood by.

"I think under these circumstances, we're not gonna hang around," Keane said. "I'll give you my number in case something changes. I'm gonna give my number to the nursing staff, too, in case your dad wakes up in the middle of the night. I live about fifteen minutes from here. I think, for now, we'll head over to Annandale and take a look at the car."

Jack didn't like the fact that Keane lived closer to the hospital than he did, but he knew he'd get called first. He could always tell the nurses he'd call Detective Keane.

"That'll be good," Jack said before taking Keane's number and adding it to his phone.

"Thanks, I appreciate it."

"I hope your dad's going to be okay," Detective Keane added.

"I guess time will tell."

They shook hands and Keane and Fatek left.

Mr. Prescott and Father Mike walked over.

"Jack, can I talk to you in private?" Mr. Prescott asked.

"Yeah, sure," Jack answered.

They walked over to an unoccupied are of the waiting room. The other couple had left during Jack's conversation with Keane.

"Jack, your father wanted me to tell you, in case he was ever incapacitated, that he wants you to take charge of the company," Mr. Prescott stated evenly.

He looked at Mr. Prescott for a moment before asking, "What is your legal authority?"

"I am the legal counsel for WISE International. I sit on the Board of Directors."

"When did this conversation take place?"

"Last week, when he knew you would come to work for him."

"Of course, I'm sure you've made it legal?"

"Yes, a succession document has already been properly filed."

"What about the vice president? There is one, isn't there?"

"Yes, but I can assure you, he wants no part of running the company. He's older, and is perfectly content with his current position. He has been in this position for several years and enjoys it, but he enjoys spending time with his family and grandkids more. I'm sure he wants to retire soon. You'll have no problem with him."

"Sounds to me like he's dead weight."

"He's quite competent. Your father and him have a great history. They go way back. His name is John Haug."

"First of all, my father's going to have a full recovery. Second, I don't know if *I* want the responsibility of running this company. My strength is being out in the field doing investigations, not paper-pushing."

"For now, I think we can wait and see what happens, but if he's incapacitated for any length of time, you'll need to address the responsibility."

Jack just nodded.

They walked back to Father Mike who was waiting patiently.

"I think we'll go now, Jack," Mr. Prescott said. "Call me if anything new develops."

Jack nodded as he shook Mr. Prescott's hand. As he was shaking Father Mike's hand, Father Mike leaned in and said quietly, "I need to speak with you as soon as possible. It's urgent. Here's my card," he said as he handed Jack his card.

Jack looked at the card, then looked up at Father Mike and asked, "When?"

Father Mike appeared troubled. He simply said, "Call me later, and we'll set up a time."

27

Jorge took the phone and sat naked in a large cushioned wing-back chair, facing the bed. A look of great concern covered his face. Luisa angrily crossed her arms as she sat up in bed. Her face was filled with disgust.

"What do you want?" he asked, speaking into the phone.

"I hope I'm not interrupting anything," Pablo Navarro stated with a contained chuckle.

"Just get to the fucking point!"

"I'm sorry. From the tone of your voice, I must have interrupted something. My apologies."

"Listen Pablo, I don't have time for your fuckin' games. Just tell me what you want."

"I was thinking we could meet Thursday at twelve o'clock at La Carreta on Calle Ocho. I've taken the liberty to reserve a room on the second floor. I will be with one other person as I've requested. I expect you will only be there with one other person as well. I don't want any trouble. Believe me, I just want to talk business and see if we can work out an agreement of mutual interest. If not, we can go our separate ways."

"You'll have my son there, too," Jorge stated, not giving Navarro any choice.

"Yes, your son will be there, but I'm giving you a heads up. I don't want any problems. If I detect a double-cross, you will never see your son again."

"There won't be any problems," Jorge said, biting his tongue.

"Good. I'm glad to hear that."

"Why are we meeting in Miami?" Jorge asked, pleased that his son had apparently been successful in steering the meeting to La Carreta.

"I thought of it as neutral ground, and I wanted to keep you from doing something stupid. I knew in the U.S., you would think twice about trying anything that would jeopardize our new relationship, and your freedom."

"Can I speak to my son now?"

"He's not with me at the moment, but he's here in Miami. You'll see him on Thursday."

"I'll be there."

"Good. There's part of me that can't wait to see you in person, and talk about our future."

"What's the other part?"

"The part that says I don't trust you completely."

"What makes you think I trust you?"

"You don't. That's what'll keep us honest."

"I'll see you, *and* my son on Thursday at twelve o'clock at La Carreta on Calle Ocho."

"See you then," Pablo said, and hung up the phone.

Jorge sat on the chair, momentarily thinking about the situation. He looked over at the bed. Luisa had gone into the bathroom. At that moment, she marched out in her bathrobe and tried to walk past him. He reached out to stop her with his arm, but she pushed it away.

"*Mi amor*, why are you mad at me?"

She continued to walk out of the room without responding.

"That was an important phone call," he called out to her. "It was about Julio!"

He decided to take a shower, but not before calling Juan and telling him to meet him downstairs in a half hour.

After his shower, he went into the bedroom fully expecting Luisa to be there, telling him what a rotten bastard he was, but she wasn't there. He took some casual clothes Luisa had brought for him out of the closet, and put them on. When he went back into the bathroom to comb his hair, he looked at himself in the mirror.

It was the first time in a long while he had examined his face closely. What he saw was disturbing. The skin around his jaws was drooping, and appeared to be pulling away from the bone, giving him jowls. His eyes had become two dark circles, recessed in deep eye sockets. The color of his skin was sallow, and his hair was thinning. It seemed as if his body was decaying right in front of his deathly dark eyes. He was no longer the handsome man he remembered.

Jorge walked out into the living area. Luisa wasn't there. She wasn't in the kitchen either. He opened the sliding doors and looked out on the balcony. She wasn't there either. Closing the door, he called out for her, but got no response. He walked over to Miguelito's room and carefully opened the door. Looking in, he saw Luisa had crawled in bed with their son, and they were both sound asleep.

Jorge closed the door softly, and went downstairs to meet Juan at the restaurant reserved for those people staying above the twenty-sixth floor. He checked in with the concierge sitting outside the restaurant ensuring nobody unwanted entered. Once she ran his room key through a security device, he was permitted to enter.

Juan had already taken a table in the back next to the sliding glass doors overlooking Biscayne Bay.

"Anything good on the menu?" Jorge asked.

Juan shrugged. "Everything looks good."

They ordered sandwiches and drinks. When the waiter left, Jorge told Juan he had heard from Pablo Navarro.

"What did he say?" Juan asked.

"He wants to meet at La Carreta on Calle Ocho on Thursday at noon. He said he's reserved a room for our meeting."

"I'll check it out."

"Try to be discreet. I don't want any unnecessary interest to develop. We don't need the feds listening to us."

"That's not a problem. We already paid off a young woman who works at La Carreta. She says someone called to reserve a room on that day. She's trying to get us more information. At least it confirms what Navarro told you."

"Maybe. We'll see if it was him who reserved it. Then we'll know for sure. I still want that place surrounded when the meeting takes place. I'm sure he'll have his people scouting the outside too. Make sure we've got enough firepower to take out his people if necessary. We have to be careful." Jorge took a moment to consider the situation. "I don't want us to draw any attention. It's delicate. If the feds find out I'm in Miami, we won't have to worry about Navarro. They'll take me down and put me away for life, but I'm not going to sit there and let the Navarros take me down either."

"I'm not going to let that happen," Juan reassured him. "You're going to live a long life. You'll die in your own bed smoking a cigar, having a drink and getting laid!"

They laughed.

"I hope you're right," Jorge told him.

After they ate and talked more business, Jorge went back to his suite, where Luisa and Miguelito were in the kitchen eating snacks. Once Miguelito saw Jorge, he came running and jumped into his arms.

"How's my little man?"

"I'm fine, Papi," Miguelito said exuberantly. "How are you?"

"I'm good," he answered, casting a glance at Luisa. "What are you and Mommy doing?"

"We just ate lunch and now Mommy said we can go to the pool. Are you coming Papi?"

"No, I think I'll take a nap," he said, walking over to Luisa who was standing there coolly. He tried to kiss her on the lips, but she turned her head, offering her cheek instead. "You and Mommy go and have a good time. You can tell me all about it when you get back, okay?"

"Okay, Papi. I hope you feel better," Miguelito said, looking at him sheepishly.

"Thank you, son. I'm sure I will." Jorge turned to Luisa. "Perhaps when you get back, we can pick up where we left off."

She leaned forward as if to kiss him, but whispered instead, "Don't hold your breath."

28
Miami

The four-door sedan with darkened windows pulled up to Luisa's mother's condo located in a gated complex in southwest Miami. Jorge had paid a handsome sum for it, making sure it was gated for his security, not his mother-in-law's. It had all the appurtenances of a well-designed community including a golf course, swimming pool, clubhouse and round-the-clock concierge.

Luisa was raised in Miami, and Jorge couldn't refuse his mother-in-law's request to live in Miami instead of Belize. Of course, Luisa exerted sexual influence over him, and he found it difficult to refuse. Since several attempts had been made on his life through the years, and he needed a place to find sanctuary, if it became necessary, it was an easy choice. Besides, who wants their mother-in-law living with them all day, every day?

Jorge had visited there only a couple of times in the past five years, although Luisa and Miguelito were there four or five times every year. He was only there now because of his meeting with the Navarros, which ironically coincided with his doctor's appointment.

"Aren't you going to come in to say hello to my mother?" Luisa asked, pouting mockingly.

Jorge looked at her with amusement. He could never get used to her mood swings. One minute she despised him, and the next she wanted to take him to bed. "No, *mi amor.* I have business to conduct, and I need to get to Dr. Casalena's."

"I was hoping you could at least say hello."

"How 'bout when I get back? Okay?"

"Are you sure I can't come with you to your doctor's appointment?" she asked eagerly. "My mother could always watch Miguelito while we're gone."

"No, you go in without me," he said. "I'm sure Miguelito wants to go to the pool, don't you, son?"

Distracted by a game on his iPad, Miguelito just nodded.

"Give your mother my best," Jorge said before leaning over to kiss Luisa. He then kissed Miguelito on the top of his head as they were getting out of the car.

"I love you, Jorge," Luisa said, leaning into the car.

"I love you, too," Jorge answered. He could hear Miguelito say "I love you Papi!" in the background. "I love you Miguelito!" he shouted back.

Luisa put her luscious lips together and made a faux kiss before shutting the door.

Jorge's driver made a hurried exit onto the highway.

"Do you think we were followed?" Jorge asked.

"No, I don't," the driver answered confidently.

Jorge had left the hotel without an entourage. He told Juan he was afraid several cars would draw attention. Nevertheless, Juan had a few cars follow from a distance without telling Jorge. He situated a few other cars along the way, knowing where Luisa's mother lived.

They made their way to Brickell Avenue, the main road through the financial district of downtown Miami, lined with towering condominiums, restaurants, banks and high-rise office buildings. The palm trees rose up equidistant along the road in a planned, orderly fashion. Biscayne Bay was visible to the left, through the breaks in the buildings. Once they pulled into the parking garage, the armed driver quickly got out and looked around for anyone suspicious. He saw Juan's vehicles and knew it was safe.

After opening Jorge's door, he escorted him to the elevator. Both men were quiet. Jorge's presence intimidated the driver. He was a new man Juan had recently elevated into the position of trust. Jorge wasn't in the mood to converse. He was in deep thought about his impending appointment.

They made their way down the hallway to Dr. Casalena's office without encountering anyone. Once they went inside, the doctor was waiting there. He had cleared his calendar, ensuring Jorge complete privacy and care.

"Jorge, how good it is to see you again." Dr. Casalena was an older man who was bald on the top of his head, while bright gray hair surrounded the rest of his head. He had an electric smile and happy eyes behind gaudy glasses.

Jorge chose Dr. Casalena not just for his superior abilities, but also because he needed someone who was discreet and could be trusted. Dr. Casalena's services had come in handy several times through the years, sometimes requiring him to travel to unsavory places where danger prowled, including the jungles of Colombia and western Belize. Of course, he was paid generously for his services.

"Henry, I'm glad you could make time for me."

"I will always make time for you, Jorge," he said. "You know that. Let's go to my office."

They walked down the hallway towards his private office, but not before Dr. Casalena introduced Jorge to his staff for the day. They were two attractive women who, Jorge was assured later, were quite competent and dependable, including maintaining his confidentiality.

They had a brief one-on-one interview where Jorge explained his symptoms. Once they were finished, Jorge was taken to a room where he removed his clothing and put on a gown. He felt insecure without his knife and gun, but he knew his driver was in the waiting room, and Dr. Casalena had cleared his calendar. There should be no one entering the office.

After performing the typical exam of looking at his eyes, ears and throat, while taking his temperature and blood pressure, the doctor told Jorge they were going to take some x-rays, and a CT scan. Next, the doctor took a sample of Jorge's sputum, telling him he was going to examine it under a microscope. Afterwards, Jorge was told to get dressed and wait in the examination room. He waited for what seemed like a half-hour before the nurse came in and escorted him to Dr. Casalena's private office.

"What's the diagnosis, Henry?" Jorge asked, trying to appear unconcerned.

Dr. Casalena took his glasses off and laid them on his desk. He wiped his face with hand. "Jorge, we go back a long way. I know you've faced countless close calls, and I know you're a strong-willed man. I don't know how to tell you this, other than to come right out and say, I'm fairly certain you have lung cancer." He looked at Jorge to gauge his reaction.

"I suspected it, so it doesn't come as a surprise."

"Of course, I can't be certain until you have a biopsy. Your shortness of breath, fatigue and spitting up blood are classic symptoms. I listened to your chest and it didn't sound healthy. After reviewing your x-rays, your CT scan, looking into your lungs and examining your sputum, I'm ninety-nine percent sure."

Jorge sat there in thought. He had faced many enemies, but he always had control of the outcome. This time he knew he didn't.

"How long do I have?"

"It's hard to say, but I think you're in Stage Four which means maybe a few months to a year. Don't count out treatment. It could add some months to your life. Modern medicine has made great strides. I recommend that you see an oncologist who will most likely recommend radiation and various medicines."

"I'm not doing that. All that will do is prolong my life, but it won't improve its quality. Eventually, we all die, Henry. I guess my time is closer than I expected. Funny, I always thought I would get shot!"

"Be careful, there's still time for that!"

They both laughed.

"I wish I had better news, and again, until you have more tests, who knows?"

"No, you got it right, Henry. I've sensed it for a while now."

Jorge stood up and so did the doctor. They shook hands and walked out to the waiting room together. The bodyguard put down the magazine he was reading, looking embarrassed.

Jorge turned to Dr. Casalena and shook his hand again.

"Thanks, Henry."

The doctor just nodded solemnly.

Jorge and his driver went to the elevator, down to the garage where his car was parked. A Jeep went by squealing its wheels. The driver reached behind his back and grabbed his pistol.

29

Washington, D.C.

Jack stood at the end of the concourse waiting for his ex-wife. Billy had offered his assistance to prevent any awkward moments, but Jack refused. He was detached from her, and knew he could handle himself professionally. Although he hadn't seen her in years, she most likely was still beautiful. Women in Hollywood don't allow themselves to wither on the vine. With all the plastic surgeons, she undoubtedly found one to maintain her youthful looks.

Jack spotted her as she came toward him pulling an expensive piece of luggage behind her, wearing a blue dress that clung to her still-vivacious curves. Her shoulder-length blonde hair was perfectly coiffed. She had a sad smile, but she was just as beautiful as he remembered her. All of a sudden he felt nervous, not because of amorous feelings, but because he knew after this crisis was over, he would have to bury the relationship again. Now, he wished Billy had come with him.

"Hello, Meg," Jack said without any sign of emotion.

"Hello, Jack," she replied as she kissed him on the cheek.

"Here, let me take your bag," he said, reaching out to take the handle, touching her hand for a brief, awkward moment.

"Thank you."

They began walking toward the baggage area. "Do you have any other luggage?"

"No, this is it," she said before asking, "I'm so sorry I didn't ask earlier when we were talking on the phone, but how is your father?"

161

"He's still in critical condition. He was shot in the back. The bullet traveled through his chest, missing his heart. Unfortunately, they had to take one of his lungs. They can't say for sure he'll recover, but for now, he's stable."

"I'm so sorry, Jack."

"Thank you," was all Jack could say.

"What about Connor?"

"The police are working very hard on it. I haven't had an update recently, but last I heard they think the kidnappers are Spanish, and they are headed south."

"What would Spanish kidnappers want with Connor, and headed south…where?"

"We think they're headed for an airport."

"Airport? Why? Where would they take him?"

"We're not certain yet."

"It still doesn't answer the question of why!"

Jack was hesitant to say more. He knew if he told her he thought they were taking him to Belize, it would just lead to more questions. Eventually, she would hate Jack for being the reason behind it. Still, Jack couldn't say for sure what the reason was, so as far as he was concerned, he wasn't lying to her.

"Do they want money? Have they given any ransom demands yet?"

"No, they haven't."

She just stared into space trying to come up with some answers.

Her eyes grew wide. Clasping her hands, she asked, "Do you think he's still alive?"

"I'm almost certain he is. They haven't contacted anyone yet with any demands, so it's likely he's still alive."

They walked out to the parking garage, and Jack placed her suitcase into the trunk before opening her door and getting in the car. Jack turned the radio down. He said, "I thought you would've come in a private jet. Doesn't your husband own a studio or something like that?"

She hesitated before saying, "We're separated."

Jack didn't know how to respond. When he didn't speak, Meg asked sheepishly, "Don't you want to know why?"

"I figure it's none of my business, but if you want to tell me, I'm all ears."

"He started cheating on me. I knew about it—well kinda, I wasn't sure, but I hired an investigator. He showed me pictures and videos. So, then I confronted Don about it. He denied it! Son of a bitch! He wouldn't admit it, at least at first, but finally he asked for forgiveness. Like an idiot, I gave in to him. After a while I just ignored it. This went on for years. I figured he was providing a good life for Connor and me so why should I rock the boat—"

"So you knew about it and let it go on. Did you have someone else too?"

Meg paused before answering, but eventually admitted to committing adultery too. "I was angry at first, so yes, I had a grudge fuck with someone who was kind to me. I could talk with him about my situation, and he would listen. He wasn't exactly handsome, but I didn't care. I wanted to get even. So, I had an affair with him for several months."

"What happened?"

"Don found out about it and confronted me. Can you believe it? He's fucking all these women in the studio, and then he's going to come down on me because I'm fucking someone else? Give me a break!"

Jack drove without speaking. He couldn't believe he was hearing her talk like this. He had never seen this side of her, but it had been almost twenty years since he had seen or talked to her.

"How did he and Connor get along?" Jack asked.

"At first, when Connor was young, they got along famously. As Connor got older, Don was never around. He was too busy. Then Connor began to ignore Don whenever he was home. He was angry. I think he could see how unhappy I was and he resented Don for it. As you know, Connor is a very intelligent young man."

"At least you should get a good settlement out of it, shouldn't you?"

"He said if I tried to take him to court, he would expose me for having an affair also. He said I wouldn't get a dime out of him."

"That doesn't sound exactly true. A judge would make sure you and Connor were taken care of, right? I mean, I know its California and everything, but it seems to me you would get some kind of nice settlement."

"I signed a pre-nup."

"So?"

"So, in California I would probably get screwed!"

Jack didn't answer.

"I guess you think I'm terrible, don't you?"

"Meg, I don't know how to answer your question. All I'm thinking about is how to get Connor back."

She started to cry. Her life had unraveled in enormous magnitudes. Her marriage had disintegrated, and now her only son was missing.

They drove in silence for a few minutes.

"I'm going to drop you off at the Four Seasons in Georgetown. I've made reservations for you, and then I'm going to catch up with the investigators to get an update. I know them, and they've kept me informed. They don't have to tell me shit, you know. I'm no longer a cop. I've retired."

"I heard," she said, turning to look at him.

"From who?"

"Your father told me. We've managed to stay in touch over the years. He's always tried to stay in Connor's life. He's the one who paid for his education, not Don."

Jack pulled up to the Four Seasons a short time later. They both exited the car. He took her suitcase and carried it into the hotel. At the front desk, Meg checked in. She offered a credit card, but Jack intervened and paid for her room. He escorted her up to her room to make sure she was situated. He brought in her suitcase and looked around. Crazy as it seemed, he wanted to make sure she was alone.

"Would you like to have a drink?" she asked.

"No. I need to get going."

Her disappointment was obvious. "Thank you for taking care of my room."

"You're welcome. I'll keep you up to date when I know anything new."

"Okay," she said, smiling.

Jack turned and left.

As he got to his car, his phone rang.

30

"**H**ello," Jack answered his phone.

"Jack, it's Brian Oliver."

"Hey Brian, what's up?"

"I think we have a lead on Jorge DePeralta."

"Really?" Jack answered.

"Jack, we think he might be in Miami."

Jack was excited. He knew it would be much easier to get Connor back if he was in the United States, instead of a foreign country.

"You are aware my father has been shot, and my son has been kidnapped?"

"Yes, I know. We just got word."

"Is there anything I can do to help catch that son of a bitch?"

"Not for the moment. Let me confirm that DePeralta is in Miami, and then I'll get back to you."

"If he's in Miami, I wanna go there," Jack said seriously. "I want to look that motherfucker in the eye, and then beat the shit out of him! Don't worry, I won't kill him. I'll give him back to you when I'm done."

"Whoa! Hold on Jack! It ain't gonna happen like that. He's not your everyday, run-of-the-mill criminal. This guy is dangerous. We need to locate him, keep him under surveillance, develop a plan, and then move on it. Once we have him safely in custody, we'll let you talk to him."

"Why not take him out now? Isn't there paper hanging on him in the U. S.?" Jack said, referring to warrants.

"Believe it or not, no. We haven't been able to tie him to any direct crimes in the U.S."

"Maybe I should go down there, and hang out until you get him."

"No, Jack. Don't do it. Let us handle it. Besides, you have your father to look after now."

"Have you informed the local investigators yet?"

"No, we haven't. Their investigation is separate from ours. We're going after Jorge DePeralta. Nobody can say for sure he's involved in the shooting of your father, and the kidnapping of your son. Our investigation is drug cartel related. It may tie in, but then again it may not. We'll let them in on it if, and when, we have reason to believe DePeralta is involved. Until then, I don't want you to say anything to anyone. I'm giving you a courtesy call because after the last fiasco you and I were involved in, I trust you, and I think I owe this to you."

"Thanks, Brian. You have my word, I won't say anything," Jack said convincingly. "But, keep me informed. I won't do anything until I receive direction from you."

"Okay, Jack. I will."

They hung up. Jack considered what his next step would be. There wasn't much he could do for his father except be there. He wasn't going to Miami against Brian Oliver's request. If he did, he knew he would never receive any more information. If, however, Detective Keane told him their investigation pointed to Connor being in Miami, he would have every right to go.

Jack called Detective Keane as he pulled out of the Four Seasons. The madness of traffic in Georgetown was just beginning. Between commuters, pedestrians and visitors, cars moved at a snail's pace. Getting to Annandale via the interstate would piss Jack off even more, but it was still the fastest way to get there, *if* he was going there.

"Hello Jack," Keane said as he answered his phone.

"Bill, any news?"

"Yes and no," Keane said cooperatively. "We're processing the van right now. There are signs of blood in the cargo area. Not a lot, but enough to be concerned about. There is a carpet back there where the blood is."

"Does it look like enough that somebody was killed?"

"No, it doesn't. It looks like someone had a significant cut, but not an amount to indicate someone was killed back there."

"I know you've checked the airports by now. What have you turned up?"

"Nothing yet. We've checked with Reagan, Dulles, Richmond, even BWI in case they decided to go north. All negative so far. We've put them on alert, and also extended it to Roanoke, Norfolk, Newport News, Charlottesville, Lynchburg and Shenandoah."

"Does that cover all of the airports in the area?"

"As far as I know."

"I'd like to drive out to the scene."

"Jack, there's nothing for you to do. It's all being processed. You know how that works. You gather evidence, and then wait for the lab results. I know you probably feel like a caged animal, but seriously Jack, you'd be wasting your time."

Jack knew Keane was right. It would accomplish nothing to stand by and watch. Still, he felt that Keane might be missing something. He didn't know exactly what it could be, but instinct told him a key element was being overlooked, yet he decided not to go to the crime scene because he didn't want to ruin the relationship he had built with Keane. He would need his help down the road, and besides, Jack was confident that he would discover any missed leads through his analytical thinking.

"Okay Bill, I guess you're right. I'm going to head for the hospital. Call me immediately if you discover anything, will you?"

"Absolutely. If anything turns up, I'll call you right away," Keane reassured him.

Jack changed direction and started for the hospital. His thoughts turned to his father. He didn't relish the thought of his father dying, particularly leaving him as the person in charge of WISE International. Jack didn't kid himself. He hardly knew his father, so the emotional attachment was weak, yet he respected him and what he had accomplished. He didn't want him to suffer, and he didn't want him to die.

When he arrived at his father's room, there was a man sitting on a chair outside the door. He was smartly dressed in a suit and was reading a newspaper. He looked to be in his thirties, well-groomed, and moderately handsome.

"Who are you?" Jack asked.

The man stood up and placed the newspaper on his seat. He smiled and extended his hand. "I'm Bruce Schofield. I was sent to guard your father. You must be his son."

"Actually, I'm here to murder Ben Dublin," Jack said as he looked the man in the eye with intent.

Bruce Schofield froze with a perplexed look. He stared at Jack trying to size him up.

"Let me see some identification," Bruce said with his left hand extended, while his right hand moved to pull his jacket back, most likely to grab his gun.

Jack just stared at him, clearly enjoying the moment. "I don't have any," he said, curious to see how the man would handle the situation.

Within five seconds, Jack felt his face against the concrete block wall of the hospital, with his hand being held behind his back.

Bruce Schofield whispered in Jack's ear, "If you think you're getting past me, you better think twice, because I will rip your arm off and shove it down your fucking throat!"

Jack quickly countered, and escaped Schofield's hold before pinning him against the wall.

Nurses looked on in astonishment as they steered clear.

"I am Jack Dublin. I was curious to see what kind of talent was watching my father," Jack said with Schofield neutralized. "Who sent you here?"

"Mr. Prescott," Schofield answered, gritting his teeth.

Jack released his hold. Schofield turned around. Pulling at the end of his sleeves and straightening his tie, he looked at Jack. He clearly wasn't happy.

"Why did Mr. Prescott send you here?" Jack asked.

"He said he was afraid whoever did this to your father might find out he was still alive, then come back to finish the job."

Jack felt foolish. Mr. Prescott was right. Assassins usually come back to complete any unfinished business. He, not Prescott, should have thought to put someone on his father's door.

"I'm glad to see he didn't put a flunky on my father's door," Jack said. Schofield didn't acknowledge him. "Sorry 'bout that. I don't take any chances."

A doctor approached with two hospital security constables, one on each side. He looked to be in his early forties. He was well-groomed, with dark hair and glasses. "Hello, my name is Dr. Stafford. Are you two related to Mr. Dublin?"

"I'm his son," Jack replied, looking strangely at the doctor as if there was something he recognized about him.

"And who are you?"

"I'm just a...bodyguard for Mr. Dublin," Schofield answered.

Dr. Stafford looked at them and said, "Mr. Dublin, please follow me." He pushed the door to Ben Dublin's room and entered. Jack followed.

The doctor approached Ben who was lying still, apparently still unresponsive with tubes everywhere. He took Ben's arm into his hand and placed his fingers on his wrist to take his pulse. Jack just stood by and watched, somewhat preoccupied. Once he was done, he took the stethoscope from around his neck, placed the rubber earpieces in his ears, and put the bell on Ben's chest. After listening for a while, he removed the bell and earpieces and placed the stethoscope around his neck.

"Mr. Dublin, your father has made some progress, but I can still hear some disturbing sounds in his remaining lung. I'm going to run some tests tomorrow. I think he's going to be okay, but I want to make sure we haven't missed anything."

"Will he fully recover?"

"I believe he will, but like I said, I want to take every precaution."

"I understand," Jack said, nodding. "And I appreciate it."

Jack stood there hearing what the doctor was saying, but there was something peculiar, something odd. He couldn't put his finger on it, but something the doctor said triggered a thought. Finally, he realized what it was.

"Would you excuse me please?"

"Certainly," Dr. Stafford said. "I have some other patients I need to visit anyway. I'll be back later. I have your number if you're not here, and I'll call you, or someone from my staff will call you, if anything changes, okay?"

"Sounds good." Jack shook his hand before walking down the hall to a quiet area in the lounge. He took his phone out and called Bill Keane.

"Hey Jack, what's up?"

"The airports you told me about...did you check the Stafford airport?"

"No, Jack. We didn't. I don't know why."

"Check it out, will you?"

31
Miami

The light morning rain gave way to the sun and white puffy clouds. It was one of the alleged benefits of living in Miami. Rains typically don't last long, but the sun is scorching hot, and the humidity is smothering. Unless you lived there year-round, you never got used to the heat.

Jorge and Juan left the Epic and began their journey to La Carreta on Calle Ocho. They rode in silence, each of them contemplating the potential for disaster, even though they had been over the plan many times. Yet, it was fool's comfort that got you killed.

Jorge's thoughts took a detour from the approaching confrontation. His mind drifted back as he reflected on his life. As he looked outside his window at the passersby, he remembered when he came here for a visit with his mother and father as a child. They were happier times that didn't last long enough. His father, a respected Cuban attorney, was gunned down in Miami, in front of Jorge and his mother in a robbery attempt. Perhaps, Jorge justified, if he'd had a stable childhood he could have become a genuine businessman, truly worthy of his wealth and stature in legitimate society. He wouldn't have to live in seclusion worried about himself, or his family getting killed, particularly in a grisly way.

Likewise, he wouldn't have killed anyone, even though he was indifferent about killing his victims. They were justified in his mind, simple casualties of war, and he enjoyed sending a message to anyone thinking about coming after him. Fear rules. To stay alive you needed to be ruthless and brutal. When someone crossed over the threshold into the drug scene, they had to expect the consequences. For him, there was an enormous sense of pride to survive the many times he faced death. Now, cancer was going to snuff him out. It was not the true warrior's death he had hoped for.

Jorge turned his gaze from outside the window to Juan, as they got on the turnpike.

"Are we being followed?" Jorge asked.

"Yes, but by our people," Juan replied.

"Let's review one more time. Was the table delivered?"

"Yes, yesterday."

"What about the security?

"Our men are all over the place as wait staff, valets and customers."

"What about the security at the door of our meeting room?"

"Got that covered too. The security firm we agreed to is an American firm with an office in Miami," Juan said. "I requested to meet the man they were sending, and I paid him a great bonus to overlook our guns. When he pats us down, he'll say we're clean."

"What about the exterior security?"

"We've got snipers on the roof of Versailles and walking the street. If anyone from the Navarro family tries anything, we'll wipe them out."

"We have to be careful. I don't want anything to happen to Julio."

"I agree, Jorge," Juan said, as he measured the gravity of the situation.

"You know, Juan, we have fought many battles together. You are my good friend. Let's not let this be our last battle. Undoubtedly, there will be more to follow, and we have to stick together."

"Absolutely!"

They made their way to La Carreta. Juan had talked to his men in position while they were en route. All of them confirmed they had not seen anyone from the Navarro family arrive, and they had not seen anyone as lookouts.

The limousine pulled up to the entrance. A valet opened the door and Juan got out. Once he surveyed the street, he leaned in to tell Jorge it was okay to get out. Jorge walked briskly to the entrance. Once inside he was taken upstairs to the meeting room. There was a tall, black male, about six-feet-three or four, in a suit that appeared to be ready to burst from the bulging muscles it restrained underneath.

Jorge and Juan were shown to seats in an alcove outside the door of the meeting room. It was agreed that everyone would enter together in order to watch each other being frisked. Juan didn't say anything, so Jorge suspected this man was the same one who had been paid off.

A half hour passed before the Navarros arrived. Jorge knew it was probably done deliberately to piss him off, but he was determined not to allow it to interfere with how he handled the meeting.

Pablo Navarro and another man, a bodyguard, walked up the steps toward Jorge. Pablo smiled broadly, displaying perfect white-capped teeth below a thick black moustache.

"It is an honor to see you again, Señor DePeralta," Pablo said, as he reached the landing outside the meeting room. He held out his hand which Jorge reluctantly shook.

"I don't recall ever meeting you before."

"We met a long time ago. I was only nine years old at the time," he said as he watched Jorge being patted down. "I accidently walked into a meeting you were having with my father. My father was not happy with me and as I remember, you asked me to come over to you. You shook my hand and put your arm around my shoulders. You talked to me for a while, asking me how old I was, and did I like sports. My father relaxed after that, and told me to be more careful about walking into a room where the door was closed, without knocking. I have not forgotten that act of kindness, Señor DePeralta."

Jorge listened with great interest. He didn't remember the encounter, even after hearing about it from Pablo.

"That's kind of you to remember, Pablo," Jorge said as he watched Pablo being patted down. Pablo's bodyguard, whose name was unknown since they weren't introduced, was also searched. No weapons were produced. Shortly thereafter, Juan and Jorge were patted down. Pablo didn't question who the security person was who patted everyone down. This bothered Jorge. Why didn't he ask? He wondered if they had been compromised.

After everyone was declared clean, they entered the room where their futures would be determined. Jorge and Juan took seats at the far end of the table. Pablo and his bodyguard sat at the other end closest to the door.

Apparently, Pablo anticipated Jorge was going to ask a question about his son. "I'm sure you're curious why Julio is not here?"

"Let's just say, I'm not happy he's not here," Jorge answered evenly.

Pablo was still smiling. "He will be here shortly. First, I wanted to talk to you about our future, without Julio being here," he said. "I think it might prevent us from having a candid discussion about our businesses if he were here. You see, Julio and I have had many conversations over the last few days. While he is a good man, he is blinded by anger. There is no place for anger here today. We cannot forge a friendship with anger being a foundation."

"We will never be friends, Pablo," Jorge said, measured enough not to incite Pablo.

"We may not become close friends, but we can become business partners. If that's the case, we must develop a trust. That won't happen with anger and hatred."

Jorge's hair bristled hearing him talk, yet he hid his discontent. He decided to let Pablo talk without trying to take control of the meeting. He knew it would feed his ego. "What do you have in mind?"

"Let's face it, there's tons of money to be made without stepping on each other's toes. Right now, our people along the distribution lines are fighting with your people. The result is people getting killed and a loss in profits for both of us. Additionally, we open ourselves up to outside scrutiny with the police in every country where we're dealing."

"We're already being watched by every law enforcement agency in existence," Jorge said unequivocally. "What do you propose?"

"I think we need to split up the territories where we do business."

Jorge suppressed a laugh, keeping it to a slight smile. "I don't think that would accomplish anything. Eventually, one of us would complain about the loss of revenue because we don't like our realigned areas."

"I understand your position, but I think we could select the territories in a fair, impartial way," Pablo said. His manner and tone were now more serious.

"I still disagree."

"Well then, maybe we need to share our mules," Pablo said, referring to the expendable people who were at risk.

"You know and I know, those people are a dime a dozen."

Pablo was starting to get more animated. "You could at least share some of your many contacts on your payroll in the governments."

Jorge now realized what it was that Pablo really wanted. "I'm not sharing my contacts. I'm sure you have paid protection throughout Mexico."

"I do, and I would be willing to share them with you."

"With all due respect, I don't do business with the swine in Mexico. They are a bunch of lowlife peasants who can't be trusted," Jorge said nonchalantly. "Present company excluded, of course. Perhaps when I can look my son straight in the eye, I may feel differently."

Pablo looked at Jorge with contempt. He glanced at his bodyguard and nodded. The bodyguard pulled out his phone and made a call.

"Jorge, I will deliver your son as promised, but first I want to give you a gift. It is a gift to show my appreciation for the respect and kindness you gave me years ago. While I am disappointed you have decided not to do business with me and my family, I will still show you the respect and honor that you deserve."

There was a knock on the door.

"Shall I open it?" the bodyguard asked.

Pablo nodded.

When the bodyguard opened the door, there was a FedEx driver standing there.

"Can we help you?" the bodyguard asked.

"I have a package for a Jorge DePeralta," he said. "Is he here?"

Pablo and the bodyguard pointed at Jorge.

"Who's it from?" Jorge asked as the driver walked toward him.

"It's from someone named Pablo, with an address in Mexico," he said as he examined the package. It was a fairly large box secured with

Amazon tape, about twenty-four inches in height and width. It wasn't very heavy. Producing a Power Pad, the driver said, "Sign here."

Jorge signed for it and the driver briskly walked out.

Jorge looked at Pablo who had a wide grin on his face. His hands were folded on his stomach. "Go ahead. Open it. I hope you like it."

Jorge pulled out his knife and cut the tape around the top. As he opened the box, he periodically looked at Pablo who was still smiling. There was a lot of gauze type paper protecting the contents. As Jorge began removing the packing paper, he again looked at Pablo. He was still smiling, but it didn't go unnoticed that his hands were no longer on his stomach. Slowly and deliberately, Jorge continued to remove the paper until he saw his gift. His eyes widened as he read what was written on his son's decapitated head. "*Singate*," the Spanish equivalent of "Fuck you!"

Pablo began to laugh hysterically.

"You motherfucker!" Jorge said as he reached for the mounted gun under the table that was pointed directly across the table at Pablo. Before Jorge could get a clear shot off, Pablo had jumped out of his chair. Juan pulled his 9mm Beretta out from behind his back. The bodyguard pulled Pablo out of the way and revealed his gun. He fired a shot at Juan, hitting him in the shoulder. He then turned to Jorge and fired a shot, but he had ducked under the table where it had been specially fortified to protect against bullets.

Quickly, the bodyguard and Pablo ran down the stairs out to a waiting car.

Jorge went over to Juan who was losing blood, but it didn't appear to be a mortal wound.

"Juan!" Jorge said excitedly. "You need to get the word out that Pablo has left, and he needs to be killed."

Juan was moaning in pain.

Jorge slapped Juan across the face. "Dammit Juan! Tell them to kill Pablo Navarro!"

Juan slowly grabbed his phone and pushed a speed dial number. "Kill Pablo Navarro," he said with as much energy as he could gather.

Soon, the crackling of gunfire could be heard outside. It sounded like too many shots to be coming from only Jorge's contingent. There were single shots accompanied by an occasional rapid fire from assault weapons.

"C'mon Juan," Jorge said, helping Juan to stand up. "We need to get out of here."

They cautiously entered the foyer outside the meeting room, first looking quickly, then ducking back into the room. Jorge was thinking they may encounter Pablo and his bodyguard, but they were gone. However, he hoped to encounter the security guard who proclaimed the Navarros were not carrying weapons. He wanted to kill him, but he too was gone.

As they traversed the steps, a Hispanic man came hurriedly through the doors of the restaurant with a gun extended in his hand. Jorge recognized him. It was the new driver. The driver's eyes widened when he saw the blood on Juan's shirt. He stuffed his gun into his pants, and then came over to Jorge.

"Let me help you," he said as he got on the other side of Juan and lifted his arm, placing it around his shoulder. Juan screamed in agony.

"We're parked out back," the driver said.

"What happened to Pablo Navarro?" Jorge asked.

Looking Jorge straight in the eye, he said, "I don't know."

32

Jack returned to his father's room. He peered down at him, examining the way he looked, as if he could determine his fate. The man was under heavy sedation, appearing peaceful. The ventilator helped his breathing.

Regardless of his father's condition, Jack knew he had to get to Miami. Connor's fate was a stronger priority. Jack's presence there could at least save his son's life.

Ben started to move slightly. It was the first time Jack had seen him move since the shooting. Ben grimaced as he tried to shift his weight. He opened his eyes, and Jack looked at him trying to read his thoughts. Ben couldn't talk with the tube down his throat.

"Don't try and talk," Jack told him. "You've been shot, but you're going to be okay. It will just take some time."

Ben just stared at Jack. He tried to talk anyway and realized he couldn't. A nurse entered the room and was surprised to see that Ben had regained consciousness. She began checking the monitors that recorded his vital signs.

"These are all good signs, Mr. Dublin," she said to her patient before turning to Jack. "Sir, I think it would be wise for you to wait outside for a moment. I need to check his wound, and I don't want him to get upset."

Ben Dublin's eyes widened and he began to move some more, clearly trying to convince the nurse that Jack should stay.

"Calm down, Mr. Dublin," she admonished. "It's not good for you to move too much. You have a serious injury, and you need to keep still. Too much moving could cause you to hemorrhage."

Jack approached the bed. "Don't worry, Dad. I'll be right outside, but when she's done I'll come back in."

Ben stopped moving and looked directly at Jack. His eyes began to mist. There seemed to be a relieved smile on his face as Jack left the room.

When Jack reached the hallway his phone buzzed. He looked at the number and realized it was from the Four Seasons Hotel.

"Hello," Jack said edgily.

"Jack, its Meg. Is there any news?"

"No, nothing new."

"You sound upset."

Jack paused. "No, I'm not upset."

"Can you pick me up? I'm going stir crazy."

"You just got there," he said with obvious frustration.

"I know, but there's nothing to do."

"Why don't you get a cab over to the hospital?"

There was silence for a moment. "Can't you come and pick me up?"

"Not at the moment. My father has just regained consciousness, and I don't want to leave."

"I thought you said there was nothing new."

Jack was beginning to remember what a pain in the ass she could be. "I thought you meant about Connor."

"I'll get a cab. I understand why you don't want to leave. How far is it from here?"

"Probably about a half hour by the time you call the cab and get here."

"Okay, I'm on my way," she said before hanging up.

Jack started to pace. It felt like he was getting hit from all directions again. He decided to call Billy.

"Get prepared to take a trip," Jack told Billy when he answered the phone.

"Miami?"

"Yep. I'm not waiting for Oliver to give me fuckin' permission. It's my son, not his."

"I'm with you, brother. What about your dad?"

"What about him?"

"Easy man, I'm just curious to see how he's doing!"

"I can't do shit for him standing around, and now that Meg's in town, she can hold his hand."

"Tell me when and where, and I'll be there."

"Let me make the arrangements, and I'll call you."

"Sounds good. Let me know."

Jack put his phone back in his pocket and it began to buzz again. He was perturbed, thinking it was Meg calling back. He looked for the number and it just said "Private Caller".

"Hello," Jack answered wearily.

"Jack, its Father Mike. We need to talk."

"Okay, you've got my attention. What do you want to talk about?"

"I don't want to talk on the phone. I want to meet you in person. Can you come to my office?"

"When?"

"If you're not doing anything at the moment, why don't you come now?"

"Mike"—he paused and then corrected himself—"I mean Father Mike. I'm at the hospital and I've got a lot going on right now. Is it important?"

"I think it is."

Jack looked at his watch. "Mike, it's late. Can we meet tomorrow?"

"If you can't come now I'll understand, but I don't care about the time. I'm up 'til late anyway."

Jack looked at his watch again. "Do you have anything going on tomorrow morning?"

"I have a dental appointment at eleven."

"Why don't we meet at your office around nine?"

Father Mike sighed. "Alright, but make sure you come. I need to talk to you."

"Why don't you text me your address and information? Make sure you include your phone number, too."

"Okay, see you tomorrow at nine."

Jack again placed his phone into his pocket. He was perplexed, but curious to hear what Father Mike urgently wanted to talk to him about.

When he returned to his father's room, he found the same nurse and Dr. Stafford hovering over his father. They had removed one of the tubes that had prevented him from talking.

"Mr. Dublin, where are you experiencing pain?" Dr. Stafford asked.

Ben was obviously having difficulty speaking, but he mustered enough strength to whisper, "All over the fucking place!"

Dr. Stafford then asked what the worst area of pain was, and to describe it from one to ten. Once they had figured out Ben Dublin was going to require more meds and what dose, they left the room.

"Dad, don't talk," Jack said. "I want you to save your energy. Let me talk and I'll fill you in on what's happening."

Jack didn't pull any punches. He told his father the whole story from the shooting at Clyde's restaurant to Connor's kidnapping. During this time, Ben's eyes were focused and he appeared to be hanging on every word. Jack didn't tell him what his plans were. He told Ben he was reluctant to leave him while he was in this condition.

"Find Connor first, then kill those bastards!" Ben whispered. "Believe me, I'm not going anywhere. I'll be here when you get back."

"Don't worry, I will," Jack responded.

The door opened and in walked Meg. She immediately came over to the bedside and kissed Ben on the forehead.

"Oh my God! I'm so happy to see you!" she said with tears in her eyes. "Thank God you're getting well."

Ben mustered a slight smile and reached out to hold her hand.

"I've still got a few years left, don't worry," he whispered before grimacing in pain.

"Are you okay?" Jack asked.

Ben closed his eyes and faintly nodded.

"Maybe we should go," Jack stated, looking at Meg. "He needs to rest."

"I just got here," she said, looking at Jack slightly perturbed. When she saw his responsive look, she replied, "But you're probably right."

"Let's go."

They said their goodbyes to Ben and told him they would be back later.

When they walked out of his room, Jack immediately went to the nurses' station. He advised the two nurses behind the counter that Ben was in pain, and to check on him. They assured him they were watching his monitors and would keep a close eye on him. They double checked his contact information.

Once inside Jack's car, Meg leaned over and kissed him on the cheek.

"What was that for?" Jack said, visibly irritated as he looked over at her.

"Relax, Jack," she said ambivalently. "I just wanted to show my appreciation for looking after me."

Jack smirked and shook his head.

"Can we go someplace to get something to eat? I'm starved."

"I don't think there's much open at this time of night."

She turned and gave him a look of disbelief. "C'mon, I used to live here, remember? This is Washington, D.C. There's plenty of places open. Just go somewhere down M Street and park. We'll find something."

"I'm sure they have room service at the Four Seasons," Jack said as he drove toward it.

"Will you eat with me?" she asked.

"No. I have an early appointment in the morning, and I've already eaten."

"I can't believe it," she said emphatically. "You're afraid of me, aren't you?"

"Why would I be afraid of you?"

"Afraid I'll try and seduce you!"

"Meg, you can't seduce me. Y'see, my father is on his deathbed, our son is with a group of kidnappers, and I have to figure out a way to get him home safely. Sex with you or anyone else for that matter is the last thing on my mind. Not to mention, I have a meeting early in the morning."

They sat in silence for a couple of minutes while Meg looked out the window.

"I'm sorry Jack," she said, detached. "I don't know what got into me. I guess I'm depressed. My husband treats me like shit, and my son, the only one who means the world to me, has been kidnapped. I guess I'm looking to you for help, to make me feel better."

Jack turned into the driveway of the Four Seasons and put the car in park. "I will make you feel better," he said, turning towards her. "As soon as I bring Connor back home."

She looked at Jack before opening her door. "You will keep me in the loop, won't you?"

"Yes. As soon as I know what's going on, I will tell you."

"Are you going to the hospital tomorrow?"

"Most likely, but I don't know what time."

"Okay, I'll get a cab to go over."

Jack nodded.

"Good night, Jack."

Jack nodded again.

33

Jack drove over to the Mount Pleasant area of D.C., where Father Mike was a priest at the Shrine of the Sacred Heart. The church was considered to be the spiritual home to the largest Hispanic section of D.C. The population contained many Asian factions as well.

Jack drove up to the large domed Byzantine-style church and found a parking spot. Following the instructions of Father Mike, he made his way around the church to a door which appeared to be at a residence. After ringing the bell and knocking on the door, Jack was met by a young man wearing a brown cassock tied around the waist with a light brown-colored rope. He looked to be in his twenties with unremarkable features.

"I'm here to see Father Delledonne," Jack said.

"You must be Mr. Dublin," the young man with a shaved head said, smiling. "He is waiting for you. Let me show the way."

He turned and began walking down a hallway. Jack followed. Their footsteps echoed against the gray stone walls which were adorned with photographs of the Pope and other members of the clergy. Some of the photographs were quite old, most likely previous priests of this parish, along with pictures of various saints. The stained glass windows were plentiful and had the usual variety of bright colors. Some of the windows seemed to depict certain historical, religious events.

They reached a large ornate oak door. After knocking, Father Mike's voice could be heard telling them to enter. The young man opened the door but didn't enter the room.

"Mr. Dublin is here to see you, Father," he said.

"Thank you Tom," Father Mike said. "Come in Jack," he said with a big smile, standing up from his desk.

"Will there be anything else, sir?"

"No, Tom, that's all. Thank you!"

Jack entered the cavernous office, looking around as he walked toward Father Mike. The ceiling seemed to be twenty feet high. There were large windows behind the desk and the curtains had been slightly drawn. The sun gleamed brightly through the slender opening. There were fully filled bookshelves and more pictures of the Pope, one of which showed Father Mike kissing his hand during a recent visit to the United States.

"Thanks for coming to see me, Jack," he said, shaking his hand.

"Not a problem, Mike."

"Sit down, sit down. Is there anything I can get you? Coffee?"

"Coffee would be fine."

"How do you like it?"

"Black."

Father Mike poured coffee for both of them and came over to a large, burgundy, tufted leather chair where he sat down, looking across at Jack who sat in a burgundy, tacked leather arm chair. The arms were also padded with leather. A cherry wood coffee table was situated between them on an expensive Oriental rug.

Father Mike stirred sugar and cream into his coffee. The cups were in saucers and were engraved with some type of English floral pattern.

"How is your father doing?" Father Mike asked.

"Last night, he regained consciousness."

"What a relief!" he responded, pleased.

"He's not out of the woods yet. He's still in a great deal of pain."

Father Mike nodded with a frown. "He's in our prayers, Jack. I have informed the congregation to pray for him."

"Thank you," Jack said, taking a sip of his coffee.

"I guess you're wondering why I asked to meet with you this morning."

Jack nodded.

"Something peculiar happened recently that I think you may be interested in. How much do you know about your father's business?"

"I know he does security for a number of Fortune 500 companies," Jack answered curiously.

"Do you know what that involves?"

"I'm sure it involves a lot of things. What do you mean specifically?"

"Do you know he has couriers who carry important documents all over the world?"

"Yes, I do."

"Do you know what these documents are?"

"I suppose they're confidential legal documents that can't be faxed or scanned for fear of interception."

Father Mike set his cup down. "Recently I attended a meeting with a couple of other priests from Roman Catholic churches in the area. The main topic of conversation was the pervasiveness of drugs in our community. Heroin is now commonplace. Once thought to be a dirty dangerous drug, it's no longer thought of in those terms. People of all colors and socio-economic backgrounds are using it. Not just the low-income people in my parish, but everywhere. As you know from our police days, there are byproducts to using. People need money to buy it; they travel out to the wealthier parts of the city to steal, rob, and kill."

"I'm well aware of everything you just said," Jack answered, annoyed.

"I know you are." Father Mike smiled. "What disturbed me was what one of the priests said. He told me a young Hispanic, all tatted up, came to him to ask for sanctuary. When he was asked for the reason, the man said he worked for a company that was transporting drugs and money. He said he didn't want to work for them anymore. He was afraid for his family and himself."

"What happened next?" Jack asked, trying to remain interested.

"The priest denied his request. He denied it because he didn't think it was valid."

"Is that the end of the story?"

"No. One week later, the man and his family were killed. Butchered would be more accurate."

"Mike, that shouldn't surprise you. You were on long enough to know this shit happens. Excuse me, crap happens."

"That's true. This shit happens every day! In fact, the ironic thing is, the Hispanic man I killed during the robbery attempt several years ago was strung-out on heroin, and he was from this area. I think it was divine intervention that sent me back here to help the people of Mount Pleasant."

Mike Delledonne had been on the Metropolitan Police Department for a year when he responded to an armed robbery in progress in the Mount Pleasant District. When he rolled up on the scene, a young Hispanic man was starting to exit a liquor store. The gun in his hand was pointed at the clerk behind the counter. He was stuffing money in his pocket with his other hand. Mike got out of his vehicle and pulled his gun. When he shouted for the armed robber to drop his gun, the man turned to point it at Mike. As he was trained, Mike fired his weapon three times at the armed man. As luck would have it, one of the bullets struck the man, not in his torso, but instead in his head. He immediately fell to the pavement, never getting a shot off.

Police training uses equipment to recreate live shooting situations. This simulator places the officer in many different complex scenarios where split-second decisions are necessary. The officer's adrenalin gets a workout. Not only is it a shoot, don't shoot situation, but the accuracy of the officer is challenged. Due to the adrenalin rush, officers often miss their target which is the center mass, the area between the chin and the waistline.

In Mike's case, his deadly shot was well placed since striking someone in the brain prevents a reflex action. The robber never got to fire back at Mike.

Once the man fell to the sidewalk, Mike ran up to him to see where he was hit, and whether or not he could render first aid. What he saw changed his life forever. The man's brains were spilling out of his head onto the concrete with profuse amounts of blood running like a river down the cracks in the sidewalk and into the street. His left eye was missing.

Mike realized he wasn't meant to be a police officer.

"Perhaps it is, Mike. Perhaps it is."

"Jack, you know what it's like. How are you doing since you shot the senator's son?"

Jack looked at Mike with a raised eyebrow. "To tell you the truth, Mike, I'm not having any problem. He deserved it."

"Jack, nobody deserves it. As the Bible says in Exodus 20:13, thou shall not kill."

"Yeah, well, I figured I would kill him before he killed me. Check your Bible, Proverbs 24:11, deliver those who are drawn toward death, and hold back those stumbling to the slaughter," Jack answered proudly. "I think the scriptures say we can defend ourselves, even if it calls for murder."

"I guess we could debate it philosophically and religiously, but I don't think we need to do that. I'm more concerned with you, and whether or not you are suffering from it."

"Not now. I did at first, but then I realized I did the right thing, the only thing. I finally became pissed off that I felt bad about it. That fucker deserved everything he got," Jack said, calmly. "Sorry, Mike."

"Getting back to the man and his family that were killed because he wasn't granted sanctuary, what disturbed me was the company he worked for."

"I'm surprised he could name a company. These companies are fronts for money laundering by drug dealers and large corporations. No legitimate company is going to be involved with anything like that."

"That's what I thought until he mentioned the company."

Jack waited.

"He mentioned your father's company. He specifically said WISE International."

"That's fuckin' bullshit!" Jack said defiantly. "My father doesn't deal in drugs. Does Mr. Prescott know about this?"

"I told him last week," Father Mike said. "He believes your uncle has a shell business that hired your father to do courier work for him.

Unknowingly, your father's couriers have been transporting drugs and money all over the world. If and when your father discovered the ruse, he would be potentially ruined. In essence, your uncle is holding your father's company hostage."

Jack set his cup on the coffee table and stood up. "I have knowledge he's in Belize. If he's there, then my son is probably there too."

"I know what you're thinking, Jack. Don't do it. Let the legal system take care of it."

"This man has taken my son—God knows what he's done to him. He's attempted to kill my father, and ruined thousands of lives with his drug business, but not for much longer." Before turning, Jack added, "Thanks for your concern, Mike," and walked toward the door without offering his hand. He didn't want to discuss it any longer.

"Jack, wait," Father Mike said, standing up. "I know what you're planning on doing. This is different than shooting in self-defense. This would be premeditated. You would be committing a cold-blooded killing. Don't do it, Jack. Let Mr. Prescott handle it."

Jack waited with his hand on the door handle, his back toward Father Mike, as he listened. He didn't respond.

Realizing he couldn't change Jack's mind, Father Mike said, "Jack, whatever you do, do it with honor."

"I will," Jack said as he opened the door and left.

34
Miami

Jorge instructed his driver to take them to his yacht. Juan was in and out of consciousness as they drove toward the Epic. The bleeding had fortunately slowed down, but he had already lost a lot of blood. Along the way, numerous Miami Police Department vehicles were speeding past them with their lights and sirens, headed in the opposite direction toward La Carreta.

"Make sure you obey the speed limits. I don't want to get pulled over," Jorge said.

Jorge got on his phone and called the captain of his yacht. He ordered him to have the yacht ready to leave for Belize in fifteen minutes. Then, he called Luisa and told her to be on the yacht when he got there because they were leaving immediately. Next he called Dr. Casalena as they continued along the toll road. He advised him about Juan's wound and asked what to do.

As luck would have it, Dr. Casalena was at the Epic with two of his girlfriends, having lunch. No doubt he was planning on some extra-curricular activity upstairs, afterwards. Dr. Casalena agreed to be on the yacht when they arrived. His *ménage a trois* would have to wait.

"Jorge," Juan whispered.

"Juan, don't talk. You need your strength."

"Jorge, they will follow us," Juan said weakly. "We need to call Javier and tell him to meet us."

"We don't have time for that."

"No, No. I don't mean meet us here. I mean meet us at sea in his plane."

Jorge remembered Javier owned a Grumman Mallard seaplane. It was a brilliant idea. If the authorities sent some officers by boat, no doubt they would be in speedy watercraft and would overtake the yacht. Realizing they would also be tracked by aircraft, they needed to get to international waters as quickly as possible.

When they arrived at the Epic, the traffic circle in front of the hotel was crowded with Mercedes, Lamborghinis, and Ferrari's. The valets and doormen were moving fast trying to get the biggest tips they could.

Jorge didn't want to wait. He wanted to get to his yacht as quickly as possible, but he didn't want anyone to see Juan in his condition.

Jorge told the driver to get a doorman to bring a wheelchair over and a blanket. He gave the driver a couple of hundred dollar bills to ensure immediate service.

Within a couple of minutes, a doorman came over dressed in his tan uniform and hat.

"Thank you my good man," Jorge said smiling. "We've got it from here. Thank you."

As the doorman walked away, they moved Juan to the chair and wrapped a blanket around him. Jorge instructed the driver to park the car while he moved Juan down the walkway to the dock which was conveniently next to the driveway. Waiting on the yacht was Dr. Casalena.

"Luisa, take Miguelito inside. I'll be with you in a minute." As soon as she disappeared inside the yacht, Dr. Casalena moved to the walkway to help bring Juan onboard.

Juan was barely conscious and about to fall out of the chair. Jorge and Dr. Casalena kept him propped up. Once they were alongside the yacht, Jorge, Dr. Casalena and one of the assistants onboard helped Juan get on the yacht.

"Take him to the first bedroom below," Jorge said to the assistant who by this point had picked Juan up in a fireman's carry.

The ship began leaving the shoreline.

Once they got to the bedroom, Juan was lowered onto the king size bed in a magnificent stateroom. The recessed lighting was bright enough to conduct a hospital operation. There was a large window on the port side which was soon covered by automated curtains that Jorge activated with a remote.

Dr. Casalena had brought along his medical bag with numerous surgical instruments. His bag also contained drugs with needles and syringes, since he always trying to maintain a readiness in case Jorge called. The likelihood was great once he arrived in Miami. Jorge always took care of him, and he never wanted to piss him off. Jorge had surgical skills of his own.

Dr. Casalena was no stranger to this type of emergency. He once had been a respected surgeon on staff at Jackson Memorial Hospital, one of the leading trauma hospitals in Miami. Patients arrived sometimes several at a time, with an array of injuries, the worst being a result of gunshots or stabbings. Life and death decisions had to be made lightning fast, sometimes without complete information. On top of that, you had to have the skills to slice and dice with expertise. It took huge balls to do it, and he had them. Rarely was he ever second-guessed. Rarely was he wrong.

"How bad is it?" Jorge asked, concerned.

"I won't know until I take a closer look," Dr. Casalena replied.

He took out his stethoscope and listened to his heart before taking his pulse. He then took scissors and cut away Juan's shirt in order to expose the wound. He was still losing blood and if it wasn't stopped soon, he would die. Dr. Casalena injected a coagulant known as Flow Seal to the site, and within a couple of minutes the bleeding stopped.

"I'm not sure of the damage that was done by the bullet, but at least the bleeding has stopped. He needs a blood transfusion, and he needs X-rays to determine the exact location of the bullet which may or may not, need to be surgically removed."

"What do you mean? Do you mean the bullet may have to stay in there?"

"Yes. It could be in a precarious position. We just don't know at this point."

Jorge motioned for the doctor to leave the room. Once they were in the hallway, he asked about the prognosis.

"It didn't have an exit wound, so it's still in the shoulder. It's hard to say, his vitals are stretched. I never gave him a physical so I don't know about his general health history. At the very least, he needs to be in a hospital to get the proper treatment."

Jorge shook his head. "That's not happening. He's not going to a hospital any time soon. I can't afford to take the risk. Can't you operate on him?"

Dr. Casalena stared back at Jorge. "Jorge, you know I can do surgery on him, but it would be very primitive. I don't have the benefit of having an X-ray or lab results. I don't have nurses to assist, and I would need more intense lighting, not to mention the sanitary situation. He would be at great risk of infection which could be more lethal than his wound."

"What happens if you do nothing?"

"He could get his strength back which would improve the odds."

"How do we do that?"

"I have some drugs to give him. It'll kill the pain, and might allow him to recover. Eventually he'll have to have the bullet removed. That's my opinion."

"You're the expert. I never doubt your opinion. Can he fly back to Belize in a seaplane?"

"I think so. He's not much more at risk than he is here," Dr. Casalena said before asking, "If you're going to fly back to Belize because you fear the police are going to take you into custody, what about me?"

"I don't think you're in any danger on the boat with Luisa and Miguelito, do you?"

"You know and I know, if they stop us and you're not on here, they're gonna be pissed. They could take all of us into custody just to get you to do something. If your wife and son are being held, and I don't give a shit whether it's legal or not, they're gonna expect you to do something, hoping to grab you."

"No offense Doc, but I'm not gonna expose myself. I'll hire an attorney to get them released, and you too if you're in custody."

"Have you contacted the seaplane?"

"As a matter of fact I have. My captain took care of it, speaking of which I need to go upstairs to check with him. Please keep an eye on

Juan. I need him," Jorge said as he began walking toward the stairs leading to the bridge.

Dr. Casalena went back to check on Juan's vitals before giving him a shot of morphine.

Within fifteen minutes, Jorge returned after talking to Luisa and Miguelito. He had convinced her to stay on the yacht.

"The seaplane will be arriving in about twenty minutes. I'm gonna need your help to get Juan on the plane, and I need you to stay behind with Luisa. What do you think I should do with Juan once we get back home?"

"Take him to Belize Medical Associates in Belize City. Register him under another name. I know a former associate who runs the place. I'll reach out to him, and let him know you're coming, and what the situation is. They have radiology capabilities and they're clean. When I get there, whenever that is, I will take it from there."

Juan gratefully nodded his head.

The captain called to Jorge on the intercom. Jorge picked up a phone and listened.

"We're being approached by what appears to be a fast moving ship on radar, believed to be a government boat sent to intercept. The captain says it's about twenty minutes from intercept."

"How close is the plane?"

"It's approaching now."

"Just in time."

Shortly thereafter, the Grumman Mallard seaplane pulled close to the yacht which had slowed down. Juan was loaded onboard without much effort, and Jorge hopped on also.

They took off while the government ship was within ten minutes of interception.

35
Belize

Billy met Jack at the Reagan airport. They were taking the company's corporate jet straight to Belize. Jack made sure his choice of weapons was packed along with a thousand rounds of ammunition. He didn't know how long or how difficult it would be to infiltrate DePeralta's compound. It didn't matter. He would get it done, or die trying.

Once they landed, they went to the Radisson hotel and checked in.

"Why don't we check out our rooms, and meet back here in fifteen minutes," Jack said.

"Sounds good to me," Billy replied.

Once he got to his room, Jack put his bags down and walked over to the sliding glass doors. He pulled the light-colored, diaphanous gauze curtains, then unlocked and opened the doors to the balcony. Outside, a light breeze carried the scent of the salty ocean water. The turquoise ocean and powdered white sand beach were only about fifty yards from the hotel property. Jack had brought a bathing suit even though he knew there wouldn't be time to use it. A blender could be heard, no doubt making an exotic drink for a thirsty tourist. After looking at his watch, Jack went back inside. Locking the door and pulling the curtains closed, he surveyed his room.

The floor was the typical twelve-by-twelve oak parquet. The furniture had been stained the same light oak color. The room had the token flat-screen TV facing the bed, but Jack's main concern was the bed. Lately, he had trouble sleeping. He sat on the edge of the bed before getting up into it. He lay with his head on the pillow and it felt comfortable. The large paddles of the fan looked like oversized tobacco leaves as they spun around, creating a pleasant breeze.

After sliding his bag of weapons and ammunition under the bed, which he had surreptitiously sneaked into the country, he went downstairs to meet Billy who was already waiting.

"How do you like your room?" Jack asked.

"Great! I like the view. It overlooks the pool, and I've already spotted some potential for later tonight," he said with a devious smile.

"Are you hungry?"

"Hungry? Man, I could eat the ass end out of a skunk," Billy declared.

"I'm not sure, but I think we can find something better than that to eat," Jack said with a slight grin. "Do you like sushi? I hear there's a great restaurant for sushi close by."

"I'm more of a meat-and-potatoes type of guy."

"Alright, let's go to the bar and see if we can order from there."

Jack and Billy walked toward the bar off the main lobby. It was small with a few square tables and about ten matching cane-style chairs situated around an L-shaped polished wood bar. The bartender was an island woman with a pretty smile and pleasant disposition. Billy started toward the bar where two men were seated. Jack tugged at his sleeve to steer him away. They went to a table situated in the back where two corner walls provided privacy.

"Why are we sitting here? I wanted to check out the bartender."

"We need to talk privately about our plan. We're going to be meeting a DEA agent here in about a half hour."

"How'd that come about?"

"I spoke with Brian Oliver. He's the one keeping us in the loop. I trust him. He knows we're here, and he wants to help. Apparently the DEA has been trying to access DePeralta's compound. They want to take him down bigtime, so we have a mutual interest."

The bartender came over and took their order for drinks. Billy didn't engage her. He was all business now.

"How are we in a position to help them?"

"Brian seems to think we might be able to gather some intelligence while we're here. They're planning to raid the compound. An agent by the name of Derek Palmer is supposed to update us when he gets here."

The bartender brought them the beer they ordered. After looking at the menu, they both ordered burgers and fries.

"We're going to be in on the raid, aren't we?" Billy asked.

"There is no way they're going in without us. Brian knows my position, and he didn't object."

"He's not the head of the DEA. What if the local office objects? They're the ones who have final say."

"Trust me. We'll be there when the shit goes down. There's no fucking way I'm leaving here without my son!"

When the waitress returned with their meals, they ate without talking about the raid.

Perfectly timed as they finished their meals, a man wearing shorts, a Hawaiian shirt, stylish straw hat and sunglasses, stopped at the entrance of the bar, and looked around. It didn't take long to figure out; Jack and Billy were the only ones sitting at a table who looked up when he entered the room. He walked over and asked if they knew Brian Oliver.

Once they answered his question, he pulled out a chair and sat down.

"Hello, gentlemen. My name is Derek Palmer. I'm sure Brian told you about me?"

"Not really," Jack answered. "He just said you would be meeting us here, and bringing us up to date on the DePeralta situation."

The bartender returned and asked Derek if he wanted anything. He told her to bring him a diet Coke with a slice of lime.

Once he took his sunglasses off, his blue eyes shone. He was a handsome man who looked to be in his late forties. Lines were beginning to crease his tanned face around his eyes and cheeks, giving him the look of an aging movie star.

"Jorge DePeralta has been a target of the DEA for several years. He is very careful and insulates himself by using anyone who is loyal to carry out his orders. Believe me, he vets out everyone to make sure they're not dangerous to his health. He's made it well known to everybody that anyone who betrays him will be tortured. He's nicknamed 'El Tiburon' because he throws traitors into a shark tank he allegedly has on his property. Sometimes his victims are alive, and sometimes they're not. The man is a heartless, ruthless, sadistic bastard! He has surrounded himself with what seems to be an impregnable fortress. It will not be easy to get inside, but we've been working an informant who may be able to provide us with the help we need to gain entry."

"How can we help?" Jack asked.

Palmer snickered. "You'd think with something of this magnitude, the government would have given us the budget allowing us to bring in a bunch of agents who can flood the place, incognito, and give us the intelligence we need, but Washington being Washington, we're shorthanded and the budget is tight. What I would like you guys to do, is make your rounds to the bars, keep your eyes open, and ears tuned, to anyone who might be able to provide us with information. We think DePeralta's men blow off steam here. I'd love to have some more intel."

Jack and Billy looked at each other dubiously.

"Do you have any pictures of these people we're supposed to be looking for?"

"I have a couple of photos," Derek said as he grabbed them from his shirt pocket before sliding them across the table. "These are two guys we've been watching. We think they're tied into the compound. We haven't been able to gather any information on them yet. It would be extremely helpful to us if you can."

Jack and Billy looked at the photos.

"Are these ours to keep?" Jack asked.

"Yes."

"What have you guys been able to put together so far?"

"We're trying to convince the local government to allow us to search the compound."

"And?"

"So far they are reluctant to let us force entry into the compound. It seems DePeralta may have already bought favor with some members of the government."

"If you've already expressed your intent to make entry onto the DePeralta compound," Jack said, "and if someone in the government is a pawn of his, don't you think it's likely he's gonna be ready and armed to the teeth?"

"We thought of that, but he's gonna be armed regardless. We haven't said anything about when we're going to strike. The element of surprise is still ours."

"How many people are involved?"

"What do you mean?"

"How many people will be involved in the raid?"

Palmer looked at Jack as if he was insulted. "Enough."

"I guess its all perception, Derek," Jack said sharply. "What you and the DEA think is enough may not be what I think is enough." He could see the frustrated look creeping on the man's face. "Look, Derek, I don't know if Brian told you, but my son is probably in there. Hopefully he hasn't been fed to the sharks by the same man you yourself described as a ruthless bastard. You just said the budget is tight which tells me Washington may not be taking this serious. The last thing I want is some half-assed, fucked-up Bay of Pigs effort."

Derek nodded. "I understand, Jack, but there's some privileged information I can't reveal right now. You'll just have to take my word for it that there will be enough firepower to take DePeralta down."

"Of course, Billy and I are gonna be a part of this raid, right?"

"As far as I know," Derek said not too convincingly.

Jack gave him a forced smile. He took the pictures and looked at them again. "Thanks, we'll see what we can do. How do we get in touch with you in case anything develops?" Jack asked.

"Let me give you my personal cell phone number," Derek said, handing them one of his business cards.

Jack took the card and looked at it. "Thanks, we'll be in touch."

Derek offered his hand as he stood up, and both Jack and Billy shook it.

"Good luck. I want to hear from you by this time tomorrow night. We need to communicate," Derek said before walking out of the bar.

"What do you think?" Billy asked after Derek disappeared.

"I think he's doing everything he can to keep us in the dark. They figure they don't need our help, so they give us these pictures to keep us busy. Who knows if these pictures are related in any way?"

"So what are we gonna do?"

"We don't have much of a choice. We'll hang out for a while and see where it takes us. I think we can develop our own information. If they think they can placate us by keeping us out of the way, they've underestimated us. As big as Jorge DePeralta is, some people gotta know where he lives and how to get in. I didn't want to say anything else to Palmer. If he knows we're antsy, he'll cut us off altogether."

"Where do we start?"

"Let's ask the concierge about hot spots in town and then we'll check them out."

36

Jorge decided not to take Juan to the hospital over the passionate objection of Dr. Casalena. Instead, they took him back to the compound where Dr. Casalena would care for him. Things were starting to heat up. He couldn't take the chance of someone seeing him in the hospital, especially with Juan's weakened condition. Everyone in the Navarro family knew that Juan was the backbone of Jorge's organization. Particularly since Jorge decided to take a back seat to allow himself the time to focus on other problems such as his health. He didn't need to be perceived as vulnerable, especially because the perception would be accurate.

Once Juan was resting in an upstairs bedroom, with Dr. Casalena at his side, Jorge decided to check on his sister and the new addition to the family.

He went into his study and saw one of his men sitting by the bookcase with an AR-15.

Once the man saw Jorge enter the room he stood up with his gun still in the ready position.

Jorge smiled as he approached.

"What's the status of my guests?" he asked.

"There is nothing new to report, sir," the guard said forcefully, even though he was scared to death of the man known as "El Tiburon." Being disloyal was not the only trait punishable by death. Weakness wasn't acceptable either.

"Is there anyone down there with them right now?" he asked.

"No sir, and they've just been fed."

"Thank you," Jorge said looking at the soldier, trying to entice a name from him.

"Alfredo," he responded, once he realized.

"*Muchas gracias*, Alfredo."

Jorge moved a couple of books on the bookshelf and it swung open like a door, revealing an open doorway with steps that descended into darkness. He reached over and flipped a switch, illuminating the tunnel below. Jorge took his time navigating down the narrow steps. When he reached the floor he could see almost thirty yards in front of him. He, of course, knew the layout quite well. He designed it. There were several turns and intersections in place to confuse anyone who followed. Not only was this an active tunnel for drug distribution, it also was meant as a path of escape.

To his immediate right was a short hallway that led to two rooms—or more appropriately, cells. These were installed to imprison anyone who may have information he needed. The isolation served to loosen the tongues of those inclined to refuse cooperation. Of course, the sparse accommodations, a dirt floor with some straw to lie on, along with restraints anchored to all four concrete walls of the ten-by-ten rooms, lent itself to quick submission. For those with a strong will, the dirt floor absorbed the blood that dripped from the lacerations inflicted by whips and knives, while their screams echoed through the subterranean tunnels.

Today, there were two very special guests staying in the two rooms which were separated by very thick concrete walls to minimize any communication between the two inhabitants. However, Jorge sometimes kept the cell door open when he was "negotiating" with one of the prisoners. Usually, this had a positive effect on the lucky prisoner who was second, because it usually convinced him to tell what he knew, temporarily sparing him from the same treatment. Jorge laughed when he talked about it. He called it the positive effect of peer pressure.

Torture was not in the plans today. These two people were valued prizes and despite their accommodations, Jorge revered them. His family was becoming more and more complete, but he had to keep them here for their own well-being. You never know when someone may come looking for them, and try to take them away. He wouldn't allow it. Nobody would be taken from him anymore. Once Luisa and Miguelito came home, he would feel complete.

He hated incarcerating them, but he couldn't risk giving them the freedom to walk easily around the compound. They could try and escape. One of them had already made the foolish attempt, although Jorge couldn't understand why anyone in their right mind would want to leave. He provided a beautiful home with a luxurious pool and spa. A personal chef who could cook whatever you wanted. Anything you wanted, you would get—within reason, of course! Perhaps in time he would loosen the reins, but not yet.

Jorge walked to the first cell and opened the door with a key. There he saw his beloved sister Bella sitting in a simple, plastic chair that he had provided. He didn't want her to sit on the floor, especially with her ailments.

"Bella," he said, smiling at her. "You look well today."

She just glared at him. She was unbroken. He could continue to demean her, but her spirit was strong. She had never thought as strongly about killing him as she did today.

"What kind of man are you?" she asked defiantly. "What kind of brother, no, what kind of human being treats people like you do? You talk about how much you love having me here, and then you treat me with so much disrespect. You're an animal!"

He smiled at her. "Bella, I have a surprise for you. Once you know what it is, you'll apologize to me. You'll understand why I do the things I do. I have always been about family, you know that. From the time I brought you here, I have loved sharing my life with you. Having my sister here to help raise my son, along with my wife, is the epitome of what families need all over the world."

"If that's so, why did you take me away from my husband, and my son? Tell me that."

"I know it was difficult for you, but your first responsibility is to me, your brother. I'm the one you left when I was barely thirteen! You left me when I no longer had a mother and father to bring me up. You left me all alone," he said, his voice rising. "How could you have done that to me?"

"I didn't know where you were. You disappeared," she said unaffected.

"Did you come looking for me? No. You were too busy to care what happened to me. You had a new life, a family!"

"When I found out years later you were making billions of dollars through the drug trade, I didn't want to confront you. I had worked for the CIA. It was best to leave you alone. I didn't want to get too close to you. Obviously, it was an extreme conflict of interest."

"Bullshit! You were covering your own ass. You were ashamed of me, but you were more ashamed of yourself. Your little brother, the one you left behind to fend for himself, was now wealthy and successful. You couldn't stand it."

"Unlike you, I don't measure success in dollars. Your success came from killing and torturing men and women. By the way, these men and women had families too. I guess that didn't matter to you. And the drugs you've manufactured and spread all over the world has destroyed thousands, if not millions, of people. Your money is stained with innocent blood. To me that's failure. Why don't you put me out of my misery, and kill me now. I can't stand the sight of you. You're disgusting!"

Jorge stared back at her. It was the dark, penetrating look he had given to many victims before they met their untimely death. After a few moments, he began to laugh.

"That's what I love about you, Bella. You've got spunk, spirit! It's no secret that you and I are a lot alike," he said proudly. Bella started to speak, but he interrupted. "I think you need to see who is next door to you. It's someone from our family you've never seen."

He could see her demeanor change. He knew she thought it was her son. He decided to play with her some more.

"Let me ask you, Bella. If there was one person in the world you'd love to see right now, right at this very moment, who would it be?"

She looked at him with trepidation, knowing his despicable capabilities.

"I would want to see my son," she said as tears began to well up in her eyes.

"If it can't be him, then who would be next?" he said, enjoying the moment.

Looking at him with apprehension, she answered. "My husband."

Jorge started shaking his head. "I'm sorry, neither one of them is here, yet, but I have someone who I think you'll love to meet. Come with me." He held his arm out, pointing to the hallway.

Bella got up and cautiously walked to the doorway.

While she stood in the hallway, outside the next cell, Jorge unlocked it.

"Stay right here," he ordered. "I'll let you know when to come in."

He entered the cell and pulled the door until it was slightly ajar. He wasn't worried about Bella going anywhere. Where could she go? Besides, he knew she was curious to see who her next door neighbor is.

37

Jorge entered the cell occupied by his nephew. Up until now, he didn't have the time to talk with the young man he hoped would lure Jack Dublin to Belize. When he entered, Connor stood up unsteadily, still trying to lose the effects of the drugs he was administered before he got on the plane. It wasn't necessarily out of respect, but of an acute awareness that this was the man who would execute him. Connor wanted to face him head-on as best he could.

"Hello, Connor," Jorge said, smiling at his young captive. "I guess you're wondering who I am, and what you're doing here. Am I right?"

"I think I know who you are," Connor said slowly. "You're my uncle, brother of my grandmother."

"Very good!" Jorge said enthusiastically. "And what do you know about your grandmother?"

"She was killed in a car accident."

"Well, some people believe that, but I never did." Jorge smiled deviously. "You see, I believe she's still alive," he said, raising his eyebrows as he paced ominously back and forth.

Connor just sat there quietly, waiting for Jorge to elaborate.

"Would you like to meet her?"

He shrugged his shoulders, not knowing what his uncle was doing.

"Stay right there," he said as he went into the hallway. He re-entered the room with Bella by his side. "Bella, I would like you to meet your grandson, Connor." Turning to Connor he said, "Connor, this is your grandmother, your father's mother. The one you thought was dead!"

211

Connor didn't know how to respond. He was confused, but Bella started to walk toward him with arms outstretched and tears in her eyes. She grabbed him, and held him tightly as she cried uncontrollably. He placed his arms around her lightly, wondering if this truly was his grandmother or an imposter.

Jorge walked over and separated them. Bella didn't want to let go. "Bella, please. You don't want any harm to come to him, do you?"

Bella turned to look at her brother pleadingly. "Please, give me some time with my grandson," she begged between sobs.

"You'll be able to visit with him again, but for now it's time for you to return upstairs. I assure you, Connor will be taken care of. No harm will come to him." Jorge grabbed her arm more forcefully, and she reluctantly let go of Connor. "Connor, I will talk with you later," he said as he pulled the door shut and turned the key.

Bella was still crying as he led her up the steps into his study. He closed the entryway to the underground labyrinth and took her into the entrance foyer. "Bella, you're free to go anywhere you want on the compound. I'm sorry I had to confine you downstairs, but I just can't trust you when I'm gone. If you try to violate this privilege, I will have no choice but to deal with Connor in a most unfortunate way," he said with great amusement. "I'm sure you would like his head to remain attached, wouldn't you?" Jorge began to laugh hysterically before walking into his study and closing the door.

Bella stood in the foyer crying softly. Shortly after Jorge had closed the door to his office, it reopened. The guard who had been inside came out and closed the door again. He now took a position by the office door.

Bella went up to her bedroom.

Jorge's cellphone vibrated. "Hello, darling," he said.

"Jorge, they are not letting us leave," Luisa said frantically before the phone was taken from her. "Hello Jorge, this is special agent Schofield with the DEA. We have your wife and son in our custody. They won't be coming home for a while. We also have your boat. How convenient that you flew off and left your wife and son behind!"

"You can't just arbitrarily hold them. They haven't done anything," he responded angrily.

THE DARK SIDE OF HONOR

"We believe your wife has. We know you were here recently, and we know you were involved in the shootings on Calle Ocho. Several men are dead and you were observed on surveillance video."

"I didn't shoot anyone, therefore I don't know what you're talking about. And, even if it was me, what does that have to do with my wife and son?"

"We think your wife was involved in the planning phase, and therefore is going to be charged with conspiracy to commit murder."

"I guess my son pulled out a machine gun!"

"Your son is free to go home. Why don't you come get him?"

Jorge bit his tongue. "What will you do with him while you have my wife in custody?"

"We'll make sure he's well provided for."

"Why don't you hand him over to his grandmother?"

"We've thought of that, but your wife prefers we don't do that. She says your mother-in-law is not mentally or physically prepared to take care of him."

"Can I talk to my wife?"

"Not at the moment."

"Why not?"

"Because she's not close by."

"She was just there a couple of minutes ago! Where the fuck could she have gone?"

"We took her to another room down the hall to be with your son. He was upset."

"Listen, you motherfucker! My wife had nothing to do with any activities on Calle Ocho. She's not involved in my business. Ask yourself, why the fuck would I bring them to Miami and put them in harm's way? You guys have nothing better to do than harass my wife and son?"

"Why *did* you bring them to Miami?"

"I brought them there to visit her mother, and let her do some shopping. We relaxed a couple of days and then I returned home. They would have been here too, if you didn't stop them from coming back with me."

"No, Jorge, that's not the way it happened. You brought them here even though you knew you were going to meet the Navarros on Calle Ocho. You set this meeting up for the sole purpose of killing your competitor because he kidnapped your oldest son. You knew the chance of your son being alive wasn't good. The Navarros came because they wanted to kill you so they could corner the drug market. They made you think your son was alive and was going to be returned to you. You figured you had to take the chance even though you were going to kill them either way."

"You think you're so smart. Let me tell you, I didn't want any trouble. I went to Miami to collect my son. That's it. That's all I wanted. Those fuckers started to talk about a lot of crazy shit and then they had a FedEx driver deliver my son's head in a box. Let me ask you, what did you say your name was?"

"Schofield."

"Do you have a family, Agent Schofield?"

There was silence.

"I'll take that as a yes. If someone cut your son's head off, delivered it in a box, and then laughed hysterically in your face, what would you do?"

Agent Schofield paused before answering. "Have you ever heard the expression, live by the sword, die by the sword? When you kill people for a living, you have to expect the same in return. It's called karma. You get no sympathy from me."

"You know what—do whatever you want with my wife and son. You're going to anyway!"

"That's it? That's how much you think of your wife and son? I never knew you to be a coward, but I guess I got it all wrong. You really are a piece of shit!"

"Let me tell you, Schofield, be careful where you walk. It's not safe out there."

"You don't scare me, Jorge. You're a scared little man. You'll never have the *cojones* to come to Miami again."

"I don't have to. I have people who work for me who'll do whatever I tell them."

"Don't be so sure. We have a couple of your men who were at Calle Ocho today and they're singing like little birds. I'd say you don't have

THE DARK SIDE OF HONOR

anyone left in Miami, Jorge. They're all talking because they don't want to go to jail."

"There's more where they came from."

"Send 'em on over. We'll be waiting," Schofield said before hanging up.

Jorge threw his phone down. He needed Juan's advice. Juan was always the one who could keep calm in the middle of the storm.

Jorge got up and left his office. He went upstairs to check on Juan. Surprisingly, when he got to his bedroom, Juan was sitting up in bed, although he looked weak. He had a gray pallor and his eyes were tired looking.

Jorge looked at Dr. Casalena who returned the look with a slight smile. "Looks like our patient is going to make it."

Jorge looked at Juan. "How do you feel?"

"Like death warmed over, but I guess it could be worse."

Jorge pulled up a chair next to the bed. "I need to tell you what's going on."

"Juan, they have Luisa and Miguelito in Miami."

"Who, the Navarros?"

"No, the DEA."

"Why?"

Jorge then told him about his conversation with Agent Schofield. "Do we have anyone in Miami we can count on?"

"Right now, after the discussion you had with the DEA, we can't trust anybody. If we talk to any of our people we had in Miami, they could be working with the government. Everything we say may be recorded. We need to call in some people from New Orleans."

Juan's phone began to vibrate. He answered the phone and listened for a few moments.

"Okay, keep me up to date," he said before ending the call.

"What was that all about?" Jorge asked.

Juan looked at Jorge with a weak smile. "He's here."

"Who?"

"Jack Dublin. That was our bartender at the hotel. She said two men, one white and one black, met another man and sat in the corner.

They talked for a while and then the one that met them got up and left. She thinks the white guy is Jack Dublin."

"Why?"

"We gave her a picture of him just in case he showed up. We gave his picture out to several businesses."

Jorge pondered the information.

"What do you think we should do?"

Juan adjusted himself in bed. He grimaced before saying, "I think you need to call Alexa and see if she can keep an eye on him. After all, she owes you, doesn't she?"

Within an hour, Alexa showed up at the front gate. The guard let her through while another escorted her to the house in a golf cart.

Jorge was waiting for her. He put on his charm as he smiled with his piano ivory teeth and welcomed her inside. "You're looking great as always."

"Thank you."

Jorge ushered her to his office.

"Can I get you a drink?"

"Just water, please."

Jorge dutifully brought her a bottle of water.

"Why did you ask me here?"

"I have a favor to ask." Jorge then told her how she could work off her debt.

38

Belize

The cool ocean breeze made the ninety-degree temperature more tolerable. Jack and Billy visited several bars looking for people in the pictures they had, but knew it was virtually futile. Billy asked, discreetly, a few members of the bars' staff about Jorge DePeralta. Nobody knew him or they were too afraid to say anything.

They made their way to the Breeze Bar and Grill, the final bar and restaurant on their list. An open air, covered bar near the water's edge, it was jam-packed with what appeared to be mostly tourists, just like all the other bars they had investigated. As they stood near the crowded bar and checked the people dancing, a DJ was playing island-themed music with steel drums, including Buffett songs and reggae music.

They ordered drinks from a roaming waitress while they continued to check the scenery. At this point, Jack was still looking for people from the photographs. Billy had pretty much given up on finding anyone in the pictures and began looking at the women. They were no longer drinking sodas. Each of them had ordered drinks with alcohol since they would be done for the night after this stop. Billy was starting to enjoy the music. Jack was still an unrelenting observer.

Once the waitress returned with their drinks, and Jack paid her, Jack turned to Billy. "What are you thinking?"

"I'm thinking we aren't going to find anyone who can provide us with any information about DePeralta. I'm looking for a friend for the evening," Billy said with an ornery smile as he took a sip of his piña colada.

"I haven't given up hope. I still think it's possible we could get lucky." Jack looked around the room. "Remember doing terrain searches?" he said, alluding to the many outdoor crime scenes where a group of officers would check an area, and then another group would search the same area.

"What about it?"

"How many times would evidence turn up with the second group? A lot," Jack said before Billy could answer. "That's all I'm saying. We can't give up. Someone with information will turn up. That's what you have to believe."

"That's true, we could get lucky," Billy said. "It's just not likely."

Out of the corner of his eye, Jack saw two women walk into the bar and take a seat where two people had just decided to leave, surrendering their seats. He didn't think they were tourists and watched them intently. Their beauty was irresistible. They wore short dresses that hugged all the curves they had, with slits that traveled up to their thighs. They appeared to be alone. Jack's priority had clearly shifted gears.

"Holy fuck! Did you see the two that just walked in?"

"Yeah, I did," Jack said, not taking his eyes away from them.

"Which one do you want?" Billy asked.

Never looking at Billy, Jack said he liked the brunette.

"Outstanding! I like blondes better anyway," Billy said excitedly. "Are we going over?"

"Let's just watch for a minute."

Jack and Billy watched while they sipped their drinks. The women ordered cocktails from the bar, laughing with the bartender. It seemed like they must be regulars the way they talked with him. When the bartender walked away to serve other customers, they talked with each other, occasionally laughing, oblivious to everyone in the bar. Once they got their drinks, they turned toward the dance floor and watched. They swayed with the music, giving signs of an invitation for the right person to connect with.

"C'mon, man. They look like they're ready."

Jack held up a hand. "Hold on, let's just watch a little longer,"

"Are you crazy? They look like they're ready to dance. If we wait much longer, someone else is going to jump in."

Jack kept his eyes on them, never looking at Billy. "Relax." Jack called the bartender over. He talked to him briefly, then handed the man a twenty-dollar bill.

Sure enough a couple of younger guys went over to them. They talked for a quick moment and then walked away.

"See what I mean," Billy said. "If we don't get our ass over there, we're gonna go home with our dicks in our hand."

Jack finished his scotch and water, and then told Billy what the bartender had said about the two women. Billy listened intently and then his manner changed. He became more businesslike. "C'mon, let's go."

They walked over to them and Jack placed his empty glass on the bar behind the brunette.

"Hi, my name is Jack and this is my friend Billy," Jack said.

"Nice to meet you, Jack and Billy." The brunette smiled as she proffered her hand to Jack.

Jack took her hand. Billy's focus was on the blonde. "Hi, I'm Billy," he said. "I just wanna tell you, you're the most beautiful woman I've ever seen. Can I buy you a drink?"

It was as if Jack and Billy were now strangers. Each of them was on their own mission.

"Do you have a name?" Jack asked.

"I do," she said smiling, not surrendering it.

"Is it top secret?"

"It is."

"How do I learn your top secrets?" Jack said with a devious smile.

She laughed. It was a throaty, sexy laugh that Jack loved. "I could tell you, but then I'd have to kill you. Besides, you don't know the password."

Jack smiled. "What are you drinking, or is that top secret?"

"Rum and coke with a slice of lime."

"Funny, I'm drinking the same thing." Jack got the bartender's attention and ordered two of her drinks. When they arrived, Jack took his and slid hers over to her since she was still working on her first drink. "We must have a lot in common!"

"What makes you think we have a lot in common? The fact that we both like rum and coke?"

"It's a start, and let's just say I'm pretty intuitive."

"What else could we possibly have in common?" she said while finishing her cocktail and turning around to replace it with the drink Jack had bought for her. "By the way, thank you." She held up her drink. "My name is Alexa."

"So's mine," he said with a sly smile.

"I thought your name was Jack?" she said with a faux smile of doubt.

"That's my middle name," he said. They stared at each other and then began to laugh.

Jack looked over at Billy who now had his back to them. It appeared he was making progress.

"Alexa," Jack repeated, looking upward. "I love your name," he said to her.

"Thank you."

"Are you here visiting?"

"I live here."

"You live here?" Jack asked, surprised.

"What's wrong with that?"

"Nothing, I just thought you were probably visiting."

"What happened to your intuition?"

"It's currently on break," Jack said before pressing on. "What does a beautiful woman like yourself do here?"

"Computers, you know, IT," she answered.

"For what company?"

"Some company you've probably never heard of."

Jack sipped his drink. "Try me," he said, knowing how she enjoyed being coy.

She paused, looking at Jack. "JDP Industries. What kind of work do you do?"

"I'm a consultant."

She began to laugh, almost spitting out her drink. "A consultant? That's a general term for somebody who doesn't have a job!"

Jack was embarrassed. Even though she was condescending, he enjoyed the chase.

He began to laugh too.

"Well, I can't tell you what my real job is."

"And why is that?"

"If I did, I'd have to kill you," he said playfully.

She smiled. "I guess I deserve that."

Billy and his new friend excused themselves and left the bar. Jack and Alexa continued talking for almost an hour.

"Looks like the bar is closing," she said. "Will you walk me home?"

"How far do you live from here?" he asked.

"About ten miles," she replied with a straight face.

Jack raised his eyebrows in disbelief. She began to laugh at his bewildered look. "I'm just kidding. I'm staying at the Radisson for the weekend."

"What a coincidence, so am I," he said. She looked at him skeptically. Jack held up his hand. "Scout's honor."

They walked out of the bar together.

39

"I have to ask you, if you live here, why are you staying at the Radisson? Why don't you just go to your home?" Jack asked as they walked along the empty street.

"Because I'm conducting business at the hotel," she answered. "I'm meeting a client there, and it's just easier for me to be prepared and ready when he arrives."

Jack nodded as if he understood. They walked the rest of the short way with general conversation about the island.

Jack walked her to her room. It wasn't on the same floor as his.

"Do you like red wine?" she asked as she looked for her key card.

"I do."

"I have a nice bottle of Cabernet Sauvignon. Would you like to come in for a drink?"

"Absolutely," Jack answered.

They entered her room and Jack was surprised at how much larger it was than his. It had a living room and full kitchen. She told him to sit anywhere and she would bring the wine. Jack looked around before taking a seat on the sofa. Surprisingly, he didn't see any computers. IT people always seem to have a computer close by and ready for use.

Alexa came out to the living room with the uncorked bottle of wine and two glasses. She set the glasses down and poured each of them a healthy serving. After offering Jack his glass, she sat close to him and held up hers. "To life!"

They clinked and took a sip. Jack noticed how great she smelled. As he looked at her up close, he thought she was more beautiful than when he first saw her. When she crossed her legs, the slit in her dress exposed them to her upper thighs. Her skin was smooth and tan.

"Y'know Jack, you really haven't told me much about yourself."

"What do you want to know?"

"Have you ever been married?" she asked, taking a sip of her wine.

"Yes, but I've been divorced for nearly twenty years."

"Any children?"

"One."

"Boy or girl?"

"Boy."

"Do you get to see him?"

"No. It's a long story," he lamented.

"Sounds like it's a sensitive subject," she said. "Are your parents still alive?"

"My father is, but my mother isn't."

"I'm sorry. How long ago?"

"About twenty years ago," Jack said. "She died in a car accident. What about you? Ever been married?"

"No," Alexa answered.

"That's hard for me to believe, a beautiful woman like you, has never been married," Jack said, taking another sip of his wine. "Why not?"

"I never found the right man."

"Maybe you need to expand your horizons and get out of Belize."

"You're probably right," she said wistfully.

Alexa placed her empty wine glass on the coffee table. Turning to Jack, she looked him straight in the eyes. She took her hand and stroked his face. She leaned into him and they began kissing, their tongues darting in each other's mouths.

"You know, I find you very attractive. What if I told you I wanted to take you to my bedroom and fuck your brains out?"

Jack took his wine glass and placed it on the table next to hers. "As Woody Allen said, that's my second favorite organ," he said.

She grabbed his crotch and felt his approval. "I think I know what your favorite organ is!"

She got up and so did Jack. She led him by the hand into her dark bedroom. There was some soft light coming from the street giving the bedroom just the perfect amount of illumination.

Jack stood by the bed. She began to undress him, taking off his shirt and his pants, before kneeling down and taking him into her mouth. Jack closed his eyes and enjoyed the moment. She teased him, and then pushed him back on the bed.

He watched her as she walked toward the bathroom. She closed the door and he saw the light come on from underneath. A few minutes later, the door opened. Alexa stood there, completely naked. Jack stared at her. She had one of the greatest bodies he had ever seen. Long legs, tiny waist, and large perfect breasts accentuated by small erect nipples. She reached behind and turned off the bathroom light.

Slowly, she walked toward the bed. She began to crawl across him from the foot of the bed. Her long hair gently touched his legs as she moved up to him. Alexa let her nipples touch his thighs as she kissed his penis. Jack could not take much more. Finally, she guided him inside her as she sat upright and moved back and forth, slowly.

It would be a long, enjoyable night.

. . .

The next morning, Jack got up and quietly dressed. He enjoyed looking at the contours of Alexa's naked body which was facing away from him. He hoped they would get to enjoy each other again, soon. He needed to find out more about her, and the married man she was secretly having an affair with. Quietly, he pulled her door closed and left.

He went back to his room, showered, dressed and went down to the restaurant. There were several tables filled with tourists. Jack found an empty table in the back. He ordered a large breakfast and coffee. He was famished. After the waitress took his order, he got the Wi-Fi password and began checking his phone for emails. Surprisingly, there was an email from his father, so he decided to call him.

"Hello," Ben Dublin said weakly.

"Hey, it's Jack," he answered.

"Where are you?"

"I'm in Belize."

"Where?"

"Belize, down in Central America."

"What are you doing down there?"

Jack brought his father up to date. "How are you feeling?"

"Like I got run over by a Mack truck, but I'll survive," Ben answered. "Do you really think Connor is down there?"

"There really isn't any positive proof yet, but my instincts tell me he is."

"Is Billy with you?"

"Yeah, he's here. I haven't spoken with him yet today, but he's here."

"Good, because your uncle is a dangerous man. Your mother and I used to have a lot of arguments about him. I wouldn't put anything past him. He'll kill you and Connor just for the sport of it. Keep Billy with you, and always look over your shoulder. You'll need to watch each other's backs."

"Don't worry, we will."

"You think the DEA is going to conduct a raid on Jorge?"

"That's what we hear. Billy and I met with the guy from the DEA, but he wasn't too helpful. If you could put some pressure on Brian Oliver from your end, I'll push from mine."

"I can do that. Did the DEA guy give you any idea when they were going to conduct the raid?"

"He didn't say, but he implied it would be soon."

"Jack, maybe you should just let the DEA handle it."

"That's not happening if I can help it. If they're going after him, I want to be there. I want to see him face to face. He tried to kill you, and took my son. I'm taking him down."

"That's very honorable, Jack, but the thing is, as long as he goes down, what does it matter?"

"It matters to me."

"Please keep me up to date, it's killing me not knowing what's going on."

"I will, in the meantime just rest and get better."

Jack got up from his table and went to the cashier to pay his check. Just as he was putting his wallet away, Billy walked in.

"Hey Jack," Billy said.

"Anything to report?" Jack asked.

"She said she works for a company called JDP. She said she just recently met Alexa, and that last night Alexa asked her if she wanted to get a drink. That's how they ended up at the bar."

"Do you know where she's from or what she does?"

"She said she's from Seattle and works with computers."

Jack considered the information. At least it matched what Alexa had told him about the company they worked for, but that could have been planned. "How was the rest of your night?"

"It couldn't have been any better," Billy said, smiling. "It's like I always say, if there's anything better than sex, the good Lord is keeping it all to himself!"

Jack just pursed his lips and shook his head.

40

Alexa was dropped off at the front gate of Jorge's compound by a friend. She found it quite irritating that she had to go through so much bullshit to enter her father's estate, a place where she used to live. She knew Luisa probably had something to do with it since they had a mutual hatred for each other. Alexa's mother, Yolanda, Jorge's first wife, was now living in exile somewhere in Paris ever since Jorge began his pursuit of Luisa. Her mother was so afraid of Jorge that she never said goodbye. She just left in the middle of the night. Alexa was very young when her mother left, and she had no direct way to get in touch with her. Yolanda always contacted Alexa, but it remained a mystery as to where she lived. She obviously feared for her life. Still, Alexa wanted to know why.

Alexa did meet with her mother secretively in Miami a few years back. It was the last time she saw her, although they still talked from time to time. When she last saw her mother, she saw a woman who was a nervous wreck. She chain-smoked and her hands shook. Her skin was ravaged from the effects of smoking and drinking, not to mention the anxiety caused by her constant vigilance of looking over her shoulder every minute of every day. Alexa was bitter with her mother for leaving her behind, but after living with her father, she understood why her mother left. Even though there were never any outward signs of affection, she intuitively knew her mother loved her. Yolanda told her that one day, she would tell her why she left.

Luis, the armed guard at the front gate, knew Alexa and allowed her to enter. She took a golf cart to the front door where she was met by Tomas, another armed guard.

"Your father is waiting for you in the study," he said while opening the front door.

Alexa smiled and went inside. Standing outside her father's study was yet another armed guard named Alberto.

"*Buenos dias,* Alexa," he said.

"*Buenos dias,* Alberto," she responded as she entered the study. Sitting behind his desk, coughing, was her father. He had an unhealthy paleness, but she had no sympathy for him.

"Come in, sit down," he said, directing her with a wave of his hand to a chair in front of him. "Were you able to make contact with Jack Dublin?"

"Yes, I was."

"What information can you tell me?"

"As you suspected, he's here looking for his son. He was in the company of another man, a black man."

"Where's he staying, the Radisson?"

"Yes."

"What does he look like? I've seen pictures, but they're not up to date."

"He looks to be in his early forties, about five feet eleven, strong build."

"Did my name come up?" Jorge asked as he lit a cigar.

"No, we never got that far."

"What did he say about his son? Does he know where he's at?"

"He said he thought he was down here on a break from college."

Jorge smiled. "I'm sorry. Would you like something to drink?"

"No, I'm good."

"Do you mind if I have something to drink?" he said, walking over to the bar.

"No."

"Did you think he was being honest about looking for his son?"

"As far as I could tell."

"What if I told you he's really looking for me?" Jorge said as he walked back to his desk with his scotch and water.

"Wouldn't surprise me either."

Jorge continued to smile at Alexa. "Did you fuck him?"

Alexa stared back with hate in her eyes. "Does it matter?"

"I'll take that as a yes, and yes it does matter to me," he answered, chuckling. "And it will matter to you too." Jorge stood up and walked over to his bookshelf. "I want to show you something." Standing with his back to her, Jorge released a lock and the bookshelf opened revealing the secret passage. "Follow me."

Alexa curiously walked over to the opening and was astonished. All the time she lived in this house, she never knew about this passageway.

"Come with me. I want to introduce someone to you."

Alexa cautiously followed Jorge down the lighted stairs until she was standing on a dirt floor in the middle of intersecting subterranean pathways. There appeared to be some rooms with locks. This scared her. At first, she wondered who he kept in these rooms before thinking it may be her final destination.

Jorge looked at her and sensed her fear. "Relax, Alexa. Nothing is going to happen to you. I want to introduce you to someone special."

They walked over to the first room which she now fully realized was a small detaining room. Jorge removed a key from his pocket and unlocked the door. Once opened, an odor emanated that made her think of farm animals. It was the smell of hay.

"Come over here," Jorge said, motioning her over. Alexa walked over with extreme trepidation. Trust was not something she ever associated with her father. "C'mon, c'mon, he won't bite you." She walked over to the doorway and carefully looked inside. Lying there on a straw mattress was a man who looked to be in his early twenties.

Jorge walked around her and faced the young man. "Stand up," he ordered. The young man stood with some difficulty. He looked emaciated and weak yet his bearing was strong.

"Alexa, I want you to meet your cousin, Connor Dublin," Jorge said, smiling widely.

Alexa looked at Connor, and didn't immediately comprehend the enormity of what Jorge had just said. As the information seeped into her conscience, a mixture of emotions took root. Her anger toward her father was tempered, but her emotion for Connor took over.

She rushed over to Connor and gave him a hug. Through tears, she whispered in his ear, "Don't worry, your father is close and is coming to save you." She backed away from Connor to minimize any suspicion by Jorge. "You are a handsome young man. I'm happy to finally meet you," she said, trying to maintain her self-control.

Jorge stood there as if he were a proud parent watching two of his children hugging each other. "Okay, Alexa, that's enough. We have to get back upstairs."

Alexa continued to look at Connor sadly with a tear in her eye. She waved to him as Jorge grabbed her arm and guided her. Once outside the detainment cell, Alexa's tears of sorrow turned to tears of anger. Her own father had become the monster she always suspected, and she was determined to eventually exterminate him from the face of the earth.

They returned to his study. Jorge locked the entryway and turned to Alexa. "Well, what are you thinking?" A deceitful grin was pasted on his face.

"Why are you keeping him locked up down there?" she demanded. "He's a young man. He doesn't deserve it. If you have something against his father, you don't need to take it out on somebody innocent."

"It's easy. It's because you're going back to town and tell Jack Dublin his son is here. When you do that, your debt is paid. You don't owe me anything."

"What is it you want to accomplish?"

"Easy. I want to talk to him."

"And you have to kidnap his son?"

"I figured it would get his attention!"

She shook her head in disbelief.

"Are you going to do it for me?" Jorge asked.

"You bet I am!"

41

Belize

Jack called Alexa's room, but she didn't answer. He decided to allow some time before calling back. Perhaps she was in the shower. He needed to see her again before he continued to search for his son. He was certain she could help him. She had lived in Belize a long time, and was aware of information that would be supportive to his cause.

He walked out to his balcony. The pool was starting to get crowded. Further out, the sun was glistening on the ocean where a variety of boats, large and small, were cutting across his view. A few couples had begun carving out their territorial piece of beach near the water's edge.

Jack decided to call Brian Oliver and pressure him for help. So far, he had nothing to go on. He had been sent out on a wild goose chase to basically keep him occupied and out of the way of the DEA. If Derek Palmer walked into the room right now, Jack would have treated him to a significant beating.

Looking out at the blue sky, the aqua ocean, and the few passing white clouds, Jack thought of the murderous deeds of his sociopathic uncle. Belize was a beautiful country starving for the legitimate source of income from tourists, yet it was seduced by the dirty drug money of Jorge DePeralta who was subsidizing most of the local economy. Not to mention his padding of the pockets of judges and politicians.

His phone rang. Caller ID didn't indicate who the caller was.

"Hello," Jack said.

"Hello, Jack. Its Brian."

"I was just going to call you."

"I hear you've spoken with Derek Palmer."

"That man is useless," Jack said derisively. "How that man can draw a paycheck is beyond me. What I want to know is, why have I been deliberately kept in the dark, and are you going to help me, or do I have to go my own way?"

"Listen, Jack, I was told you were going to be involved. I don't know why you weren't given clearance to be included on this mission, or why Agent Palmer kept you in the dark, but I'm here now, and I promise you, things are going to change."

"You're in town?"

"Yes, I want to get together with you, and bring you up to date. When can we meet?"

"Whenever you want."

"Tell you what. I've got to talk with the team down here, and be fully informed before we get together. I want to give you the most complete information I have. Why don't we meet at your hotel around eighteen hundred hours?"

"It's probably not a good idea to meet at the hotel. Why don't we meet at the Celebrity Restaurant? It's on Marine Parade Boulevard near the ocean. I've heard it's good and better yet, they have a private room we should be able to get. I'll call to confirm. If there's a problem, I'll call you back. I'm bringing Billy too."

"No problem. I'll see you there at six."

Jack called the restaurant and reserved the private room for six o'clock. He tried to get a hold of Billy, but didn't get an answer, so he left a message. Jack then called Alexa again, but still didn't get an answer. He thought about walking up to her room, but decided against it.

It was six hours until he would meet with Brian Oliver. Thoughts of the mission and getting Connor back safely were all he could focus on. He decided to put on a bathing suit and walk to the ocean. If he was being watched he would at least send the message, "Here I am, come get me!"

He sat on a white, hotel chaise lounge on their private beach and read a *Time* magazine he had picked up in the hotel convenience store to bide his time. He had looked for Billy at the pool before opting for the ocean. Jack adjusted his chaise, laid back, and unintentionally fell asleep.

"Hello Jack," said a female voice standing over him.

Jack slowly opened his eyes and tried to see who was addressing him by shading the sun with his hand. It was difficult to see who it was, particularly since he had been asleep for about half an hour.

"Alexa?" Jack said, squinting. She pulled another chaise lounge next to him and sat down. "I tried calling your room."

"I had to run out," she said. "Jack, I have to ask you. What is your son's name?" she asked tentatively.

Jack noticed how serious she became. "It's Connor, why?"

She stared out to the horizon.

"What's wrong?"

"I don't know how to tell you this, but I know where he is. I just saw him at my father's house."

"Who's your father, and where does he live?"

She turned to him and looked into his eyes with sadness. She knew the impact of what she was going to say would devastate him as it did her. "My father is Jorge DePeralta. Have you heard of him?"

Jack stared at her as the information slowly permeated his thought process. "You were going to set me up for your father, weren't you?"

"No, Jack. That's not true."

"Your father sent you to find me, didn't he?"

"No," Alexa lied. She liked Jack and didn't want to alienate him.

"When you went into that bar, you knew who I was."

"No I didn't. I didn't know who you were. I never saw any pictures of you. Don't forget, last night you came over to me. I didn't come over to you," she answered in her defense, looking into Jack's disbelieving eyes. "Okay, I admit my father did want me to make contact with you, but I didn't know why. The only description I had was that you were a white man in your forties and you were traveling with a black man. I also knew you were staying at the Radisson. When you and your friend approached me, I figured you were the Jack Dublin my father had sent me for."

"I didn't know you were his daughter. I mistakenly thought you were his mistress," Jack said with no emotion. "That was information I was told."

She looked at him in disbelief. "So, you knew who I was the whole time, didn't you?"

"Obviously, I didn't, otherwise I wouldn't have gone back to your room. You, on the other hand, didn't care."

"You knew who Jorge DePeralta was and that I had a connection with him!"

"Yes."

Alexa reached over and tried to slap Jack, but he quickly grabbed her arm in self-defense.

"You're not exactly innocent either. You were sent to find me and ask around about me for your father. I didn't know you would take it to the extreme. Only a ruthless whore would fuck her cousin!"

She tried to wrest her arm away. "Let go, let go!"

Jack released her arm. She looked at him with disgust. "I didn't know who you were until he introduced me to your son today. He told me he was my cousin. It was then and only then that I knew we were related. If I knew we were cousins, things would have been different. Listen, do you think I would have allowed what happened last night if I knew we were related? What kind of person do you think I am?"

"So, my son is in his compound?" Jack asked, avoiding her question.

"Yes, he is, and he's being kept in a small room that's underground," she answered, still rubbing her arms where Jack had grabbed her.

"Underground?"

"Yes."

"How many people does your father have for security?"

"Why the hell should I tell you anything else?"

"Because your father is a murderer. He's selling drugs and killing people. He doesn't care about women or children, and he tortures people. Obviously, he doesn't care about you either! He's a sick man who needs to be stopped. I can't do it by myself. If you're any kind of decent human being you'll answer my questions."

"Probably about twenty-five."

"Heavily armed?"

"Yes."

"What kind of weapons, do you know?"

"They have automatic weapons all over the place, and my father keeps a helicopter close by, in case he needs to escape."

"Any rocket-propelled grenades?"

"Yes."

"You're sure?"

"Yes," she answered indignantly.

Jack considered the options. He would definitely need to get with Brian Oliver now.

"Listen, I'm sorry," she said as she began to cry. "I never would have let last night happen. It was a mistake. I didn't know."

"You had known me for only a couple of hours, and yet you had no reservations about taking me back to your room for sex. You were setting me up and I was a fool not to see it. You're someone who's just like her father, someone who doesn't have a soul."

She slapped Jack across the face. "I'm nothing like my father. I detest him. You have no idea what he's done to me. I was in trouble and I needed money. He gave it to me under one condition, that I find you. How was I to know what the purpose was? I had no ties to you. I didn't know you or why you were here. For all I knew, you were here to conduct business with him."

Jack gave her a hard, expressionless stare. "Thanks for your help," he said as he stood up and started walking back to the hotel.

42

Belize

Jack and Billy met in the lobby of the hotel early in the morning. Jack had received a call from Brian Oliver, his contact with the DEA, stating he couldn't make dinner the previous night because some new information was being developed, and he would call them the next day.

Brian called early and told Jack and Billy it was urgent for them to come to Belize Police Headquarters. He didn't provide any additional information.

Jack and Billy got into a cab and headed over.

"Could you put some music on?" Jack asked the driver.

Once the music started, Jack and Billy talked quietly in the back seat.

"What do you think is going on?" Billy asked in a hushed voice.

"I don't know."

"This is getting weird."

"Did you have any more contact with the woman from the other night?" Jack queried.

"No, she left the hotel," Billy said. "She didn't leave a note, a number, nothing. What about you?"

Jack stared momentarily out the window. "Yeah, I had contact with her."

"Did you...you know, get laid?"

"Is that all you think about?"

"Most of the time, but I think it could lead to some valuable information. Don't you agree? I mean, isn't that what we're doing? Going on a fact-finding mission?"

"Billy, all you need to know is she is the daughter of JD."

Billy hesitated and then got it. "You mean you were with the daughter of the guy we're looking for?"

Jack nodded.

"Wow!" he said, then as the connection sank in, "Holy shit! That means she's your cousin!"

"Yes."

"Man, I hope you didn't get laid!"

They rode in silence for a couple of minutes before arriving at Police Headquarters. Jack paid the driver and they got out.

The building looked like an old elementary school from the sixties back in the States. Once they got inside they approached the front desk and gave their names. They were told to sit on a bench and someone would come for them.

A black man, who looked to be in his mid-thirties, dressed in casual clothes came within a couple of minutes and greeted them.

"Are you Dublin and Dawkins?" he asked.

"Yes we are."

"Come with me," he said as he turned to walk down the hallway.

They followed him to a stairway that led upstairs to the second floor. As they walked down the hall, they could see Brian and Derek Palmer talking outside a classroom. It definitely made Jack feel like he was back in junior high school.

"Here they are, sir," the plainclothes police officer said.

"Thank you, Paul," Brian said.

The officer turned and left.

"Hello Jack, Billy," Brian said, shaking their hands. "You remember Agent Palmer."

"Yes, we remember," Jack said without offering his hand.

"How are you guys doing?" Palmer asked.

"Great." Jack looked him in the eyes, his glare cold and hard.

"Jack, can I talk to you in private for a moment?" Brian asked as he motioned Jack to step away a few feet. "Listen Jack, today we received some sensitive information."

"Shouldn't Billy hear this?"

"We'll fill him in, but I don't think you want him to hear what I'm about to say," Brian told him. "We've had an informant who contacted us last night and then showed up early this morning with valuable information about DePeralta. She said she's your cousin." Brian looked at Jack for any sign of recognition.

"What else did she say?"

"Just that she was your cousin."

"So, how's that important?"

"She said you two had drinks last night. Is there anything you want to tell me?"

"What are you implying, Brian?"

"Jack, why didn't you tell me about this development?"

"I didn't have a chance, until now. I would have informed you last night at dinner. Since it didn't happen, and you wanted me and Billy here this morning, I was going to tell you when I got here. Now you know."

"What else should I know?"

"All I know is my son is being held at Jorge DePeralta's compound. I don't know where it is. He has a small contingent of about twenty-five men for security and they are heavily armed. He also has a helicopter for escape if necessary. That's it. I don't know anything else."

"When you were talking with her, did you get any more information about your uncle?"

"It's complicated. I was going to ask her, but we had a disagreement."

"What kind of disagreement?"

"Why the hell are you interrogating me? Don't you think you should be asking her these questions?"

"I have, Jack. I'm just concerned that maybe you have a conflict."

"Don't give me that shit! You know how I operate. I have one objective and one objective only—that's to get my son out of there safely."

"Jack, I trust you. I needed to talk with you before the locals ask you any questions. They don't want outsiders involved, especially someone who has a son being held captive. They think it could cloud your ability to perform. They're worried about the safety of everyone involved in this operation. I've told them about you and I think I have them convinced, but your relationship with Alexa is troubling."

"There is no relationship. She's my cousin who I met for the first time last night. As far as I'm concerned we should be worried about any information she offers. After all, she is the daughter of the most notorious drug dealer in the world."

"She's provided us with information that confirms other information we've received that nobody else would know except Alexa and another informant who lived there. We got the same layout of the compound from two separate, independent parties, not to mention other details."

"I can handle it."

"Alexa said you were hostile towards her."

"Why is that a concern? She's not part of the operation."

"Well, Jack, she is."

"How?"

"She's going to get us in the compound. Since it's heavily fortified, if we don't have an easy way in, we would have to take it by force from the get-go. This would alert them early of our presence and lead to more casualties. Alexa is known there and can get us past the guard at the front gate. Once we're in the compound we can operate more freely since we have a layout."

"I'll be fine. I'll do whatever they want, except stay behind."

"C'mon, let's go talk with them. We're getting ready to make final plans. I'll introduce you."

As they began to walk towards the meeting room, Jack and Billy caught eye contact. Billy grabbed Jack's arm. "What's going on?" he asked, concerned.

"Don't worry about it. Everything's under control," Jack said. "C'mon, let's go in and listen to their plan to take down DePeralta."

They entered the room. It was occupied by approximately fifty men. Jack didn't see any women and thought it was a mistake. His experience told him it was always, unequivocally better to have trained and seasoned women officers involved, but it wasn't his operation. Standing at the front of the room was Brian Oliver representing the DEA and Colonel Jose Herrera of the Belize Police.

Colonel Herrera asked everyone to take a seat so they could make their presentation. The equipment they were using was out-of-date.

It consisted of an overhead projector and screen, but it was still suffi- cient. Jack and Billy took seats near the front. Alexa was sitting not far from them. She was the only woman in the room.

"Before we get started, I want to acknowledge the presence of two people who have a distinct interest in the outcome of tomorrow's operation," Col. Herrera said. Looking at Jack, he continued, "Jorge DePeralta has kidnapped the son of an American police officer and is holding him captive on the compound. We must make every effort that not only is he rescued without harm, but also any other innocent person who is reluctantly working on the premises. I'm gonna ask Mr. Jack Dublin to please stand up so our officers can see you and know who you are."

Jack stood up, surprised, and turned around so he could be seen by everyone in the room.

"Thank you, Mr. Dublin," the colonel continued. "I want to assure you that every officer in here will fight for you and your son. Now, I'm going to ask you and Mr. Dawkins to leave this briefing so we can begin our presentation."

"Excuse me, Colonel, but Mr. Dawkins and I have come here to assist you with this operation."

"I appreciate your willingness to help us, but you're a liability. I mean no disrespect, but since you have a relative—particularly a son— who could be in harm's way throughout our execution of the extrac- tion, your thinking could be distorted."

"Sir, I was a member of our SWAT Unit in Washington, D.C. We were utilized many times in harm's way. I worked the street and dealt with the worst kind of scum that inhabits this earth. Billy here," Jack said, pointing at Billy, "in addition to working the streets of Washington, is a Gulf War veteran who was exposed to frontline warfare of the worst kind. We respectfully request that you reconsider your position."

Colonel Herrera thoughtfully deliberated over Jack's statement. "Mr. Dublin, I understand your position. If I were in your shoes, I would be making the same case. Since I'm removed from the personal connection to this case, I think I can see more clearly than you. Your presence still presents a potential danger. With that in mind, I'm going to have to ask you and Mr. Dawkins to leave. I assure you, we will keep you updated as the operation progresses. Thank you again for your willingness to help."

Jack's face was flushed with anger. He knew he had to bite his tongue, but it wasn't one of his strengths. His veins bulged in his neck and arms. His eyes narrowed with an intensity not shown before. Fuck Herrera! He would find another way in.

Jack and Billy stood up slowly and started to leave the room.

"Wait! I have something to say." Alexa stood up. "If they can't be a part of this operation, then I'm not either." Alexa began to clear her way between a couple of desks, and make her way for the front door.

Brian leaned over and whispered in Colonel Herrera's ear. He nodded and then said, "Wait a minute! It's obvious everyone in this room wants a successful outcome. We need someone to provide us with access to the DePeralta compound, otherwise more lives would be put in harm's way. Since Ms. DePeralta is the only person who can provide us with that advantage, and since she is adamant that Mr. Dublin and Dawkins also be present during this operation, I'll acquiesce."

Alexa, Jack, and Billy went back to their seats.

43

As planned, Alexa and Jack arrived at the front gate at seven o'clock in the morning on a Harley motorcycle. It was generously acquired from one of the Belize officers. Alexa knew all the guards at the gate and they all loved her. When she lived there full-time, she always made sure they were taken care of with refreshments. The fact that she was so beautiful didn't go unnoticed by them either.

She went up to the guard at the gate who looked like he just woke up. It was Carlos. Unfortunately, he had always been one of her favorites.

"Carlos, can you let us in?" she asked sweetly.

He came to the gate with his rifle slung over his shoulder. Wiping his eyes, he opened the gate. "Who's this?" he asked while looking at Jack.

"He's someone my father wants to meet."

"I'll have to call the main house and let them know. Kinda early, isn't it," he said as he turned to the booth which had a display of cameras. He started to reach for the button to close the gate.

Jack reached behind his back, grabbed his gun with suppressor and shot Carlos in the back of the head with a single shot. A red cloud of blood and brains splashed against the inside of the glass booth. Alexa averted her eyes. She had seen many displays of death while living here, but still didn't want to see someone she knew lying on the ground with his brains on display.

Jack ran out of the gate and signaled the access was open. Within seconds, officers in camouflage gear stormed the compound. Brian

Oliver was not among the initial wave of men. He and the colonel were close by in a mobile command unit monitoring the situation. Billy appeared, decked-out in SWAT gear. He brought Jack a headset and radio.

"Thanks, Billy, but you're going to have to hold on to it," Jack said. "We still have to go to the front door. I can't raise any suspicion until we're in the house. By then, it won't matter." He looked up at the sky. In the distance, the hum of helicopters could be heard. "Are you ready for this?"

"I can't wait to meet this dude," Billy replied. "I hope I get to light him up!"

"We'll see him soon enough. You've got your assignment. Stay in touch."

Billy nodded and ran off with a group of soldiers who were still unnoticed by DePeralta's security team. The area was heavily wooded from the gate until you were about fifty yards from the house. This was going to present the most dangerous and difficult situation. Once their presence was known, all hell would break loose. Close to the house, the sound of dogs barking reminded everyone this was no rehearsal. Jack was dumbfounded how light the security was. Why wasn't anyone patrolling the premises?

Jack and Alexa secured a golf cart by the security shack. She felt it would be more inconspicuous if they arrived at the front door on a cart instead of the Harley. They traversed the driveway, looking into the woods, and observed the troops on each side of the driveway moving forward, toward the edge of the tree line where the assault would begin.

"Are you okay?" Jack asked Alexa who was driving the cart.

"I'm good!" she said, masking her thoughts.

Jack wondered what she was thinking. She knew her father was most likely going to die, yet she appeared unusually calm. Perhaps she had become emotionless toward her father as a result of the trauma she had experienced over the years. He could never underestimate the horrors she witnessed in her lifetime. Nothing in the line of police work was as terrifying as seeing people tortured, garroted, or decapitated in front of you.

Perhaps she was thinking of the night they spent together unaware they were first cousins. Jack tried to push those thoughts out of his mind. He needed to have a clear head once they got to the house. They could talk about it later, after the mission was completed.

"Thanks for sticking up for me and Billy at the meeting yesterday," Jack said as he began to re-focus.

"You're welcome," she answered before adding, "You have a right to be here."

Jack nodded.

As they approached the end of the tree line, the dogs' barking grew louder. It sounded like they were no longer in their pens. Moments later, several Doberman pinschers came running from behind the house toward the golf cart. They continued to bark and show their teeth. Alexa called to them and they soon calmed down. It was perfect timing. If they hadn't intercepted the dogs, they would have gone into the woods and created a maelstrom for the officers waiting there.

They pulled up to the front door and were met immediately by a man named Alejandro. He was a short man but powerfully built. He carried an AR-15 by his side. A few other men appeared as well, all armed and none were smiling.

"Alejandro, I've brought this man to meet my father," she said with confidence. "He wants to meet him."

"Funny, I don't remember your father ever telling me that you were bringing a stranger to his house," he said with no emotion. "Especially at this time of day! Did Carlos know about this?"

"He must have, he let us in the gate," Alexa said.

"Stay right here, I have to talk to Carlos," he said.

"Why don't you just call my father?"

"Because your father is very sick, and I don't think he wants any interruptions."

"I'll call him myself," Alexa said, while she took out her phone, trying to avert any attempt by Alejandro to call Carlos, who wouldn't be accepting any more calls.

"Papi, it's me, Alexa," she said warmly. "I have brought Jack Dublin to the house to meet you." She listened to his response. "Could you please tell Alejandro to let us in?" She listened again and then handed the phone to Alejandro.

After listening for a few moments, he said, "Yes sir, I will take care of it." He handed the phone back to Alexa.

At that moment, an alarm went off. It was learned later that there were trip wires in the woods and one of the officers set it off.

"Take your positions!" Alejandro yelled to the men assembled at the front of the house.

As soon as the command was given, men seemed to appear from everywhere. Shots began to ring out. Jack turned on Alejandro, and before Alejandro could take a shot, Jack fired his gun and shot him right between the eyes. Jack reached over and grabbed Alejandro's AR-15 and ammo clip. Quickly, Alexa grabbed Jack's arm and pulled him into the house. She bolted the door and told him to follow her. Multiple shots could be heard outside. Some of them could be heard hitting the heavy front door.

Jack and Alexa began running across the foyer when one of DePeralta's men appeared at the top of the steps and began shooting his AR-15 in their direction. Jack found a doorway to take cover. Alexa kept running safely toward a hallway. Jack saw the shooter's silhouette on the opposite wall. There was room to kneel down. The shooter probably had his gun aimed expecting Jack to emerge at head level. It would give Jack a split-second advantage. Jack darted out and fired a quick burst, hitting his target in the chest and head. The man fell over the railing onto the tile floor.

How many more men were upstairs? he wondered. The rotor wash of helicopters grew louder. It sounded like Black Hawks. This would bring a new wave of men to counter any defense mounted by DePeralta. Jack wasn't going to sit and wait for backup. He realized going in, it was going to require taking chances.

At that moment there was an explosion at the front door. Some men from the security team were backing into the living room keeping cover by firing out the door at the approaching troops. Unfortunately for them it wasn't a safe haven. Jack ripped off the remaining ammunition in his clip and took out four men. Smoke began to fill the room, giving him the advantage to move under cover. The problem was he couldn't see where to run even though he had been thoroughly briefed on the layout of the mansion. He took the other ammo clip he had taken from Alejandro and slapped it in place. It felt like it was a thirty-cartridge clip.

He thought he heard more voices at the front door, but was unable to discern whether it was part of his team. It was time to get out of the foyer. He made the choice to keep his back against the wall until he could feel his way to an opening. Once he made it to a hallway, the air was clearer and he could see where he was going. He had no idea where Alexa was, and he couldn't call out to her because it would give his position. DePeralta's room was upstairs and most likely he was too, since Alejandro alluded to it when they arrived at the front door.

Most importantly, he had no idea where Connor was and whether or not his life was in deep jeopardy. Jack believed DePeralta would now try to use Connor as a bargaining chip. He had to find him before DePeralta did.

The gunfire was still heavy outside. If the plan were executed properly, three Black Hawks would have landed on the property by now. The gunfire and explosions were so loud, Jack wasn't sure.

As he made his way stealthily down the hallway, an explosion rocked the house. He heard the whirring of one of the Black Hawk engines after it took a hit from a rocket-propelled grenade. It struck the back of the house. Flames began their way rapidly down the hallway. Jack was able to dive into a room out of the path of the firestorm. Apparently, DePeralta's men were well equipped and not giving up.

Fire began to creep into the room where Jack hid. He surveyed his surroundings and realized the only door he could exit from was becoming engulfed in flames. He went to the furthest point in the room away from the approaching fire. Smoke seeped into the room as well.

Behind him he heard breaking glass. He then realized there was an adjoining room with what once was a glass door. Not knowing how the glass broke and whether or not the enemy was on the other side, Jack made a split-second decision to enter low and scan the area.

One man stood in the room, dressed in camouflage. His gun was pointed at Jack.

"Jack, where the fuck have you been?" Billy asked.

"Just trying to mind my own business, looking for a blender so I could make myself a drink," Jack said sarcastically.

"Man, I don't know where the fuck we are, but we need to get out of here."

"Has my son been located?"

"I don't know. The radio has been silent. I don't know if we lost a signal or what?"

"We need to split up. There isn't much time. We need to get to DePeralta's study before he does. If he gets to Connor first, we'll have a hostage situation…or worse."

"Sounds like they got one of our birds!"

"I know," Jack said as he listened. "I think the fight is slowing down. We need to get out of here before the place burns down. I'm gonna go out first. Give me cover. Once I'm out, head in the opposite direction. Since we have a small window of time, we'll have a better chance working independently."

"Alright, let's get moving," Billy said.

44

Jack popped his head out, took a quick look and ducked back. He gave Billy a hand signal indicating one of DePeralta's fighters was in the hallway.

Billy nodded and counted to three silently by using his fingers.

Jack ran across the hallway to another room. Billy quickly looked around the doorway and fired, taking out the distracted enemy. Looking at each other, Jack went down the hallway in the direction of the dying fighter who was lying face down. Jack felt the man's neck for a pulse. It was slight and weakening.

"I'm gonna go back and secure the rest of the area," Billy whispered. "I'll find the study and meet you there."

Jack picked up the man's AR-15 and removed the clip. He then continued down the hallway, leaving the man to die, hoping to find the study.

During all the fighting, he had become confused. Trying to remember the layout of the home was of no value, because he didn't know where he was on the first floor. He turned around and Billy was gone.

Movement could be heard on the second floor. Without a radio and headset, Jack had no idea whether it was a team member or a security force. He knew the priority was to find the study. Once he found it, he could sit tight because he knew DePeralta would make it there.

Moving quickly but cautiously from room to room, Jack looked back out toward the fire. For some reason it didn't appear to be spreading as fast as he thought it would. Still, he wanted to get his son and get the hell out of there. Some gunfire was still heard outside. Hopefully, by the time he made his exit with Connor, it would be safe.

Jack found himself back in the foyer where he last saw Alexa. It was littered with several bodies, all of them members of the security team. Broken glass and chips of wood from the front door along with small pieces of concrete from the pockmarked walls were scattered from wall to wall.

An older woman screamed from upstairs, but Jack was undeterred. His son was first priority. He went to the opposite side of the foyer from where he first took cover upon entering the house. Opening the tall wood door, at first he stepped back before entering the room. It was DePeralta's study. This is where the access to the underground cell was. Not far from here, he hoped to find his son.

Taking precaution, he kneeled down, and then quickly poked his head in to scan the room before ducking back. He didn't see anyone in the room, but with the short glance he knew it was impossible to scan the entire room. Still, he had to take a chance and enter the room, prepared to defend himself.

He took another quick glance and then entered the room with his rifle leveled. He moved around the room. There was nobody there. Knowing time was short, he knew somewhere in the bookcase was the secret to gaining access to the underground escape route, and the location where DePeralta held people captive. He leaned his rifle against the wall while he examined the shelves. Frantically, he looked everywhere, occasionally looking back toward the door and also the other doors at the far end of the room. One entire wall was four sets of French doors which led outside to a patio in the rear of the house. Gunfire was still active in the outside near the patio doors. Gunshots were also heard inside the home on the ground floor.

Jack turned his attention again to the bookcase. Alexa had advised at the briefing, she saw her father reach into the shelf and manipulate a switch of some kind, releasing a lock causing the bookshelf to swing open, allowing access to the underground.

Someone running in the direction of the study diverted Jack's attention. He reached for the rifle, but it slid down the wall to the floor. He tried to grab it blindly while watching the door, but had to leave it to take cover. He decided to hide behind the sofa until he could determine who was entering the room. Fortunately, he still had his Glock secured in the belt holster. Watching surreptitiously, Jack saw a man he knew was Jorge DePeralta enter the room. He was coughing violently.

Standing not fifteen feet away from Jack was the man who tortured, executed, and ruined the lives of hundreds of thousands of people. A man who was a billionaire created by the misery he caused. It was the man who kidnapped his son and almost killed his father. It was a man who had to die!

Jack watched and waited while DePeralta went to the bookcase and maneuvered it to open.

"Hold it right there," Jack said before DePeralta could bend over and grab the rifle Jack had left on the floor. His back was facing Jack. "Turn around!"

Jorge slowly turned around and looked at his nephew for the first time.

"Well, what a pleasure to finally meet my nephew," he said, smiling. He looked frail. He was no longer the handsome man who women begged to be with. He was a living shadow.

"Move over, away from the opening," Jack ordered.

Jorge moved slowly toward the center of the room until Jack told him to stop in front of cushioned chair. Jack watched Jorge casually look left and right as if he was trying to find a way out.

A shot rang out in the room. Jack flinched then looked around. Billy D had quietly entered the room through one of the French doors and shot one of Jorge's men who was aiming at Jack.

"Thanks, Billy," he said.

Jorge tried to bolt out of the room but Jack screamed at him to halt. Jack's gun was trained on him.

"Jack, we've got to get going," Billy said. "There's a bird waiting for us. It's still not secure here and they want to get one out of here. Connor is on board, and so is a woman who says she's his grandmother. Don't waste a bullet on him. He's dying anyway. Let him rot!"

Jack continued looking at Jorge who put his hands up in mock surrender.

Smiling, he said, "That's right Jack, I've got terminal cancer!"

With his Glock still aimed at DePeralta, Jack slowly squeezed the trigger. The bullet hit him in the chest, propelling him against the chair he was standing in front of, with enough force causing the chair and him to fall backwards.

Jack slowly walked over and looked down at the empty, gazing eyes of Jorge DePeralta. "Not anymore."

Billy ran over and looked down at DePeralta. "Nice shot, Jack. Are you okay?"

Jack just looked at Billy without a hint of any emotion.

"C'mon man, we need to get our asses out of here!" Billy said as he ran toward the door. Jack looked one more time at his uncle, and then turned to follow Billy through the open door.

An explosion quaked the house. Pictures on the wall fell and the ceiling started cracking. Jack stumbled, but was able to keep his balance. He haphazardly ran to the door Billy had left open.

Not far from the patio, the helicopter rotors were in full rotation. The sound was more like a jet, because of its turbo engines. Jack ran low to the open side door and was helped on board by one of the soldiers. Once Jack moved to his seat and buckled in, he noticed Connor sitting next to an elderly woman. Their backs faced him. Jack wasn't able to talk with Connor. Conversation was impossible due to the noise of the aircraft. Sitting next to Jack was Billy D who appeared to be deep in thought.

Jack looked out the window wondering if Alexa made it. Without her involvement and commitment, the mission would have never been successful, or at the least, casualties would have been worse. He hoped nobody was killed or severely injured.

The helicopter lifted off the ground and Jack suspected they would head back to Police Headquarters. As they lifted skyward, he looked down and saw one half of the DePeralta compound was now engulfed in flames. Many security men's bodies littered the area around the house. Sadly, the remains of the downed helicopter continued to burn. There were a couple of soldiers lying there too. Still, the mission was a success. One of the most notorious drug dealers was wiped out, and Jack got his son back. The elderly woman was still an uncomfortable mystery to him.

45

The chopper touched down as expected at Belize Headquarters. There was a landing area behind it that once was a school yard. Jack was one of the first persons off. He was ushered into a small room on the ground floor. It looked like an officer's lounge. There were sofas and cushioned chairs, vending machines, and a flat-screen television.

Nobody else arrived in the room with him. He was curious as to where everyone else went, not to mention Billy who he thought would be right behind him. Within five minutes, the door opened. An officer led Connor, and the woman who accompanied them on the flight from the compound, into the room. It was as if Jack was looking at a ghost. The woman was undeniably his mother.

He had not seen Isabella Dublin in over twenty years. She still had the same look and size, but with the expected changes one experiences over time. Her hair was gray and pulled back. Her face was still beautiful with gleaming eyes somewhat faded with age, but her skin was no longer flawless. It was wrinkled and creased, no doubt expedited from the stress of living with a maniac.

Isabella ran over to Jack and put her arms around him. She looked at him with tears in her eyes.

"Jack, my Jack," she sobbed. "It's been so long!"

Jack held her loosely while gazing at Connor with an even look. How do you explain seeing your mother, who you thought was dead, for the first time after twenty years?

Connor watched his father with the same uncertainty as the day they met at the restaurant in D.C. Perhaps he was still in shock as well.

Finally, Connor walked over to his father and grandmother and put his arms around them. It felt good.

Brian Oliver, after giving them a few minutes of private time, approached and stood in the doorway.

"Hello, Jack," he said formally. "I just wanted to give you a brief update on the mission. Can I see you in the hallway?"

Jack released his embrace and followed Brian into the hallway.

"You okay?" Brian asked.

"Yeah, sure."

"Jack, I know right now you have a lot on your plate. I'll just take a couple of minutes to give you an update, and then you can go back to your family. Everyone in the residence, with the exception of your son and mother, was killed including Jorge DePeralta and his main adviser, Juan Ruiz. I'm told that you were the one who took out DePeralta," he stated, pausing to get a reaction.

Jack nodded.

"Good job, Jack. You personally took out a global terrorist. You may not appreciate the totality of your actions right now, but let me tell you, you have done the world a great service!"

Jack nodded, staring blankly.

"Alexa is safe and is being debriefed upstairs. It had to be difficult for her, knowing, most likely, her father was going to be killed. Yet she knew he was, for all intents and purposes, a terrorist. She said they didn't really have a good relationship for years. Still hard on her anyway, I'm sure."

"I'd like a moment with her, if I could," Jack said.

"No problem. Why don't you go back and spend some time with Connor and your mother? I'll bring her down here in a few minutes."

Jack turned to the door and then stopped. "Hey Brian, I'm curious about something that was said in the briefing. You said the information Alexa gave you was confirmed by another source. The mission's over. Who was the other source?"

Brian smiled. "The other source was Jorge's wife. She's been working with us for some time. She told us about the compound, his deteriorating health, and the escape tunnel. She told us a lot! Alexa just confirmed it."

Jack acknowledged, and went back in the room to join his mother and Connor. He had a lot of questions that needed to be answered. There would be plenty of time to talk on the flight back to the States. In the meantime, nothing needed to be said. It was time to appreciate the moment.

Brian Oliver brought Alexa down to the hallway outside the room where Jack was. He went in and retrieved Jack.

"I'll let you two talk while I round up a ride to the airport for you, your mother, and Connor. I'm told your company jet is arriving and will be ready to take you home within the hour," Brian said before turning to walk down the hallway.

"How're you doing?" Jack asked.

"I'm fine," Alexa replied.

"You know I'm the one, don't you?"

"Yes, I know," she said. "I'm not angry with you. He was my father, but he was a terrible man. A terrible human being."

They stood in silence, awkwardly, for a few moments.

"Listen, I know you're upset with me about the other night, but I truly didn't know we were related until the next day," she said as tears formed in her eyes.

"I know. I believe you."

They stood there looking at each other.

"What are your plans now?" Jack asked.

"I'm gonna find my mother in Paris, and tell her what happened."

Jack said, "Well listen, I need to get back to my son and mother, but I want to thank you for all you did."

"You're welcome," she said as she wiped away her tears. "I'd like for us to stay in touch. After all, we're related," she said as she laughed through her tears.

"Okay," Jack said.

"I have your number."

"Okay." Jack held out his hand. "I guess I'll be talking to you."

She looked at it and dismissed it. Instead, she gave him a warm embrace. "Goodbye, Jack."

"Goodbye, Alexa."

They were delayed one day in Belize because the company plane needed some repairs. On the flight home, Jack was able to talk with his mother about her situation. She explained to him that Jorge DePeralta was angry about his life. He felt abandoned by his family since their parents died while he was still relatively young.

Since Isabella was his big sister, he felt the only way he could restore his sense of family was to have her back in his life. As he got older and powerful, he reached out to her. But there were complications. Working for the government, she knew he had become a priority target of surveillance. They wanted to infiltrate his organization and knew Isabella might be the perfect ticket to gain access. She refused and then took an early retirement.

When her brother showed up on her doorstep, she was no longer a protected government employee. From the classified information she read before she left, she knew her brother was demonic.

"He threatened me, telling me if I didn't come to live with him at his estate, he would kill you and your father. I felt confident that your father could take care of himself since he was CIA, but I was afraid for you," she said. "There was no way I could protect you twenty-four seven. He could follow you to school, there could be a thousand ways he could get to you. In fact, I don't know if you remember, but he brought you home one day. So, I made the most difficult decision of my life, and agreed to go to Belize. I wanted to spare you from being tortured and killed. If this was the way I was going to spend the rest of my life, I was resigned to it. I just prayed he would die, so I could come back to you and your father. I tried to escape a couple of times, but they found me, and kept me isolated. The last time they caught me, Jorge said the next time I tried to escape, he would kill me. I believed him!"

"The police said they found your body in a car that had been in an accident and caught fire," Jack said.

Isabella smirked. "My brother had so many resources. He murdered someone who was about the same size as me, planted false evidence, and paid off the police."

Connor sat next to them and heard everything.

When they landed, a limousine was waiting to take them to the hospital to see Ben Dublin. After arriving at the hospital, they went up to the waiting area where Ben sat in his wheelchair. He had been informed about the events in Belize and was anxiously waiting. He looked like he was well on his way to recovery. Standing next to him was Meg, Jack's ex-wife.

Isabella ran over to Ben and hugged him. Connor ran to his mother. Tears were flowing everywhere. Jack stood back and watched before his phone rang.

Stepping away, Jack answered it.

"Jack, is that you?"

"Yes."

"Jack, its Alexa. I have some great news!"

Jack listened.

"Jack, are you still there?"

"Yes, I'm here."

"I've just spoken with my mother and she told me that Jorge DePeralta was not my father. She said that's the reason she's been in hiding all these years. She was afraid he would find out and kill her. Jack, we're not related. I'm not your cousin!" she said joyfully.

"That's interesting. Did she tell you who your father is?"

"Yes, she did. It was Juan, my father's number one adviser."

Jack didn't respond.

"Jack, I hope that brings some relief for you about our night together!"

"Yes, it does. I hope it brings closure for you as well."

"It does. It's great news!"

"Thanks for calling, Alexa. It was nice talking to you. I wish you the best." He could hear her saying something as he terminated the call.

Jack sighed, turned around, and walked back to his family.

Acknowledgments

Writing a second novel is seductive, yet there is a tendency to fear the sophomore slump. It feels like the insecure teenager asking for a second date. Speaking of those tender teenage years, I would like to thank many friends from MTPHS and NCCPD who offered their time to read, proof, offer insight and opinions. I am indebted to them for their time and thoughts, but more so, for their unwavering support.

Thanks particularly to Mike Maier, Steve Zimmerman, Ron Morris, John Haug and Vincent Kowal for your encouragement and advice.

To my editor Michelle Josette who did an outstanding job of keeping me on track with the proper amount of push and pull.

Providing me with medical advice was Gerard Hogan M.D., a graduate of Johns Hopkins now practicing at several hospitals in Maryland and Delaware. Aside from being an expert, he always brought humor to a serious situation. Being Irish didn't hurt either! Any mistakes are mine, pure and simple.

I took poetic license with the heroin overdose of the Waverly character. A fatal heroin overdose is instantaneous. A victim would not be able to mutter any words. Thanks again to Vincent Kowal, NCCPD (ret.) and LT. Karl Hitchens, NCC Paramedic.

Thanks to Jake Sacher, Laura Phillips, Jaxson, Chase and Harper. Love you guys!

Finally, thanks to my family for giving me the momentum I needed. For my brother Wayne and sister Vicki who always bragged about the book. To my son Scotty, daughters Rachel, Chloe and Monica who make me proud. Most of all, to my wife and best friend Maria who rocks my world!

S.T. Phillips is a former New Castle County Police
Officer who served in Patrol and Criminal Investigations.
He was also a member of SWAT as a sniper.
Currently he serves as a Deputy Sheriff in
New Castle County, Delaware.
The Dark Side of Honor is a sequel to his award winning book,
The Dark Side of Death.
Look for the next Dark Side Book in 2017.

Made in the USA
Middletown, DE
11 September 2017